Lamb's Tales
From
Shakespeare

CHILDREN'S
CLASSICS

LAMB'S TALES
FROM
SHAKESPEARE

Charles and Mary Lamb

Bloomsbury Books
London

This edition published 1994 by Bloomsbury Books, an
imprint of The Godfrey Cave Group, 42 Bloomsbury Street,
London, WC1B 3QJ.

ISBN 1 85471 297 7

Printed and bound by Firmin-Didot (France),
Group Herissey. No d'impression : 27840.

Contents

Romeo And Juliet

The two chief families in Verona were the rich Capulets and the Montagues. There had been an old quarrel between these families, which was grown to such a height, and so deadly was the enmity between them, that it extended to the remotest kindred, to the followers and retainers of both sides, insomuch that a servant of the house of Montague could not meet a servant of the house of Capulet, nor a Capulet encounter a Montague by chance, but fierce words and sometimes bloodshed ensued; and frequent were the brawls, from such accidental meetings, which disturbed the happy quiet of Verona's estate.

Old Lord Capulet made a great supper, to which many fair ladies and many noble guests were invited. All the admired beauties of Verona were present, and all comers were made welcome if they were not of the house of Montague. At this feast of Capulet's, Rosaline, beloved of Romeo, son to the old Lord Montague, was present, and though it was dangerous for a Montague to be seen in this assembly, yet Benvolio, a friend of Romeo, persuaded the young lord to go to this assembly in the disguise of a mask that he might see his Rosaline, and seeing her, compare her with some choice beauties of Verona, who, he said, would make him think his swan a crow. Romeo had small faith in Benvolio's words; nevertheless, for the love of Rosaline, he was persuaded to go. For Romeo was a sincere and passionate lover, and one that lost his sleep for love, and fled society to be alone, thinking on Rosaline, who disdained him, and never requited his love with the least show of courtesy or affection; and Benvolio wished to cure his friend of this love by showing him diversity of ladies and company. To this feast of Capulet's, then, young Romeo, with Benvolio and their friend Mercutio, went masked. Old Capulet bid them welcome, and told them that ladies, who had their toes unplagued with corns, would dance with them. And the old man was light-hearted and merry, and said that he had worn a mask when he was young, and could have told a whispering tale in a fair lady's ear. And they fell to dancing, and Romeo was suddenly struck with the exceeding beauty of a lady that danced there, who seemed to him to teach the torches to burn bright, and her beauty to show by night like a rich jewel worn by a blackamoor: beauty too rich for use, too dear for earth; like a snowy dove trooping with crows, he said, so richly did her beauty and perfection shine above the ladies her companions. While he uttered these praises, he was overheard by Tybalt, a nephew of Lord Capulet, who knew him by his voice to be Romeo. And this Tybalt, being of a fiery and passionate temper, could not endure that a Montague should come, under cover of a mask, to fleer and scorn, as he said, at their solemnities. And he stormed and raged exceedingly, and would have struck young Romeo dead. But his uncle, the old Lord Capulet, would not suffer him to do any injury at that time both out of respect to his guests, and because Romeo had borne himself like a gentleman, and all tongues in Verona bragged of him to be a virtuous and well-governed youth. Tybalt, forced to be patient against his will, restrained himself, but vowed that this vile Montague should at another time dearly pay for his intrusion.

The dancing being done, Romeo watched the place where the lady stood, and, under favour of his masking habit, which might seem to excuse in part the liberty, he presumed, in the gentlest manner, to take her by the hand, calling it a shrine, which, if he profaned by touching it, he was a blushing pilgrim, and would kiss it for atonement. "Good pilgrim," answered the lady, "your devotion shows by far too mannerly and too courtly: saints have hands, which pilgrims may touch, but kiss not." "Have not saints lips, and pilgrims too?" said Romeo. "Ay," said the lady, "lips which they must use in prayer." "O then, my dear saint," said Romeo, "hear my prayer and grant it, lest I despair." In such like allusions and loving conceits they were engaged, when the lady was called away to her mother. And Romeo, inquiring who her mother was, discovered that the lady, whose peerless beauty he was so much struck with, was young Juliet, daughter and heir to the Lord Capulet, the great enemy of the Montagues, and that he had unknowingly engaged his heart to his foe. This troubled him, but it could not dissuade him from loving. As little rest had Juliet when she found that the gentleman that she had been talking with was Romeo and a Montague, for she had been suddenly smit with the same hasty and inconsiderate passion for Romeo which he had conceived for her; and a prodigious birth of love it seemed to her, that she must love her enemy, and that her affections should settle there, where family considerations should induce her chiefly to hate.

It being midnight, Romeo with his companions departed; but they soon missed him, for, unable to stay away from the house where he had left his heart, he leaped the wall of an orchard which was at the back of Juliet's house. Here he had not remained long, ruminating on his new love, when Juliet appeared above at a window, through which her exceeding beauty seemed to break like the light of the sun in the east; and the moon, which shone in the orchard with a faint light, appeared to Romeo as if sick and pale with grief at the superior lustre of this new sun. And she leaning her hand upon her cheek, he passionately wished himself a glove upon that hand, that he might touch her cheek. She all this while, thinking herself alone, fetched a deep sigh, and exclaimed, "Ah me!" Romeo was enraptured to hear her speak, and said softly, unheard by her, "O speak again, bright angel, for such you appear, being over my head like a winged messenger from heaven whom mortals fall back to gaze upon." She, unconscious of being overheard, and full of the new passion which that night's adventure had given birth to, called upon her lover by name (whom she supposed absent): "O Romeo, Romeo!" said she, "wherefore art thou Romeo? Deny thy father, and refuse thy name, for my sake; or if thou wilt not, be but my sworn love, and I no longer will be a Capulet." Romeo, having this encouragement, would fain have spoken, but he was desirous of hearing more, and the lady continued her passionate discourse with herself (as she thought), still chiding Romeo for being Romeo and a Montague, and wishing him some other name, or that he would put away the hated name, and for that name, which was no part of himself, he should take all herself. At this loving word Romeo could no longer refrain, but, taking up the dialogue as if her words had been addressed to him personally, and not merely in fancy, he bade her call him Love, or by whatever other name she pleased, for he was no longer Romeo, if that name was displeasing to her. Juliet, alarmed to hear a man's voice in the garden, did not at first know who it was that, by favour of the night and darkness, had thus stumbled upon the discovery of her secret; but when he spoke again, though her ears had not yet drunk a hundred words of that tongue's uttering, yet so nice is a lover's hearing that she immediately knew him to be young Romeo, and she expostulated with him on the danger to which he had exposed himself by climbing the orchard walls, for if any of her kinsmen should find him there it would be death to him, being a Montague.

"Alack," said Romeo, "there is more peril in your eye than in twenty of their swords. Do you but look kind upon me, lady, and I am proof against their enmity. Better my life should be ended by their hate than that hated life should be prolonged to live without your love." "How came you into this place," said Juliet, "and by whose direction?" "Love directed me," answered Romeo: "I am no pilot, yet wert thou as far apart from me as that vast shore which is washed with the farthest sea, I should adventure for such merchandise." A crimson blush came over the face of Juliet, yet unseen by Romeo by reason of the night, when she reflected upon the discovery which she had made, yet not meaning to make it, of her love to Romeo. She would fain have recalled her words, but that was impossible; fain would she have stood upon form and have kept her lover at a distance (as the custom of discreet ladies is), to frown and be perverse and give their suitors harsh denials at first; to stand off and affect a coyness or indifference where they most love, that their lovers may not think them too lightly or too easily won, for the difficulty of attainment increases the value of the object. But there was no room in her case for denials, or puttings off, or any of the customary arts of delay and protractive courtship. Romeo had heard from her own tongue, when she did not dream that he was near her, a confession of her love. So, with an honest frankness, which the novelty of her situation excused, she confirmed the truth of what he had before heard, and addressing him by the name of *fair Montague* (love can sweeten a sour name) she begged him not to impute her easy yielding to levity or an unworthy mind, but that he must lay the fault of it (if it were a fault) upon the accident of the night which had so strangely discovered her thoughts. And she added that, though her behaviour to him might not be sufficiently prudent, measured by the custom of her sex, yet that she would prove more true than many whose prudence was dissembling, and their modesty artificial cunning.

Romeo was beginning to call the heavens to witness that nothing was farther from his thoughts than to impute a shadow of dishonour to such an honoured lady, when she stopped him, begged him not to swear; for although she joyed in him, yet she had no joy of that night's contract; it was too rash, too unadvised, too sudden. But he being urgent with her to exchange a vow of love with her that night, she said that she already had given him hers before he requested it, meaning when he overheard her confession; but she would retract what she then bestowed for the pleasure of giving it again, for her bounty was as infinite as the sea, and her love as deep. From this loving conference she was called away by her nurse, who slept with her, and thought it time for her to be in bed, for it was near to day-break; but hastily returning, she said three or four words more to Romeo, the purport of which was, that if his love was indeed honourable and his purpose marriage, she would send a messenger to him tomorrow, to appoint a time for their marriage, when she would lay all her fortunes at his feet, and follow him as her lord through the world. While they were settling this point, Juliet was repeatedly called for by her nurse, and went and returned, and went in and returned again, for she seemed as jealous of Romeo going from her as a young girl of her bird, which she will let hop a little from her hand, and pluck it back with a silken thread; and Romeo was as loath to part as she; for the sweetest music to lovers is the sound of each other's tongues at night. But at last they parted, wishing mutually sweet sleep and rest for that night.

The day was breaking when they parted, and Romeo, who was too full of thoughts of his mistress and that blessed meeting to allow him to sleep, instead of going home, bent his course to a monastery hard by to find Friar Lawrence. The good friar was already up at his devotions, but seeing young Romeo abroad so early, he conjectured rightly that he had not been abed that night, but that some distemper of youthful affection had kept him waking. He was right in imputing the cause of Romeo's wakefulness to love, but he made a wrong guess at the object, for he thought that his love for Rosaline had kept him waking. But when Romeo revealed his new passion for Juliet, and requested the assistance of the friar to marry them that day, the holy man lifted up his eyes and hands in a sort of wonder at the sudden change in Romeo's affections, for he had been privy to all Romeo's love for Rosaline, and his many complaints of her disdain; and he said that young men's love lay not truly in their hearts, but in their eyes. But Romeo replying that he himself had often chidden him for doting on Rosaline, who could not love again, whereas Juliet both loved and was beloved by him, the friar assented in some measure to his reasons; and thinking that a matrimonial alliance between young Juliet and Romeo might happily be the means of making up the long breach between the Capulets and the Montagues, which no one more lamented than this good friar, who was a friend to both the families, and had often interposed his mediation to make up the quarrel without effect; partly moved by policy, and partly by his fondness for young Romeo, to whom he could deny nothing, the old man consented to join their hands in marriage.

Now was Romeo blessed indeed, and Juliet, who knew his intent from a messenger which she had despatched according to promise, did not fail to be early at the cell of Friar Lawrence, where their hands were joined in holy marriage; the good friar praying the heavens to smile upon that act, and in the union of this young Montague and young Capulet to bury the old strife and long dissensions of their families.

The ceremony being over, Juliet hastened home, where she stayed impatient for the coming of night, at which time Romeo promised to come and meet her in the orchard, where they had met the night before; and the time between seemed as tedious to her as the night before some great festival seems to an impatient child that has got new finery which it may not put on till the morning.

The same day about noon, Romeo's friends, Benvolio and Mercutio, walking through the streets of Verona, were met by a party of the Capulets with the impetuous Tybalt at their head. This was the same angry Tybalt who would have fought with Romeo at old Lord Capulet's feast. He, seeing Mercutio, accused him bluntly of associating with Romeo, a Montague. Mercutio, who had as much fire and youthful blood in him as Tybalt, replied to this accusation with some sharpness; and in spite of all Benvolio could say to moderate their wrath, a quarrel was beginning, when Romeo himself passing that way, the fierce Tybalt turned from Mercutio to Romeo, and gave him the disgraceful appellation of villain. Romeo wished to avoid a quarrel with Tybalt above all men, because he was the kinsman of Juliet, and much beloved by her; besides this, young Montague had never thoroughly entered in the family quarrel, being by nature wise and gentle, and the name of a Capulet, which was his dear lady's name, was now rather a charm to allay resentment than a watchword to excite fury. So he tried to reason with Tybalt, whom he saluted mildly by the name of *good Capulet*, as if he, though a Montague, had some secret pleasure in uttering that name; but Tybalt, who hated all Montagues as he hated sin, would hear no reason, but drew his weapon; and Mercutio, who knew not of Romeo's secret motive for desiring peace with Tybalt, but looked upon his present forbearance as a sort of calm dishonourable submission, with many disdainful words provoked Tybalt to the prosecution of his first quarrel with him; and Tybalt and Mercutio fought till Mercutio fell, receiving his death wound while Romeo and Benvolio were vainly endeavouring to part the combatants. Mercutio being dead, Romeo kept his temper no longer, but returned the scornful appellation of villain which Tybalt had given him, and they fought till Tybalt was slain by Romeo. This deadly broil falling out in the midst of Verona at noonday, the news of it quickly brought a crowd of citizens to the spot, and among them the old Lords Capulet and Montague with their wives and soon after arrived the prince himself, who, being related to Mercutio, whom Tybalt had slain, and having had the peace of his government often disturbed by these brawls of Montagues and Capulets, came determined to put the law in strictest force against those who should be found to be offenders. Benvolio, who had been eye-witness to the fray, was commanded by the prince to relate the origin of it, which he did, keeping as near the truth as he could without injury to Romeo, softening and excusing the part which his friends took in it. Lady Capulet, whose extreme grief for the loss of her kinsman Tybalt made her keep no bounds in her revenge, exhorted the prince to do strict justice upon his murderer, and to pay no attention to Benvolio's representation, who, being Romeo's friend and a Montague, spoke partially. Thus she pleaded against her new son-in-law, but she knew not yet that he was her son-in-law and Juliet's husband. On the other hand was to be seen Lady Montague pleading for her child's life, and arguing with some justice that Romeo had done nothing worthy of punishment in taking the life of Tybalt, which was already forfeited to the law by his having slain Mercutio. The prince, unmoved by the passionate exclamations of these women, on a careful examination of the facts, pronounced his sentence, and by that sentence Romeo was banished from Verona.

Heavy news to young Juliet, who had been but a few hours a bride, and now by this decree seemed everlastingly divorced! When the tidings reached her, she at first gave way to rage against Romeo, who had slain her dear cousin: she called him a beautiful tyrant, a fiend angelical, a ravenous dove, a lamb with a wolf's nature, a serpent-heart hid with a flowering face and other like contradictory names, which denoted the struggles in her mind between her love and her resentment; but in the end love got the mastery, and the tears which she shed for grief that Romeo had slain her cousin, turned to drops of joy that her husband lived whom Tybalt would have slain. Then came fresh tears, and they were altogether of grief for Romeo's banishment. That word was more terrible to her than the death of many Tybalts.

Romeo, after the fray, had taken refuge in Friar Lawrence's cell, where he was first made acquainted with the prince's sentence, which seemed to him far more terrible than death. To him it appeared there was no world out of Verona's walls, no living out of the sight of Juliet. Heaven was there where Juliet lived, and all beyond was purgatory and torture. The good friar would have applied the consolation of philosophy to his griefs; but this frantic young man would hear of none, but like a madman he tore his hair, and threw himself all along upon the ground, as he said, to take the measure of his grave. From this unseemly state he was roused by a message from his dear lady, which a little revived him, and then the friar took the advantage to expostulate with him on the unmanly weakness which he had shown. He had slain Tybalt, but would he also slay himself, slay his dear lady who lived but in his life? The noble form of man, he said, was but a shape of wax when it wanted the courage which should keep it firm. The law had been lenient to him, that instead of death, which he had incurred, had pronounced by the prince's mouth only banishment. He had slain Tybalt, but Tybalt would have slain him; there was a sort of happiness in that. Juliet was alive, and beyond all hope had become his dear wife; therein he was most happy. All these blessings, as the friar made them out to be, did Romeo put from him like a sullen, misbehaved wench. And the friar bade him beware, for such as despaired, he said, died miserable. Then, when Romeo was a little calmed, he counselled him that he should go that night and secretly take his leave of Juliet, and thence proceed straightways to Mantua, at which place he should sojourn till the friar found a fit occasion to publish his marriage, which might be a joyful means of reconciling their families, and then he did not doubt but the prince would be moved to pardon him, and he would return with twenty times more joy than he went forth with grief. Romeo was convinced by these wise counsels of the friar, and took his leave to go and seek his lady, proposing to stay with her that night, and by daybreak pursue his journey alone to Mantua; to which place the good friar promised to send him letters from time to time, acquainting him with the state of affairs at home.

That night Romeo passed with his dear wife, gaining secret admission to her chamber from the orchard in which he had heard her confession of love the night before. That had been a night of unmixed joy and rapture; but the pleasures of this night, and the delight which these lovers took in each other's society, were sadly allayed with the prospect of parting, and the fatal adventures of the past day. The unwelcome daybreak seemed to come too soon, and when Juliet heard the morning song of the lark, she would fain have persuaded herself that it was the nightingale, which sings by night: but it was too truly the lark which sung, and a discordant and unpleasing note it seemed to her; and the streaks of day in the east too certainly pointed out that it was time for these lovers to part. Romeo took his leave of his dear wife with a heavy heart, promising to write to her from Mantua every hour in the day, and when he had descended from her chamber window, as he stood below her on the ground, in that sad foreboding state of mind in, which she was, he appeared to her eyes as one dead in the bottom of a tomb. Romeo's mind misgave him in like manner; but now he was forced hastily to depart, for it was death for him to be found within the walls of Verona after daybreak.

This was but the beginning of the tragedy of this pair of star-crossed lovers. Romeo had not been gone many days before the old Lord Capulet proposed a match for Juliet. The husband he had chosen for her, not dreaming that she was married already, was Count Paris, a gallant, young, and noble gentleman, no unworthy suitor to the young Juliet if she had never seen Romeo.

The terrified Juliet was in a sad perplexity at her father's offer. She pleaded her youth unsuitable to marriage, the recent death of Tybalt, which had left her spirits too weak to meet a husband with any face of joy, and how indecorous it would show for the family of the Capulets to be celebrating a nuptial feast when his funeral solemnities were hardly over; she pleaded every reason against the match but the true one, namely, that she was married already. But Lord Capulet was deaf to all her excuses, and in a peremptory manner ordered her to get ready, for by the following Thursday she should be married to Paris; and having found her a husband rich, young, and noble, such as the proudest maid in Verona might joyfully accept, he could not bear that out of an affected coyness, as he construed her denial, she should oppose obstacles to her own good fortune.

In this extremity Juliet applied to the friendly friar, always her counsellor in distress, and he asking her if she had resolution to undertake a desperate remedy and she answering that she would go into the grave alive rather than marry Paris, her own dear husband living, he directed her to go home and appear merry, and give her consent to marry Paris, according to her father's desire, and on the next night, which was the night before the marriage, to drink off the contents of a phial which he then gave her, the effect of which would be, that for two-and-forty hours after drinking it she would appear cold and lifeless; that when the bridegroom came to fetch her in the morning he would find her to appearance dead; that then she would be borne, as the manner in that country was, uncovered on a bier to be buried in the family vault; that if she could put off womanish fear, and consent to this terrible trial, in forty-two hours after swallowing the liquid (such was its certain operation) she would be sure to awake as from a dream; and before she should awake he would let her husband know their drift, and he should come in the night and bear her thence to Mantua. Love, and the dread of marrying Paris, gave young Juliet strength to undertake this horrible adventure; and she took the phial of the friar, promising to observe his directions.

Going from the monastery, she met the young Count Paris, and, modestly dissembling, promised to become his bride. This was joyful news to the Lord Capulet and his wife. It seemed to put youth into the old man; and Juliet, who had displeased him exceedingly by her refusal of the count, was his darling again, now she promised to be obedient. All things in the house were in a bustle against the approaching nuptials. No cost was spared to prepare such festival rejoicings as Verona had never before witnessed.

On the Wednesday night Juliet drank off the potion. She had many misgivings lest the friar, to avoid the blame which might be imputed to him for marrying her to Romeo, had given her poison; but then he was always known for a holy man; then lest she should awake before the time that Romeo was to come for her; whether the terror of the place, a vault full of dead Capulets' bones, and where Tybalt, all bloody, lay festering in his shroud, would not be enough to drive her distracted; again she thought of all the stories she had heard of spirits haunting the places where their bodies were bestowed. But then her love for Romeo and her aversion for Paris returned, and she desperately swallowed the draught, and became insensible.

When young Paris came early in the morning with music to awaken his bride, instead of a living Juliet, her chamber presented the dreary spectacle of a lifeless corpse. What death to his hopes! What confusion then reigned through the whole house! Poor Paris lamenting his bride, whom most detestable death had beguiled him of, had divorced him even before their hands were joined. But still more piteous it was to hear the mournings of the old Lord and Lady Capulet, who, having but this one—one poor loving child to rejoice and solace in—cruel death had snatched her from their sight, just as these careful parents were on the point of seeing her advanced, as they thought, by a promising and advantageous match. Now all things that were ordained for the festival were turned from their properties to do the office of a black funeral. The wedding cheer served for a sad burial feast, the bridal hymns were changed to sullen dirges, the sprightly instruments to melancholy bells, and the

flowers that should have been strewed in the bride's path now
served but to strew her corpse. Now instead of a priest to marry her,
a priest was needed to bury her; and she was borne to church indeed, not to augment the cheerful hopes of the living, but to swell
the dreary numbers of the dead.

Bad news, which always travel faster than good, now brought the
dismal story of his Juliet's death to Romeo at Mantua before the
messenger could arrive who was sent from Friar Lawrence to ap-
prise him that these were mock funerals only, and but the shadow
and representation of death, and that his dear lady lay in the tomb
but for a short while, expecting when Romeo should come to re-
lease her from that dreary mansion. Just before, Romeo had been
unusually joyful and light-hearted. He had dreamed in the night
that he was dead (a strange dream, that gave a dead man leave to
think), and that his lady came and found him dead, and breathed
such life with kisses in his lips, that he revived, and was an emperor! And now that a messenger came from Verona, he thought
surely it was to confirm some good news which his dreams had
presaged. But when the contrary to this flattering vision appeared,
and that it was his lady who was dead in truth, whom he could not
revive by any kisses, he ordered horses to be got ready, for he determined that night to visit Verona, and to see his lady in her tomb.
And as mischief is swift to enter into the thoughts of desperate men,
he called to mind a poor apothecary whose shop in Mantua he had
lately passed, and from the beggarly appearance of the man, who
seemed famished, and the wretched show in his shop of empty
boxes ranged on dirty shelves, and other tokens of extreme wretchedness, he had said at the time (perhaps having some misgivings
that his own disastrous life might haply meet with a conclusion so
desperate), "If a man were to need poison, which by the law of
Mantua it is death to sell, here lives a poor wretch who would sell it
him." These words of his now came into his mind, and he sought
out the apothecary, who after some pretended scruples, Romeo of-
fering him gold which his poverty could not resist, sold him a poison, which, if he swallowed, he told him, if he had the strength of
twenty men, would quickly despatch him.

With this poison he set out for Verona to have a sight of his dear
lady in her tomb, meaning, when he had satisfied his sight, to swal-

low the poison, and be buried by her side. He reached Verona at midnight, and found the churchyard, in the midst of which was situated the ancient tomb of the Capulets. He had provided a light, and a spade, and wrenching iron, and was proceeding to break open the monument, when he was interrupted by a voice, which, by the name of *vile Montague,* bade him desist from his unlawful business. It was the young Count Paris, who had come to the tomb of Juliet at that unseasonable time of night to strew flowers and to weep over the grave of her that should have been his bride He knew not what an interest Romeo had in the dead, but knowing him to be a Montague, and, as he supposed, a sworn foe to all the Capulets, he judged that he was come by night to do some villainous shame to the dead bodies; therefore in angry tone he bade him desist, and as a criminal, condemned by the laws of Verona to die if he were found within the walls of the city, he would have apprehended him. Romeo urged Paris to leave him, and warned him by the fate of Tybalt, who lay buried there, not to provoke his anger, or draw down another sin upon his head by forcing him to kill him. But the count in scorn refused his warning, and laid hands on him as a felon, which Romeo resisting, they fought, and Paris fell. When Romeo, by the help of a light, came to see who it was that he had slain, that it was Paris, who (he learned in his way from Mantua) should have married Juliet, he took the dead youth by the hand, as one whom misfortune had made a companion, and said that he would bury him in a triumphal grave, meaning in Juliet's grave, which he now opened; and there lay his lady, as one whom death had no power upon to change a feature or complexion in her matchless beauty, or as if Death were amorous, and the lean, abhorred monster kept her there for his delight; for she lay yet fresh and blooming, as she had fallen to sleep when she swallowed that benumbing potion; and near her lay Tybalt in his bloody shroud, whom Romeo seeing, begged pardon of his lifeless corpse, and for Juliet's sake called him *cousin,* and said that he was about to do him a favour by putting his enemy to death. Here Romeo took his last leave of his lady, kissing her; and here he shook the burden of his cross stars from his weary body, swallowing that poison which the apothecary had sold him, whose operation was fatal and real, not like that dissembling potion which Juliet had swallowed, the effect of which was now nearly expiring, and she about to awake to complain that Romeo had not kept his time, or that he had come too soon.

For now the hour was arrived at which the friar had promised that she should awake; and he, having learned that his letters which he had sent to Mantua, by some unlucky detention of the messenger, had never reached Romeo, came himself, provided with a pickaxe and lantern, to deliver the lady from her confinement; but he was surprised to find a light already burning in the Capulets' monument, and to see swords and blood near it, and Romeo and Paris lying breathless by the monument.

Before he could entertain a conjecture, to imagine how these fatal accidents had fallen out, Juliet awoke out of her trance, and seeing the friar near her, she remembered the place where she was, and the occasion of her being there, and asked for Romeo; but the friar, hearing a noise, bade her come out of that place of death and of unnatural sleep, for a greater power than they could contradict had thwarted their intents; and, being frightened by the noise of people coming he fled; but when Juliet saw the cup closed in her true love's hands, she guessed that poison had been the cause of his end, and she would have swallowed the dregs if any had been left, and she kissed his still warm lips to try if any poison yet did hang upon them; then hearing a nearer noise of people coming, she quickly unsheathed a dagger which she wore, and, stabbing herself, died by her true Romeo's side.

The watch by this time had come up to the place. A page belonging to Count Paris, who had witnessed the fight between his master and Romeo, had given the alarm, which had spread among the citizens, who went up and down the streets of Verona confusedly, exclaiming, a Paris, a Romeo, a Juliet, as the rumour had imperfectly reached them, till the uproar brought Lord Montague and Lord Capulet out of their beds, with the prince, to inquire into the causes of the disturbance. The friar had been apprehended by some of the watch coming from the churchyard, trembling, sighing, and weeping, in a suspicious manner. A great multitude being assembled at the Capulets' monument, the friar was demanded by the prince to deliver what he knew of these strange and disastrous accidents.

And there, in the presence of the old Lords Montague and

Capulet, he faithfully related the story of their children's fatal love, the part he took in promoting their marriage, in the hope in that union to end the long quarrels between their families: how Romeo, there dead, was husband to Juliet, and Juliet, there dead, was Romeo's faithful wife; how before he could find a fit opportunity to divulge their marriage, another match was projected for Juliet, who to avoid the crime of a second marriage swallowed the sleeping draught, as he advised, and all thought her dead; how meantime he wrote to Romeo to come and take her thence when the force of the potion should cease, and by what unfortunate miscarriage of the messenger the letters never reached Romeo; further than this the friar could not follow the story, nor knew more than that, coming himself to deliver Juliet from that place of death, he found the Count Paris and Romeo slain. The remainder of the transactions was supplied by the narration of the page who had seen Paris and Romeo fight, and by the servant who came with Romeo from Verona, to whom this faithful lover had given letters to be delivered to his father in the event of his death, which made good the friar's words, confessing his marriage with Juliet, imploring the forgiveness of his parents, acknowledging the buying of the poison of the poor apothecary, and his intent in coming to the monument to die and lie with Juliet. All these circumstances agreed together to clear the friar from any hand he could be supposed to have had in these complicated slaughters, further than as the unintended consequences of his own well-meant, yet too artificial and subtle contrivances.

And the prince, turning to these old lords, Montague and Capulet, rebuked them for their brutal and irrational enmities, and showed them what a scourge Heaven had laid upon such offences, that it had found means, even through the love of their children, to punish their unnatural hate. And these old rivals, no longer enemies, agreed to bury their long strife in their children's graves; and Lord Capulet requested Lord Montague to give him his hand, calling him by the name of brother, as if in acknowledgment of the union of their families by the marriage of the young Capulet and Montague, and saying that Lord Montague's hand (in token of reconcilement) was all he demanded for his daughter's jointure. But Lord Montague said he would give him more, for he would raise her a statue of pure gold, that while Verona kept its name no figure should be so esteemed for its richness and workmanship as that of the true and faithful Juliet. And Lord Capulet, in return, said that he would raise another statue to Romeo. So did these poor old lords, when it was too late, strive to outgo each other in mutual courtesies; while so deadly had been their rage and enmity in past times, that nothing but the fearful overthrow of their children (poor sacrifices to their quarrels and dissensions) could remove the rooted hates and jealousies of the noble families.

King Lear

Lear, King of Britain, had three daughters—Gonerill, wife to the Duke of Albany; Regan, wife to the Duke of Cornwall; and Cordelia, a young maid, for whose love the King of France and Duke of Burgundy were joint suitors, and were at this time making stay for that purpose in the court of Lear.

The old king, worn out with age and the fatigues of government, he being more than fourscore years old, determined to take no further part in state affairs, but to leave the management to younger strengths, that he might have time to prepare for death, which must at no long period ensue. With this intent he called his three daughters to him, to know from their own lips which of them loved him best, that he might part his kingdom among them in such proportions as their affection for him should seem to deserve.

Gonerill, the eldest, declared that she loved her father more than words could give out, that he was dearer to her than the light of her own eyes, dearer than life and liberty, with a deal of such professing stuff, which is easy to counterfeit where there is no real love, only a few fine words delivered with confidence being wanted in that case. The king, delighted to hear from her own mouth this assurance of her love, and thinking truly that her heart went with it, in a fit of fatherly fondness bestowed upon her and her husband one-third of his ample kingdom.

Then calling to him his second daughter, he demanded what she had to say. Regan, who was made of the same hollow metal as her sister, was not a whit behind in her professions, but rather declared that what her sister had spoken came short of the love which she professed to bear for his highness; insomuch that she found all other joys dead in comparison with the pleasure which she took in the love of her dear king and father.

Lear blessed himself in having such loving children, as he

thought, and could do no less, after the handsome assurances which Regan had made, than bestow a third of his kingdom upon her and her husband, equal in size to that which he had already given away to Gonerill.

Then turning to his youngest daughter Cordelia, whom he called his joy, he asked what she had to say, thinking, no doubt, that she would glad his ears with the same loving speeches which her sisters had uttered, or rather that her expressions would be so much stronger than theirs, as she had always been his darling, and favoured by him above either of them. But Cordelia, disgusted with the flattery of her sisters, whose hearts she knew were far from their lips, and seeing that all their coaxing speeches were only intended to wheedle the old king out of his dominions, that they and their husbands might reign in his lifetime, made no other reply but this, that she loved his majesty according to her duty, neither more nor less.

The king, shocked with this appearance of ingratitude in his favourite child, desired her to consider her words and to mend her speech, lest it should mar her fortunes.

Cordelia then told her father that he was her father, that he had given her life and loved her, that she returned those duties back as was most fit, and did obey him, love him, and most honour him, but that she could not frame her mouth to such large speeches as her sisters had done, or promise to love nothing else in the world. Why had her sisters husbands, if, as they said, they had no love for anything but their father? If she should ever wed, she was sure the lord to whom she gave her hand would want half her love, half of her care and duty; she should never marry like her sisters.

Cordelia, who in earnest loved her old father even almost as extravagantly as her sisters pretended to do, would have plainly told him so at any other time, in more daughter-like and loving terms and without those qualifications which did indeed sound a little ungracious; but, after the crafty, flattering speeches of her sisters, which she had seen draw such extravagant rewards, she thought the handsomest thing she could do was to love and be silent. This put her affection out of suspicion of mercenary ends, and showed that she loved, but not for gain, and that her professions, the less ostentatious they were, had so much the more of truth and sincerity than her sisters'.

This plainness of speech, which Lear called pride so enraged the monarch—who in his best of times always showed much of spleen and rashness, and in whom the dotage incident to old age had so clouded over his reason that he could not discern truth from flattery, nor a gay painted speech from words that came from the heart—that in a fury of resentment he retracted the third part of his kingdom which yet remained, and which he had reserved for Cordelia, and gave it away from her, sharing it equally between her two sisters and their husbands, the Dukes of Albany and Cornwall, whom he now called to him, and in the presence of all his courtiers, bestowing a coronet between them, invested them jointly with all the power, revenue, and execution of government, only retaining to himself the name of king; all the rest of royalty he resigned, with this reservation, that himself, with a hundred knights for his attendants, was to be maintained by monthly course in each of his daughters' palaces in turn.

So preposterous a disposal of his kingdom, so little guided by reason, and so much by passion, filled all his courtiers with astonishment and sorrow; but none of them had the courage to interpose between this incensed king and his wrath except the Earl of Kent, who was beginning to speak a good word for Cordelia, when the passionate Lear, on pain of death, commanded him to desist; but the good Kent was not so to be repelled. He had been ever loyal to Lear, whom he had honoured as a king, loved as a father, followed as a master; and had never esteemed his life further than a pawn to wage against his royal master's enemies, nor feared to lose it when Lear's safety was the motive; nor now that Lear was most his own enemy did this faithful servant of the king forget his old principles, but manfully opposed Lear to do Lear good, and was unmannerly only because Lear was mad. He had been a most faithful counsellor, in times past to the king, and he besought him now that he would see with his eyes (as he had done in many weighty matters), and go by his advice still, and in his best consideration recall this hideous rashness; for he would answer with his life, his judgment, that Lear's youngest daughter did not love him least, nor were those empty-hearted whose low sound gave no token of hollowness. When power bowed to flattery, honour was bound to plainness. For Lear's threats, what could he do to him, whose life was already at his service? That should not hinder duty from speaking.

The honest freedom of this good Earl of Kent only stirred up the king's wrath the more, and, like a frantic patient who kills his physician, and loves his mortal disease, he banished this true servant, and allotted him but five days to make his preparations for departure; but if on the sixth his hated person was found within the realm of Britain, that moment was to be his death. And Kent bade farewell to the king, and said, that since he chose to show himself in such fashion, it was but banishment to stay there; and before he went, he recommended Cordelia to the protection of the gods, the maid who had so rightly thought and so discreetly spoken; and only wished that her sisters' large speeches might be answered with deeds of love, and then he went, as he said, to shape his old course to a new country.

The King of France and Duke of Burgundy were now called in to hear the determination of Lear about his youngest daughter, and to know whether they would persist in their courtship to Cordelia, now that she was under her father's displeasure, and had no fortune but her own person to recommend her; and the Duke of Burgundy declined the match, and would not take her to wife upon such conditions; but the King of France, understanding what the nature of the fault had been which had lost her the love of her father, that it was only a tardiness of speech, and the not being able to frame her tongue to flattery like her sisters, took this young maid by the hand, and saying that her virtues were a dowry above a kingdom, bade Cordelia to take farewell of her sisters and of her father, though he had been unkind, and she should go with him, and be queen of him and of fair France, and reign over fairer possessions than her sisters; and he called the Duke of Burgundy in contempt a waterish duke, because his love for this young maid had in a moment run all away like water.

Then Cordelia with weeping eyes took leave of her sisters, and besought them to love their father well, and make good their professions; and they sullenly told her not to prescribe to them, for they knew their duty, but to strive to content her husband, who had taken her (as they tauntingly expressed it) as Fortune's alms. And Cordelia with a heavy heart departed, for she knew the cunning of her sisters, and she wished her father in better hands than she was about to leave him in.

Cordelia was no sooner gone than the devilish dispositions of her sisters began to show themselves in their true colours. Even before the expiration of the first month, which Lear was to spend by agreement with his eldest daughter Gonerill, the old king began to find out the difference between promises and performances. This wretch, having got from her father all that he had to bestow, even to the giving away of the crown from off his head, began to grudge even those small remnants of royalty which the old man had reserved to himself to please his fancy with the idea of being still a king. She could not bear to see him and his hundred knights. Every time she met her father she put on a frowning countenance; and when the old man wanted to speak with her, she would feign sickness, or anything to be rid of the sight of him; for it was plain that she esteemed his old age a useless burden, and his attendants an unnecessary expense; not only she herself slackened in her expressions of duty to the king, but by her example, and, it is to be feared, not without her private instructions, her very servants affected to treat him with neglect, and would either refuse to obey his orders, or still more contemptuously pretend not to hear them. Lear could not but perceive this alteration in the behaviour of his daughter, but he shut his eyes against it as long as he could, as people commonly are unwilling to believe the unpleasant consequences which their own mistakes and obstinacy have brought upon them.

True love and fidelity are no more to be estranged by *ill*, than falsehood and hollow-heartedness can be conciliated by *good usage*. This eminently appears in the instance of the good Earl of Kent, who, though banished by Lear, and his life made forfeit if he were found in Britain, chose to stay and abide all consequences, as long as there was a chance of his being useful to the king his master. See to what mean shifts and disguises poor loyalty is forced to submit sometimes; yet it counts nothing base or unworthy, so as it can but do service where it owes an obligation! In the disguise of a serving-man, all his greatness and pomp laid aside, this good earl proffered his services to the king, who, not knowing him to be Kent in that disguise, but pleased with a certain plainness, or rather bluntness, in his answers which the earl put on (so different from that smooth, oily flattery which he had so much reason to be sick of, having found the effects not answerable in his daughter), a bargain was quickly struck, and Lear took Kent into his service by the name of Caius, as he called himself, never suspecting him to be his once great favourite, the high and mighty Earl of Kent.

This Caius quickly found means to show his fidelity and love to his royal master; for Gonerill's steward that same day behaving in a disrespectful manner to Lear, and giving him saucy looks and language, as no doubt he was secretly encouraged to do by his mistress, Caius, not enduring to hear so open an affront put upon majesty, made no more ado but presently tripped up his heels, and laid the unmannerly slave in the kennel; for which friendly service Lear became more and more attached to him.

Nor was Kent the only friend Lear had. In his degree, and as far as so insignificant a personage could show his love, the poor fool, or jester, that had been of his palace while Lear had a palace, as it was the custom of kings and great personages at that time to keep a fool (as he was called) to make them sport after serious business; this poor fool clung to Lear after he had given away his crown, and by his witty sayings would keep up his good humour, though he could not refrain sometimes from jeering at his master for his imprudence in uncrowning himself and giving all away to his daughters; at which time, as he rhymingly expressed it, these daughters

> For sudden joy did weep,
> And he for sorrow sung,
>   That such a king should play bo-peep,
> And go the fools among.

And in such wild sayings and scraps of songs, of which he had plenty, this pleasant, honest fool poured out his heart, even in the presence of Gonerill herself, in many a bitter taunt and jest, which cut to the quick: such as comparing the king to the hedge-sparrow, who feeds the young of the cuckoo till they grow old enough, and then has its head bit off for its pains, and saying that an ass may know when the cart draws the horse (meaning that Lear's daughters, that ought to go behind, now ranked before their father), and that Lear was no longer Lear, but the shadow of Lear, for which free speeches he was once or twice threatened to be whipped.

The coolness and falling off of respect which Lear had begun to perceive were not all which this foolish fond father was to suffer from his unworthy daughter; she now plainly told him that his staying in her palace was inconvenient so long as he insisted upon keeping up an establishment of a hundred knights; that this establishment was useless and expensive, and only served to fill her court with riot and feastings; and she prayed him that he would lessen their number, and keep none but old men about him, such as himself, and fitting his age.

Lear at first could not believe his eyes or ears, nor that it was his daughter who spoke so unkindly. He could not believe that she who had received a crown from him could seek to cut off his train, and grudge him the respect due to his old age. But she persisting in her undutiful demand, the old man's rage was so excited, that he called her a detested kite, and said that she had spoken an untruth; and so indeed she did, for the hundred knights were all men of choice behaviour and sobriety of manners, skilled in all particulars of duty, and not giving to rioting and feasting as she said. And he bid his horses to be prepared, for he would go to his other daughter Regan, he and his hundred knights; and he spoke of ingratitude, and said it was a marble-hearted fiend, and showed more hideous in a child than the sea-monster. And he cursed his eldest daughter Gonerill so as was terrible to hear, praying that she might never have a child, or, if she had, that it might live to return that scorn and contempt upon her which she had shown to him, that she might feel how sharper than a serpent's tooth it was to have a thankless child. And Gonerill's husband, the Duke of Albany, beginning to excuse himself for any share which Lear might suppose he had in the unkindness, Lear would not hear him out, but in a rage ordered his horses to be saddled, and set out with his followers for the abode of Regan, his other daughter. And Lear thought to himself how small the fault of Cordelia (if it was a fault) now appeared in comparison with her sister's, and he wept; and then he was ashamed that such a creature as Gonerill should have so much power over his manhood as to make him weep.

Regan and her husband were keeping their court in great pomp and state at their palace; and Lear despatched his servant Caius with letters to his daughter, that she might be prepared for his reception, while he and his train followed after. But it seems that

Gonerill had been beforehand with him, sending letters also to Regan, accusing her father of waywardness and ill-humours, and advising her not to receive so great a train as he was bringing with him. This messenger arrived at the same time with Caius, and Caius and he met, and who should it be but Caius's old enemy the steward, whom he had formerly tripped up by the heels for his saucy behaviour to Lear. Caius not liking the fellow's look, and suspecting what he came for, began to revile him, and challenged him to fight, which the fellow refusing, Caius, in a fit of honest passion beat him soundly, as such a mischief-maker and carrier of wicked messages deserved, which coming to the ears of Regan and her husband, they ordered Caius to be put in the stocks, though he was a messenger from the king her father, and in that character demanded the highest respect; so that the first thing the king saw when he entered the castle was his faithful servant Caius sitting in that disgraceful situation.

This was but a bad omen the reception which he was to expect; but a worse followed, when, upon inquiry for his daughter and her husband, he was told they were weary with travelling all night, and could not see him; and when lastly, upon his insisting, in a positive and angry manner, to see them, they came to greet him, whom should he see in their company but the hated Gonerill, who had come to tell her own story, and set her sister against the king their father!

This sight much moved the old man, and still more to see Regan take her by the hand; and he asked Gonerill if she was not ashamed to look upon his old white beard. And Regan advised him to go home again with Gonerill and live with her peaceably, dismissing half of his attendants, and to ask her forgiveness; for he was old and wanted discretion, and must be ruled and led by persons that had more discretion than himself. And Lear showed how preposterous that would sound if he were to down on his knees and beg of his own daughter for food and raiment, and he argued against such an unnatural dependence, declaring his resolution never to return with her, but to stay where he was with Regan, he and his hundred knights; for he said that she had not forgot the half of the kingdom which he had endowed her with, and that her eyes were not fierce like Gonerill's, but mild and kind. And he said that rather than return to Gonerill with half his train cut off, he would go over to France, and beg a wretched pension of the king there, who had married his youngest daughter without a portion.

But he was mistaken in expecting kinder treatment of Regan than he had experienced from her sister Gonerill. As if willing to outdo her sister in unfilial behaviour, she declared that she thought fifty knights too many to wait upon him; that five-and-twenty were enough. Then Lear, nigh heart-broken, turned to Gonerill, and said that he would go back with her, for her fifty doubled five-and-twenty, and so her love was twice as much as Regan's. But Gonerill excused herself and said, what need of so many as five-and-twenty, or even ten, or five, when he might be waited upon by her servants, or her sister's servants? So these two wicked daughters, as if they strove to exceed each other in cruelty to their old father who had been so good to them, by little and little would have abated him of all his train, all respect (little enough for him that once commanded a kingdom) which was left him to show that he had once been a king! Not that a splendid train is essential to happiness, but from a king to a beggar is a hard change, from commanding millions to be without one attendant; and it was the ingratitude in his daughters denying it, more than what he would suffer by the want of it, which pierced this poor old king to the heart; insomuch that, with this double ill-usage and vexation for having so foolishly given away a kingdom, his wits began to be unsettled, and while he said he knew not what, he vowed revenge against those unnatural hags, and to make examples of them that should be a terror to the earth!

While he was thus idly threatening what his weak arm could never execute, night came on, and a loud storm of thunder and lightning with rain; and his daughters still persisting in their resolution not to admit his followers, he called for his horses, and chose rather to encounter the utmost fury of the storm abroad than stay under the same roof with these ungrateful daughters; and they, saying that the injuries which wilful men procure to themselves are their just punishment, suffered him to go in that condition, and shut their doors upon him.

The winds were high, and the rain and storm increased when the old man sallied forth to combat with the elements, less sharp than his daughters' unkindness. For many miles about there was scarce a bush; and there upon a heath, exposed to the fury of the storm in a dark night, did King Lear wander out, and defy the winds and the thunder; and he bid the winds to blow the earth into the sea, or swell the waves of the sea, till they drowned the earth, that no token might remain of any such ungrateful animal as man. The old king was now left with no other companion than the poor fool, who still abided with him, with his merry conceits striving to outjest misfortune, saying, it was but a naughty night to swim in, and truly the king had better go in and ask his daughter's blessing:

> But he that has a little tiny wit,
> With heigh ho, the wind and the rain!
> Must make content with his fortunes fit,
> Though the rain it raineth every day;

and swearing it was a brave night to cool a lady's pride.

Thus poorly accompanied, this once great monarch was found by his ever-faithful servant the good Earl of Kent, now transformed to Caius, who ever followed close at his side, though the king did not know him to be the earl; and he said, "Alas! sir, are you here? Creatures that love night love not such nights as these. This dreadful storm has driven the beasts to their hiding-places. Man's nature cannot endure the affliction or the fear." And Lear rebuked him and said, these lesser evils were not felt where a greater malady was fixed. When the mind is at ease, the body has leisure to be delicate; but the tempest in his mind did take all feeling else from his senses, but of that which beat at his heart. And he spoke of filial ingratitude, and said it was all one as if the mouth should tear the hand for lifting food to it; for parents were hands and food and everything to children.

But the good Caius, still persisting in his entreaties that the king would not stay out in the open air, at last persuaded him to enter a little wretched hovel which stood upon the heath, where the fool first entering suddenly ran back terrified, saying that he had seen a spirit. But upon examination this spirit proved to be nothing more than a poor Bedlam beggar, who had crept into this deserted hovel for shelter, and with his wild talk frightened the fool—one of those poor lunatics who are either mad, or feign to be so, the better to extort charity from the compassionate country people; who go about the country, calling themselves poor Tom and poor Turlygood, saying, "Who gives anything to poor Tom?" sticking pins and nails and sprigs of rosemary into their arms to make them bleed; and with such horrible actions, partly by prayers and partly with lunatic curses, they move or terrify the ignorant country-folks into giving them alms. This poor fellow was such a one; and the king seeing him in so wretched a plight, with nothing but a blanket about his loins to cover his nakedness, could not be persuaded but that the fellow was some father who had given all away to his daughters, and brought himself to that pass; for nothing, he thought, could bring a man to such wretchedness but the having unkind daughters.

And from this and many such wild speeches which he uttered, the good Caius plainly perceived that he was not in his perfect mind, but that his daughters' ill-usage had really made him go mad. And now the loyalty of this worthy Earl of Kent showed itself in more essential services than he had hitherto found opportunity to perform. For with the assistance of some of the king's attendants who remained loyal, he had the person of his royal master removed at daybreak to the castle of Dover, where his own friends and influence, as Earl of Kent, chiefly lay; and himself embarking for France, hastened to the court of Cordelia, and did there in such moving terms represent the pitiful condition of her royal father, and set out in such lively colours the inhumanity of her sisters, that this good and loving child, with many tears, besought the king her husband that he would give her leave to embark for England with a sufficient power to subdue these daughters and their husbands, and restore the king her father to his throne; which being granted she set forth, and with a royal army landed at Dover.

Lear, having by some chance escaped from the guardians which the good Earl of Kent had put over him to take care of him in his lunacy, was found by some of Cordelia's train wandering about the fields near Dover, in a pitiable condition, stark mad and singing aloud to himself, with a crown upon his head which he had made of straw and nettles and other wild weeds that he had picked up in the corn-fields. By the advice of the physicians, Cordelia, though earnestly desirous of seeing her father, was prevailed upon to put off the meeting, till, by sleep and the operation of herbs which they gave him, he should be restored to greater composure. By the aid of these skilful physicians, to whom Cordelia promised all her gold and jewels for the recovery of the old king, Lear was soon in a condition to see his daughter.

A tender sight it was to see the meeting between this father and daughter; to see the struggles between the joy of this poor old king at beholding again his once darling child, and the shame at receiving such filial kindness from her whom he had cast off for so small a fault in his displeasure; both these passions struggling with the remains of his malady, which in his half-crazed brain sometimes made him that he scarce remembered where he was, or who it was that so kindly kissed him and spoke to him; and then he would beg the standers-by not to laugh at him if he were mistaken in thinking this lady to be his daughter Cordelia. And then to see him fall on his knees to beg pardon of his child; and she, good lady, kneeling all the while to ask a blessing of him, and telling him that it did not become him to kneel, but it was her duty, for she was his child, his true and very child Cordelia. And she kissed him, as she said, to kiss away all her sisters' unkindness, and said that they might be ashamed of themselves to turn their old kind father, with his white beard, out into the cold air, when her enemy's dog, though it had bit her (as she prettily expressed it), should have stayed by her fire such a night as that, and warmed himself. And she told her father how she had come from France with purpose to bring him assistance; and he said, that she must forget and forgive, for he was old and foolish, and did not know what he did; but that, to be sure, she had great cause not to love him, but her sisters had none. And Cordelia said that she had no cause, no more than they had.

So we will leave this old king in the protection of this dutiful and loving child, where, by the help of sleep and medicine, she and her physicians at length succeeded in winding up the untuned and jarring senses which the cruelty of his other daughters had so violently shaken. Let us return to say a word or two about those cruel daughters.

These monsters of ingratitude, who had been so false to their own father, could not be expected to prove more faithful to their own husbands. They soon grew tired of paying even the appearance of duty and affection, and in an open way showed they had fixed their loves upon another. It happened that the object of their guilty loves was the same. It was Edmund, a natural son of the late Earl of Gloucester, who by his treacheries had succeeded in disinheriting his brother Edgar, the lawful heir, from his earldom, and by his wicked practices was now earl himself: a wicked man, and a fit object for the love of such wicked creatures as Gonerill and Regan. It falling out about this time that the Duke of Cornwall, Regan's husband, died, Regan immediately declared her intention of wedding this Earl of Gloucester, which rousing the jealousy of her sister, to whom as well as to Regan this wicked earl had at sundry times professed love, Gonerill found means to make away with her sister by poison; but being detected in her practices, and imprisoned by her husband, the Duke of Albany, for this deed, and for her guilty passion for the earl which had come to his ears, she, in a fit of disappointed love and rage, shortly put an end to her own life. Thus the justice of Heaven at last overtook these wicked daughters.

While the eyes of all men were upon this event, admiring the justice displayed in their deserved deaths, the same eyes were suddenly taken off from this sight to admire at the mysterious ways of the same Power in the melancholy fate of the young and virtuous daughter, the lady Cordelia, whose good deeds did seem to deserve a more fortunate conclusion; but it is an awful truth that innocence and piety are not always successful in this world. The forces which Gonerill and Regan had sent out, under the command of the bad Earl of Gloucester, were victorious, and Cordelia, by the practices of this wicked earl, who did not like that any should stand between him and the throne, ended her life in prison. Thus Heaven took this innocent lady to itself in her young years, after showing her to the world an illustrious example of filial duty. Lear did not long survive this kind child.

Before he died, the good Earl of Kent, who had still attended his old master's steps from the first of his daughters' ill-usage to this sad period of his decay, cried to make him understand that it was he who had followed him under the name of Caius, but Lear's care-crazed brain at that time could not comprehend how that could be, or how Kent and Caius could be the same person; so Kent thought it needless to trouble him with explanations at such a time; and Lear soon after expiring, this faithful servant to the king, between age and grief for his old master's vexations, soon followed him to the grave.

How the judgment of Heaven overtook the bad Earl of Gloucester, whose treasons were discovered, and himself slain in single combat with his brother the lawful earl, and how Gonerill's husband, the Duke of Albany, who was innocent of the death of Cordelia, and had never encouraged his lady in her wicked proceedings against her father, ascended the throne of Britain after the death of Lear, is needless here to narrate, Lear and his three daughters being dead, whose adventures alone concern our story.

Othello

Brabantio, the rich senator of Venice, had a fair daughter, the gentle Desdemona. She was sought, too, by diverse suitors, both on account of her many virtuous qualities and for her rich expectations. But among the suitors of her own clime and complexion she saw none whom she could affect; for this noble lady, who regarded the mind more than the features of men, with a singularity rather to be admired than imitated, had chosen for the object of her affections a Moor, a black, whom her father loved, and often invited to his house.

Neither is Desdemona to be altogether condemned for the unsuitableness of the person whom she selected for her lover. Bating that Othello was black, the noble Moor wanted nothing which might recommend him to the affections of the greatest lady. He was a soldier, and a brave one, and by his conduct in fierce wars against the Turks had risen to the rank of general in the Venetian service, and was esteemed and trusted by the State.

He had been a traveller, and Desdemona (as is the manner of ladies) loved to hear him tell the story of his adventures, which he would run through from his earliest recollection; the battles, sieges, and encounters which he had passed through; the perils he had been exposed to by land and by water; his hairbreadth escapes when he had entered a breach, or marched up to the mouth of a cannon; and how he had been taken prisoner by the insolent enemy, and sold to slavery; how he demeaned himself in that state, and how he escaped; all these accounts, added to the narration of the strange things he had seen in foreign countries, the vast wildernesses and romantic caverns, the quarries, the rocks and mountains, whose heads are in the clouds; of the savage nations, the cannibals who are man-eaters, and a race of people in Africa whose heads do grow beneath their shoulders; these travellers' stories would so enchain the attention of Desdemona, that if she were called off at any time by household affairs, she would despatch with all haste that business, and return, and with a greedy ear devour Othello's discourse. And once he took advantage of a pliant hour, and drew from her a prayer that he would tell her the whole story of his life at large, of which she had learned so much, but only by parts; to which he consented, and beguiled her of many a tear, when he spoke of some distressful stroke which his youth suffered.

His story being done, she gave him for his pains a world of sighs; she vowed that it was all passing strange, and pitiful, wondrous pitiful; she wished, she said, she had not heard it, yet she wished that Heaven had made her such a man; and then she thanked him, and told him if he had a friend who loved her, he had only to teach him how to tell his story, and that would woo her. Upon this hint, delivered with not more frankness than modesty, accompanied with a certain bewitching prettiness and blushes, which Othello could not but understand, he spoke more openly of his love, and in this golden opportunity gained the consent of the generous lady Desdemona privately to marry him.

Neither Othello's colour nor his fortune were such that it could be hoped Brabantio would accept him for a son-in-law. He had left his daughter free; but he did expect that, as the manner of noble Venetian ladies was, she would choose ere long a husband of senatorial rank or expectations. But in this he was deceived; Desdemona loved the Moor, though he was black, and devoted her heart and fortunes to his valiant parts and qualities; so was her heart subdued to an implicit devotion to the man she had selected for a husband, that his very colour, which to all but this discerning lady would have proved an insurmountable objection, was by her esteemed above all the white skins and clear complexions of the young Venetian nobility, her suitors.

Their marriage, which, though privately carried out, could not long be kept a secret, came to the ears of the old man Brabantio, who appeared in a solemn council of the senate as an accuser of the Moor Othello, who by spells and witchcraft, he maintained, had seduced the affections of the fair Desdemona to marry him without the consent of her father, and against the obligations of hospitality.

At this juncture of time it happened that the state of Venice had immediate need of the services of Othello, news having arrived that the Turks, with mighty preparation, had fitted out a fleet, which was bending its course to the Island of Cyprus, with intent to regain that strong post from the Venetians, who then held it. In this emergency the State turned its eyes upon Othello, who alone was deemed adequate to conduct the defence of Cyprus against the Turks. So that Othello, now summoned before the senate, stood in their presence at once as a candidate for a great State employment, and as a culprit, charged with offences which by the laws of Venice were made capital.

The age and senatorial character of old Brabantio commanded a most patient hearing from that grave assembly; but the incensed father conducted his accusations with so much intemperance, producing likelihoods and allegations for proofs, that when Othello was called upon for his defence he had only to relate a plain tale of the course of his love, which he did with such an artless eloquence, recounting the whole story of his wooing, as we have related it above, and delivered his speech with so noble a plainness (the evidence of truth), that the duke, who sat as chief judge, could not help confessing that a tale so told would have won his daughter too; and the spells and conjurations which Othello had used in his courtship plainly appeared to have been no more than the honest arts of men in love, and the only witchcraft which he had used, the faculty of telling a soft tale to win a lady's ear.

This statement of Othello was confirmed by the testimony of the lady Desdemona herself, who appeared in court, and professing a duty to her father for life and education, challenged leave of him to profess a yet higher duty to her lord and husband, even so much as her mother had shown in preferring him (Brabantio) above her father.

The old senator, unable to maintain his plea, called the Moor to him with many expressions of sorrow, and, as an act of necessity, bestowed upon him his daughter, whom, if he had been free to withhold her, he told him, he would with all his heart have kept from him, adding that he was glad at soul that he had no other child, for this behaviour of Desdemona would have taught him to be a tyrant, and hang clogs on them for her desertion.

This difficulty being got over, Othello, to whom custom had rendered the hardships of a military life as natural as food and rest are to other men, readily undertook the management of the wars in Cyprus; and Desdemona, preferring the honour of her lord (though with danger) before the indulgence of those idle delights in which new-married people usually waste their time, cheerfully consented to his going.

No sooner were Othello and his lady landed in Cyprus than news arrived that a desperate tempest had dispersed the Turkish fleet, and thus the island was secure from any immediate apprehension of an attack. But the war which Othello was to suffer was now beginning, and the enemies which malice stirred up against his innocent lady proved in their nature more deadly than strangers or infidels.

Among all the general's friends no one possessed the confidence of Othello more entirely than Cassio. Michael Cassio was a young soldier, a Florentine, gay, amiable, and of pleasing address, favourite qualities with women; he was handsome and eloquent, and exactly such a person as might alarm the jealousy of a man advanced in years (as Othello in some measure was), who had married a young and beautiful wife; but Othello was as free from jealousy as he was noble, and as incapable of suspecting as of doing a base action. He had employed this Cassio in his love affair with Desdemona, and Cassio had been a sort of go-between in his suit; for Othello, fearing that himself had not those soft parts of conversation which please ladies, and finding these qualities in his friend, would often depute Cassio to go, as he phrased it, a-courting for him—such innocent simplicity being an honour rather than a blemish to the character of the valiant Moor. So that no wonder if, next to Othello himself (but at far distance as beseems a virtuous wife), the gentle Desdemona loved and trusted Cassio. Nor had the marriage of this couple made any difference in their behaviour to Michael Cassio. He frequented their house, and his free and rattling talk was no unpleasing variety to Othello, who was himself of a more serious temper; for such tempers are observed often to delight in their contraries, as a relief from the oppressive excess of their own; and Desdemona and Cassio would talk and laugh together, as in the days when he went a-courting for his friend.

Othello had lately promoted Cassio to be the lieutenant, a place of trust, and nearest to the general's person. This promotion gave great offence to Iago, an older officer, who thought he had a better claim than Cassio, and would often ridicule Cassio, as a fellow fit only for the company of ladies, and one that knew no more of the art of war, or how to set an army in array for battle, than a girl. Iago hated Cassio, and he hated Othello, as well for favouring Cassio, as for an unjust suspicion, which he had lightly taken up against Othello, that the Moor was too fond of Iago's wife Emilia. From these imaginary provocations the plotting mind of Iago conceived a horrid scheme of revenge, which should involve both Cassio, the Moor, and Desdemona in one common ruin.

Iago was artful, and had studied human nature deeply, and he knew that of all the torments which afflict the mind of man (and far beyond bodily torture) the pains of jealousy were the most intolerable, and had the sorest sting. If he could succeed in making Othello jealous of Cassio, he thought it would be an exquisite plot of revenge, and might end in the death of Cassio or Othello, or both; he cared not.

The arrival of the general and his lady in Cyprus, meeting with the news of the dispersion of the enemy's fleet, made a sort of holiday in the island. Everybody gave themselves up to feasting and making merry.

Cassio had the direction of the guard that night, with a charge from Othello to keep the soldiers from excess in drinking, that no brawl might arise to fright the inhabitants, or disgust them with the newly-landed forces. That night Iago began his deep-laid plans of mischief. Under cover of loyalty and love to the general, he enticed Cassio to make rather too free with the bottle (a great fault in an officer upon guard). Cassio for a time resisted, but he could not long hold out against the honest freedom which Iago knew how to put on, but kept swallowing glass after glass (as Iago still plied him with drink and encouraging songs), and Cassio's tongue ran over in praise of the lady Desdemona, whom he again and again toasted, affirming that she was a most exquisite lady, until at last the enemy which he put into his mouth stole away his brains; and upon some provocation given him by a fellow whom Iago had set on, swords were drawn, and Montano, a worthy officer who interfered to appease the dispute, was wounded in the scuffle. The riot now began to be general and Iago, who had set on foot the mischief, was foremost in spreading the alarm, causing the castle-bell to be rung (as if some dangerous mutiny, instead of a slight drunken quarrel, had arisen). The alarm-bell ringing awakened Othello, who, dressing in a hurry, and coming to the scene of action, questioned Cassio of the cause. Cassio was now come to himself, the effect of the wine having a little gone off, but was too much ashamed to reply; and Iago, pretending a great reluctance to accuse Cassio, but as it were forced into it by Othello, who insisted to know the truth, gave an account of the whole matter (leaving out his own share in it, which Cassio was too far gone to remember) in such a manner, as while he seemed to make Cassio's offence less, did indeed make it appear greater than it was. The result was, that Othello, who was a strict observer of discipline, was compelled to take away Cassio's place of lieutenant from him.

Thus did Iago's first artifice succeed completely: he had now undermined his hated rival, and thrust him out of his place; but a further use was hereafter to be made of the adventure of this disastrous night.

Cassio, whom this misfortune had entirely sobered, now lamented to his seeming friend Iago that he should have been such a fool as to transform himself into a beast. He was undone, for how could he ask the general for his place again; he would tell him he was a drunkard. He despised himself. Iago, affecting to make light of it, said that he or any man living might be drunk upon occasion; it remained now to make the best of a bad bargain; the general's wife was now the general, and could do anything with Othello; that he were best to apply to the Lady Desdemona to mediate for him with her lord; that she was of a frank, obliging disposition and would readily undertake a good office of this sort, and set Cassio right again in the general's favour; and then this crack in their love would be made stronger than ever—a good advice of Iago, if it had not been given for wicked purposes, which will after appear.

Cassio did as Iago advised him, and made application to the Lady Desdemona, who was easy to be won over in any honest suit; and she promised Cassio that she would be his solicitor with her lord, and rather die than give up his cause. This she immediately set about in so earnest and pretty a manner, that Othello, who was mortally offended with Cassio, could not put her off. When he pleaded delay, and that it was too soon to pardon such an offender, she would not be beat back, but insisted that it should be the next night, or the morning after, or the next morning to that at farthest. Then she showed how penitent and humbled poor Cassio was, and that his offence did not deserve so sharp a check. And when Othello still hung back, "What! my lord," said she, "that I should have so much to do to plead for Cassio, Michael Cassio, that came a-courting for you, and oftentimes when I have spoken in dispraise of you, has taken your part? I count this but a little thing to ask of you. When I mean to try your love indeed I shall ask a weighty matter." Othello could deny nothing to such a pleader, and only requesting that Desdemona would leave the time to him, promised to receive Michael Cassio again into favour.

It happened that Othello and Iago had entered into the room where Desdemona was just as Cassio, who had been imploring her intercession, was departing at the opposite door; and Iago who was full of art, said in a low voice, as if to himself, "I like not that." Othello took no great notice of what he said; indeed, the conference which immediately took place with his lady put it out of his head, but he remembered it afterwards. For when Desdemona was gone, Iago, as if for mere satisfaction of his thought, questioned Othello whether Michael Cassio, when Othello was courting his lady, knew of his love. To this the general answering in the affirmative, and adding, that he had gone between them very often during the courtship, Iago knitted his brow, as if he had got fresh light of some terrible matter, and cried, "Indeed!" This brought into Othello's mind the words which Iago had let fall upon entering the room, and seeing Cassio with Desdemona; and he began to think there was some meaning in all this; for he deemed Iago to be a just man, and full of love and honesty, and what in a false knave would be tricks, in him seemed to be the natural workings of an honest mind, big with something too great for utterance, and Othello prayed Iago to speak what he knew, and to give his worst thoughts words. "And what," said Iago, "if some thoughts very vile should have intruded into my breast, as where is the palace into which foul things do not enter?" Then Iago went on to say, what a pity it were if any trouble should arise to Othello out of his imperfect observations; that it would not be for Othello's peace to know his thoughts; that people's good names were not to be taken away for slight suspicions; and when

Othello's curiosity was raised almost to distraction with these hints and scattered words, Iago, as if in earnest care for Othello's peace of mind, besought him to beware of jealousy. With such art did this villain raise suspicions in the unguarded Othello, by the very caution which he pretended to give him against suspicion. "I know," said Othello, "that my wife is fair, loves company and feasting, is free of speech, sings, plays, and dances well; but where virtue is, these qualities are virtuous. I must have proof before I think her dishonest." Then Iago, as if glad that Othello was slow to believe ill of his lady, frankly declared that he had no proof, but begged Othello to observe her behaviour well when Cassio was by, not to be jealous nor too secure neither, for that he (Iago) knew the dispositions of the Italian ladies, his countrywomen, better than Othello could do. Then he artfully insinuated that Desdemona deceived her father in marrying with Othello, and carried it so closely that the poor old man thought that witchcraft had been used. Othello was much moved with this argument, which brought the matter home to him, for if she had deceived her father, why might she not deceive her husband?

Iago begged pardon for having moved him; but Othello, assuming an indifference, while he was really shaken with inward grief at Iago's words begged him to go on, which Iago did with many apologies, as if unwilling to produce anything against Cassio, whom he called his friend. He then came strongly to the point, and reminded Othello how Desdemona had refused many suitable matches of her own clime and complexion, and had married him, a Moor, which showed unnatural in her, and proved her to have a headstrong will; and when her better judgment returned, how probable it was she should fall upon comparing Othello with the fine forms and clear white complexions of the young Italians her countrymen. He concluded with advising Othello to put off his reconcilement with Cassio a little longer, and in the meanwhile to note with what earnestness Desdemona should intercede in his behalf, for that much would be seen in that; so mischievously did this artful villain lay his plots to turn the gentle qualities of this innocent lady into her destruction, and make a net for her out of her own goodness to entrap her—first setting Cassio on to entreat her mediation, and then, out of that very mediation, contriving stratagems for her ruin.

The conference ended with Iago's begging Othello to account his wife innocent until he had more decisive proof, and Othello promised to be patient, but from that moment the deceived Othello never tasted content of mind. Poppy, nor the juice of mandragora, nor all the sleeping potions in the world, could ever again restore to him that sweet rest which he had enjoyed but yesterday. His occupation sickened upon him. He no longer took delight in arms. His heart, that used to be roused at the sight of troops, and banners, and battle-array, and would stir and leap at the sound of a drum, or a trumpet, or a neighing war-horse, seemed to have lost all that pride and ambition, which are a soldier's virtue, and his military ardour and all his old joys forsook him. Sometimes he thought his wife honest, and at times he thought her not so; sometimes he thought Iago just, and at times he thought him not so; then he would wish that he had never known of it; he was not the worse for her loving Cassio, so long as he knew it not. Torn in pieces with these distracting thoughts, he once laid hold on Iago's throat, and demanded proof of Desdemona's guilt, or threatened instant death for his having belied her. Iago, feigning indignation that his honesty should be taken for a vice, asked Othello if he had not sometimes seen a handkerchief spotted with strawberries in his wife's hand. Othello answered that he had given her such a one, and that it was his first gift. "That same handkerchief," said Iago, "did I see Michael Cassio wipe his face with." "If it be as you say," said Othello, "I will not rest till a wide revenge swallow them up; and first, for a token of your fidelity, I expect that Cassio shall be put to death within three days; and for that fair wretch (meaning his lady), I will withdraw and devise some swift means of death for her."

Trifles light as air are to the jealous proofs as strong as holy writ. A handkerchief of his wife's seen in Cassio's hand was motive enough to the deluded Othello to pass sentence of death upon them both, without once inquiring how Cassio came by it. Desdemona had never given such a present to Cassio, nor would this constant lady have wronged her lord with doing so naughty a thing as giving his presents to another man; both Cassio and Desdemona were innocent of any offence against Othello; but the wicked Iago, whose spirits never slept in contrivance of villainy, had made his wife (a good but a weak woman) steal this handkerchief from Desdemona, under pretence of getting the work copied, but in reality to drop it in Cassio's way, where he might find it, and give a handle to Iago's suggestion that it was Desdemona's present.

Othello, soon after meeting his wife, pretended that he had a headache (as he might indeed with truth), and desired her to lend him her handkerchief to hold his temples. She did so. "Not this," said Othello, "but that handkerchief I gave you." Desdemona had it not about her (for indeed it was stolen as we have related).

"How," said Othello; "this is a fault indeed. That handkerchief an Egyptian woman gave to my mother; the woman was a witch and could read people's thoughts; she told my mother while she kept it it would make her amiable, and my father would love her; but if she lost it or gave it away, my father's fancy would turn, and he would loathe her as much as he had loved her. She dying, gave it me, and bade me, if I ever married, to give it to my wife. I did so; take heed of it. Make it a darling as precious as your eye." "Is it possible?" said the frighted lady. "'Tis true," continued Othello; "It is a magical handkerchief; a sibyl, that had lived in the world two hundred years, in a fit of prophetic fury worked it, the silk-worms that furnished the silk were hallowed, and it was dyed in mummy of maidens' hearts conserved." Desdemona, hearing the wondrous virtues of the handkerchief, was ready to die with fear, for she plainly perceived she had lost it, and with it she feared the affections of her husband. Then Othello started, and looked as if he were going to do some rash thing, and still he demanded the handkerchief, which, when she could not produce, she tried to divert her husband from too serious thoughts, and cheerfully told him she saw all his talk about the handkerchief was only to put her off from her suit about Michael Cassio, whom she went on to praise (as Iago had foretold), till Othello, in perfect distraction, burst out of the room, and then Desdemona, though unwillingly, began to suspect her lord was jealous.

What cause she could have ministered to him she knew not, and then she accused herself for accusing the noble Othello, and thought, to be sure, that some untoward news from Venice or some State troubles had puddled his spirits and made his temper not so sweet as formerly. And she said, "Men are not gods, and we must not look for that observance from them when they are married which they show us on the bridal day." And she beshrewed herself for so unkindly judging of his unkindness.

Again Othello and Desdemona met, and he accused her more plainly of being unfaithful and of loving another man, but he did not name whom; and Othello wept, and Desdemona said, "Alas, the heavy day! why do you weep?" And Othello told her he could have borne all sorts of evils with fortitude—poverty, and disease, and disgrace—but her infidelity had broken his heart, and he called her a weed that looked so fair, and smelled so sweet, that the sense ached at it, and wished she had never been born. And when he had left her, this innocent lady was so stupefied with wonder at her lord's untrue suspicion of her that a weight-like sleep came over her, and she only desired her attendant to make her bed, and to lay her wedding-sheets upon it, saying that when people teach their babes they do it by gentle means and easy tasks, and Othello might have chided her so, for in good faith she was but a child when she was chidden. And this was all the complaint which this gentle lady made.

Desdemona being retired to bed, expecting her lord would follow her, soon fell into a slumber, the effect of her troubled spirits, when Othello entered the chamber full of the black purpose which he had meditated of putting his lady to death; but when he saw her asleep he thought he would not shed her blood, nor scar that white skin of hers, more white than alalabaster. But he was resolved she should die, else, as he said, she would live to betray more men as she had done him; then he kissed her for the last time, as he said, and that kiss was so sweet he must needs kiss her again, and he wept, but he said they were cruel tears.

Desdemona was awakened with his kisses, and she looked upon Othello, and she saw him gnaw his underlip and roll his eyes, and she knew he was always fatal when he looked so; and he bade her prepare for death, and to say her prayers, for he would not kill her soul. And this innocent wife, as she lay at his mercy, begged for compassion and to know her fault; and then he named Cassio, and the handkerchief which, he said, she had given him; and as the guiltless lady was proceeding to clear herself, he suddenly would hear no more, but covering her up in the bedclothes, stifled her till she died.

In this instant of time was brought into the house Cassio, wounded and bleeding, whom Iago had set one of his creatures on to assassinate; but the fellow not succeeding in his attempt to kill Cassio (whom he wounded, but not mortally), and being himself killed by Iago to prevent discovery, in his pockets were found certain letters which made the guilt of Iago and the innocence of Cassio clear beyond all doubt; and Cassio now came to beg pardon of Othello, and to ask wherein he had offended him that he had employed Iago to murder him.

This discovery was as a thunderstroke to Othello, who now plainly saw that he was no better than a murderer, and that his wife (poor innocent lady) had been ever faithful to him; the extreme anguish of which discovery making life insupportable, he fell upon his sword, and, throwing himself upon the body of his dear injured lady, expired.

These rash acts raised much passion of horror and amazement in the bystanders, for Othello had borne a fair reputation, and till he was wrought upon by the arts of a villain which his own noble nature never gave him leave to suspect, he was a loving and doting husband. He had loved, not wisely, but too well; and his manly eyes, when he learned his mistake, though not used to weep on every small occasion, dropped tears as fast as the Arabian trees their gum. And when he was dead all his former merits and his valiant acts were remembered. Nothing now remained for his successor but to put the utmost censure of the law in force against Iago, who was executed with strict tortures, and to send word to the State of Venice of the lamentable death of their renowned general.

Macbeth

When Duncan the Meek reigned king of Scotland, there lived a great thane, or lord, called Macbeth. This Macbeth was a near kinsman to the king, and in great esteem at court for his valour and conduct in the wars, an example of which he had lately given in defeating a rebel army, assisted by the troops of Norway, in terrible numbers.

The two Scottish generals, Macbeth and Banquo, returning victorious from this great battle, their way lay over a blasted heath, where they were stopped by the strange appearance of three figures like women, except that they had beards, and their withered skins and wild attire made them look not like any earthly creatures. Macbeth first addressed them, when they, seemingly offended, laid each one her choppy finger upon her skinny lips, in token of silence, and the first of them saluted Macbeth with the title of Thane of Glamis. The general was not a little startled to find himself known by such creatures, but how much more, when the second of them followed up that salute by giving him the title of Thane of Cawdor, to which honour he had no pretensions; and again the third bid him "All hail! king that shall be hereafter!" Such a prophetic greeting might well amaze him, who knew that while the king's sons lived he could not hope to succeed to the throne. Then, turning to Banquo, they pronounced him, in a sort of riddling terms, to be *lesser than Macbeth and greater! not so happy, but much happier*! and prophesied that though he should never reign yet his sons after him should be kings in Scotland. They then turned into air and vanished, by which the generals knew them to be the weird sisters, or witches.

While they stood pondering on the strangeness of this adventure, there arrived certain messengers from the king, who were empowered by him to confer upon Macbeth the dignity of Thane of Cawdor. An event so miraculously corresponding with the prediction of the witches astonished Macbeth, and he stood wrapped in amazement, unable to make reply to the messengers; and in that point of time swelling hopes arose in his mind that the prediction of the third witch might in like manner have its accomplishment, and that he should one day reign king in Scotland.

Turning to Banquo, he said, "Do you not hope that your children shall be kings, when what the witches promised to me has so wonderfully come to pass?" "That hope," answered the general, "might enkindle you to aim at the throne; but oftentimes these ministers of darkness tell us truths in little things to betray us into deeds of greatest consequence."

But the wicked suggestions of the witches had sunk too deep into the mind of Macbeth to allow him to attend to the warnings of the good Banquo. From that time he bent all his thoughts how to compass the throne of Scotland.

Macbeth had a wife, to whom he communicated the strange prediction of the weird sisters, and its partial accomplishment. She was a bad, ambitious woman, and so long as her husband and herself could arrive at greatness, she cared not much by what means. She spurred on the reluctant purpose of Macbeth, who felt compunction at the thoughts of blood, and did not cease to represent the murder of the king as a step absolutely necessary to the fulfilment of the flattering prophecy.

It happened at this time that the king, who out of his royal condescension would oftentimes visit his principal nobility upon gracious terms, came to Macbeth's house, attended by his two sons, Malcolm and Donalbain, and a numerous train of thanes and attendants, the more to honour Macbeth for the triumphal success of his wars.

The castle of Macbeth was pleasantly situated, and the air about it was sweet and wholesome, which appeared by the nests which the martlet or swallow had built under all the jutting friezes and buttresses of the building, wherever it found a place of advantage; for where those birds most breed and haunt, the air is observed to be delicate. The king entered well pleased with the place, and not less so with the attentions and respect of his honoured hostess, Lady Macbeth, who had the art of covering treacherous purposes with smiles, and could look like the innocent flower, while she was indeed the serpent under it.

The king, being tired with his journey, went early to bed, and in his state-room two grooms of his chamber, as was the custom, slept beside him. He had been unusually pleased with his reception, and had made presents before he retired to his principal officers, and among the rest had sent a rich diamond to Lady Macbeth, greeting her by the name of his most kind hostess.

Now was the middle of night, when over half the world nature seems dead, and wicked dreams abuse men's minds asleep, and none but the wolf and the murderer is abroad. This was the time when Lady Macbeth waked to plot the murder of the king. She would not have undertaken a deed so abhorrent to her sex, but that she feared her husband's nature, that it was too full of the milk of human kindness to do a contrived murder. She knew him to be ambitious, but withal to be scrupulous, and not yet prepared for that height of crime which commonly in the end accompanies inordinate ambition. She had won him to consent to the murder, but she doubted his resolution, and she feared that the natural tenderness of his disposition (more humane than her own) would come between and defeat the purpose. So with her own hands, armed with a dagger, she approached the king's bed, having taken care to ply the grooms of his chamber so with wine that they slept intoxicated, and careless of their charge. There lay Duncan in a sound sleep after the fatigues of his journey, and as she viewed him earnestly, there was something in his face, as he slept, which resembled her own father, and she had not the courage to proceed.

She returned to confer with her husband. His resolution had begun to stagger. He considered that there were strong reasons against the deed. In the first place, he was not only a subject, but a near kinsman to the king; and he had been his host and entertainer that day, whose duty, by the laws of hospitality, it was to shut the door against his murderers, not bear the knife himself. Then he considered how just and merciful a king this Duncan had been, how clear of offence to his subjects, how loving to his nobility, and in particular to him; that such kings are the peculiar care of Heaven, and their subjects doubly bound to revenge their deaths; besides, by the favours of the king, Macbeth stood high in the opinion of all sorts of men, and how would those honours be stained by the reputation of so foul a murder!

In these conflicts of the mind, Lady Macbeth found her husband, inclining to the better part, and resolving to proceed no farther. But she, being a woman not easily shaken from her evil purpose, began to pour in at his ears words which infused a portion of her own spirit into his mind, assigning reason upon reason why he should not shrink from what he had undertaken; how easy the deed was, how soon it would be over, and how the action of one short night would give to all their nights and days to come a sovereign sway and royalty! Then she threw contempt on his change of purpose, and accused him of fickleness and cowardice, and declared that she had given suck, and knew how tender it was to love the babe that fondled her, but she would, while it was smiling in her face, have plucked it from her breast and dashed its brains out if she had so sworn to do it, as he had sworn to perform that murder. Then she added, how practicable it was to lay the guilt of the deed upon the drunken, sleepy grooms. And with the valour of her tongue she so chastised his sluggish resolutions, that he once more summoned up courage to the bloody business.

So, taking the dagger in his hand, he softly stole in the dark to the room where Duncan lay; and as he went, he thought he saw another dagger in the air, with the handle towards him, and on the blade and at the point of it drops of blood; but when he tried to grasp at it, it was nothing but air, a mere phantasm proceeding from his own hot and oppressed brain and the business he had in hand.

Getting rid of this fear he entered the king's room, whom he despatched with one stroke of his dagger. Just as he had done the murder one of the grooms who slept in the chamber laughed in his sleep, and the other cried "Murder", which woke them both; but they said a short prayer. One of them said, "God bless us!" and the other answered, "Amen," and addressed themselves to sleep again. Macbeth, who stood listening to them, tried to say "Amen" when the fellow said "God bless us!" but though he had most need of a blessing, the word stuck in his throat, and he could not pronounce it.

Again he thought he heard a voice which cried, "Sleep no more! Macbeth doth murder sleep, the innocent sleep that nourishes life!" Still it cried, "Sleep no more!" to all the house. "Glamis hath murdered sleep, and therefore Cawdor shall sleep no more, Macbeth shall sleep no more!"

With such horrible imaginations Macbeth returned to his listening wife, who began to think he had failed of his purpose, and that the deed was somehow frustrated. He came in so distracted a state that she reproached him with his want of firmness, and sent him to wash his hands of the blood which stained them, while she took his dagger with purpose to stain the cheeks of the grooms with blood, to make it seem their guilt. Morning came, and with it the discovery of the murder, which could not be concealed; and though Macbeth and his lady made great show of grief, and the proofs against the grooms (the dagger being produced against them and their faces smeared with blood) were sufficiently strong, yet the entire suspicion fell upon Macbeth, whose inducements to such a deed were so much more forcible than such poor silly grooms could be supposed to have; and Duncan's two sons fled. Malcolm, the eldest, sought for refuge in the English court; and the youngest, Donalbain, made his escape to Ireland.

The king's sons, who should have succeeded him, having thus vacated the throne, Macbeth, as next heir, was crowned king, and thus the prediction of the weird sisters was literally accomplished.

Though placed so high, Macbeth and his queen could not forget the prophecy of the weird sisters that, though Macbeth should be king, yet not his children, but the children of Banquo should be kings after him. The thought of this, and that they had defiled their hands with blood and done so great crimes only to place the posterity of Banquo upon the throne, so rankled within them, that they determined to put to death both Banquo and his son, to make void the predictions of the weird sisters, which in their own case had been so remarkably brought to pass.

For this purpose they made a great supper, to which they invited all the chief thanes, and among the rest, with marks of particular respect, Banquo and his son Fleance were invited. The way by which Banquo was to pass to the palace at night was beset by murderers appointed by Macbeth, who stabbed Banquo; but in the scuffle Fleance escaped. From that Fleance descended a race of monarchs who afterwards filled the Scottish throne, ending with James the Sixth of Scotland and the First of England, under whom the two crowns of England and Scotland were united.

At supper the queen, whose manners were in the highest degree affable and royal, played the hostess with a gracefulness and attention which conciliated every one present, and Macbeth discoursed freely with his thanes and nobles, saying that all that was honourable in the country was under his roof if he had but his good friend Banquo present, whom yet he hoped he should rather have to chide for neglect than to lament for any mischance. Just at these words the ghost of Banquo, whom he had caused to be murdered, entered the room and placed himself on the chair which Macbeth was about to occupy. Though Macbeth was a bold man, and one who could have faced death without trembling, at this horrible sight his cheeks turned white with fear, and he stood quite unmanned with his eyes fixed upon the ghost. His queen and all the nobles, who saw nothing, but perceived him gazing, as they thought, upon an empty chair, took it for a fit of distraction, and she reproached him, whispering that it was but the same fancy which had made him see the dagger in the air when he was about to kill Duncan. But Macbeth continued to see the ghost and gave no heed to all they could say, while he addressed it with distracted words, yet so significant, that his queen, fearing the dreadful secret would be disclosed, in great haste dismissed the guests, excusing the infirmity of Macbeth as a disorder he was often troubled with.

To such dreadful fancies Macbeth was subject. His queen and he had their sleeps afflicted with terrible dreams, and the blood of Banquo troubled them not more than the escape of Fleance, whom now they looked upon as father to a line of kings who should keep their posterity out of the throne. With these miserable thoughts they found no peace, and Macbeth determined once more to seek out the weird sisters, and know from them the worst.

He sought them in a cave upon the heath where they, who knew by foresight of his coming, were engaged in preparing their dreadful charms by which they conjured up infernal spirits to reveal to them futurity. Their horrid ingredients were toads, bats, and serpents, the eye of a newt, and the tongue of a dog, the leg of a lizard, and the wing of the night-owl, the scale of a dragon, the tooth of a wolf, the maw of the ravenous salt-sea shark, the mummy of a witch, the root of the poisonous hemlock (this to have effect must be digged in the dark), the gall of a goat, and the liver of a Jew, with slips of the yew-tree that roots itself in graves, and the finger of a dead child; all these were set on to boil in a great kettle or caldron which, as fast as it grew too hot, was cooled with a baboon's blood. To these they poured in the blood of a sow that had eaten her young, and they threw into the flame the grease that had sweaten from a murderer's gibbet. By these charms they bound the infernal spirits to answer their questions.

It was demanded of Macbeth whether he would have his doubts resolved by them or by their masters, the spirits. He, nothing daunted by the dreadful ceremonies which he saw, boldly answered, "Where are they?—let me see them." And they called the spirits, which were three. And the first arose in the likeness of an armed head, and he called Macbeth by name and bid him beware of the Thane of Fife, for which caution Macbeth thanked him, for Macbeth had entertained a jealousy of Macduff, the Thane of Fife.

And the second spirit arose in the likeness of a bloody child, and he called Macbeth by name, and bid him have no fear, but laugh to scorn the power of man, for none of woman born should have power to hurt him; and he advised him to be fierce, bold, and resolute. "Then live, Macduff!" cried the king; "what need I fear of thee? But yet I will make assurance doubly sure. Thou shalt not live, that I may tell pale-hearted Fear it lies, and sleep in spite of thunder." That spirit being dismissed, a third arose in the form of a child crowned, with a tree in his hand. He called Macbeth by name, and comforted him against conspiracies, saying that he should never be vanquished until the wood of Birnam to Dunsinane Hill should come against him. "Sweet bodements, good!" cried Macbeth; "who can unfix the forest, and move it from its earthbound roots? I see I shall live the usual period of man's life, and not be cut off by a violent death. But my heart throbs to know one thing. Tell me, if your art can tell so much, if Banquo's issue shall ever reign in this kingdom?" Here the caldron sunk into the ground, and a noise of music was heard, and eight shadows, like kings, passed by Macbeth, and Banquo last, who bore a glass which showed the figures of many more, and Banquo all bloody smiled upon Macbeth, and pointed to them, by which Macbeth knew that these were the posterity of Banquo, who should reign after him in Scotland; and the witches, with a sound of soft music and with dancing, making a show of duty and welcome to Macbeth, vanished, and from this time the thoughts of Macbeth were all sanguinary and dreadful.

The first thing he heard when he got out of the witches' cave was that Macduff, Thane of Fife, had fled to England to join the army which was forming against him under Malcolm, the eldest son of the late king, with intent to displace Macbeth and set Malcolm the right heir, upon the throne. Macbeth, stung with rage, set upon the castle of Macduff, and put his wife and children, whom the thane had left behind, to the sword, and extended the slaughter to all who claimed the least relationship to Macduff.

These and such like deeds alienated the minds of all his chief nobility from him. Such as could fled to join with Malcolm and Macduff, who were now approaching with a powerful army which they had raised in England, and the rest secretly wished success to their arms, though, for fear of Macbeth, they could take no active part. His recruits went on slowly. Everybody hated the tyrant, nobody loved or honoured him, but all suspected him, and he began to envy the condition of Duncan, whom he had murdered, who slept soundly in his grave, against whom treason had done its worst; steel nor poison, domestic malice nor foreign levies could hurt him any longer.

While these things were acting, the queen, who had been the sole partner in his wickedness, in whose society he could sometimes seek a momentary repose from those terrible dreams which afflicted them both nightly, died, it is supposed, by her own hands, unable to bear the remorse of guilt and public hate; by which event he was left alone, without a soul to love or care for him, or a friend to whom he could confide his wicked purposes.

He grew careless of life, and wished for death; but the near approach of Malcolm's army roused in him what remained of his ancient courage, and he determined to die, as he expressed it, "with armour on his back." Besides this, the hollow promises of the witches had filled him with false confidence, and he remembered the sayings of the spirits, that none of woman born was to hurt him, and that he was never to be vanquished till Birnam wood should come to Dunsinane, which he thought could never be. So he shut himself up in his castle, whose impregnable strength was such as defied a siege; here he sullenly awaited the approach of Malcolm, when upon a day there came a messenger to him, pale and shaking with fear, almost unable to report that which he had seen; for he averred that, as he had stood upon his watch on the hill, he looked towards Birnam, and to his thinking the wood began to move! "Liar and slave!" cried Macbeth; "if thou speakest false, thou shalt hang alive upon the next tree, till famine end thee. If thy tale be true, I care not if thou dost as much by me"; for Macbeth now began to faint in resolution, and to doubt the equivocal speeches of the spirits. He was not to fear till Birnam wood should come to Dunsinane; and now a wood did move! "However," said he, "if this which he avouches be true, let us arm and out. There is no flying hence, nor staying here. I begin to be weary of the sun, and wish my life at an end." With these desperate speeches he sallied forth upon the besiegers, who had now come up to the castle.

The strange appearance which had given the messenger an idea of a wood moving is easily solved. When the besieging army marched through the wood of Birnam, Malcolm, like a skilful general, instructed his soldiers to hew down every one a bough and bear it before him, by way of concealing the true numbers of his host. This marching of the soldiers with boughs had at a distance the appearance which had frightened the messenger. Thus were the words of the spirit brought to pass, in a sense different from that in which Macbeth had understood them, and one great hold of his confidence was gone.

And now a severe skirmishing took place, in which Macbeth, though feebly supported by those who called themselves his friends, but in reality hated the tyrant and inclined to the party of Malcolm and Macduff, yet fought with the extreme of rage and valour, cutting to pieces all who were opposed to him, till he came to where Macduff was fighting. Seeing Macduff, and remembering the caution of the spirit who had counselled him to avoid Macduff above all men, he would have turned, but Macduff, who had been seeking him through the whole fight, opposed his turning, and a fierce contest ensued, Macduff giving him many foul reproaches for the murder of his wife and children. Macbeth, whose soul was charged enough with blood of that family already, would still have declined the combat, but Macduff still urged him to it, calling him tyrant, murderer, and villain.

Then Macbeth remembered the words of the spirit, how none of woman born should hurt him, and, smiling confidently, he said to Macduff, "Thou losest thy labour, Macduff. As easily thou mayest impress the air with thy sword as make me vulnerable. I bear a charmed life, which must not yield to one of woman born."

"Despair thy charm," said Macduff, "and let that lying spirit whom thou hast served tell thee that Macduff was never born of woman, never, that is, as the ordinary manner of men is to be born."

"Accursed be the tongue which tells me so," said the trembling Macbeth who felt his last hold of confidence give way, "and let never man in future believe the lying equivocations of witches and juggling spirits, who deceive us in words which have double senses, and while they keep their promise literally, disappoint our hopes with a different meaning. I will not fight with thee."

"Then live!" said the scornful Macduff; "we will have a show of thee, as men show monsters, and a painted board, on which shall be written, ' Here men may see the tyrant!'"

"Never," said Macbeth, whose courage returned with despair; "I will not live to kiss the ground before young Malcolm's feet, and to be baited with the curses of the rabble. Though Birnam wood be come to Dunsinane, and thou opposed to me wast never born of woman, yet will I try the last." With these frantic words he threw himself upon Macduff, who, after a severe struggle, in the end overcame him, and cutting off his head, made a present of it to the young and lawful king, Malcolm, who took upon him the government which, by the machinations of the usurper, he had so long been deprived of, and ascended the throne of Duncan the Meek amid the acclamations of the nobles and the people.

The Merchant Of Venice

Shylock, the Jew, lived at Venice; he was a usurer, who had amassed an immense fortune by lending money at great interest to Christian merchants. Shylock, being a hardhearted man, exacted the payment of the money he lent with such severity that he was much disliked by all good men, and particularly by Antonio, a young merchant of Venice; and Shylock as much hated Antonio, because he used to lend money to people in distress, and would never take any interest for the money he lent; therefore there was great enmity between this covetous Jew and the generous merchant Antonio. Whenever Antonio met Shylock on the Rialto (or Exchange) he used to reproach him with his usuries and hard dealings, which the Jew would bear with seeming patience, while he secretly meditated revenge.

Antonio was the kindest man that lived, the best conditioned, and had the most unwearied spirit in doing courtesies; indeed, he was one in whom the ancient Roman honour more appeared than in any that drew breath in Italy. He was greatly beloved by all his fellow-citizens; but the friend who was nearest and dearest to his heart was Bassanio, a noble Venetian, who, having but a small patrimony, had nearly exhausted his little fortune by living in too expensive a manner for his slender means, as young men of high rank with small fortunes are too apt to do. Whenever Bassanio wanted money, Antonio assisted him, and it seemed as if they had but one heart and one purse between them.

One day Bassanio came to Antonio, and told him, that he wished to repair his fortune by a wealthy marriage with a lady whom he dearly loved, whose father, that was lately dead, had left her sole heiress to a large estate; and that in her father's lifetime he used to visit at her house, when he thought he had observed this lady had sometimes from her eyes sent speechless messages that seemed to say he would be no unwelcome suitor; but not having money to furnish himself with an appearance befitting the lover of so rich an heiress, he besought Antonio to add to the many favours he had shown him by lending him three thousand ducats.

Antonio had no money by him at that time to lend his friend; but expecting soon to have some ships come home laden with merchandise, he said he would go to Shylock, the rich money-lender, and borrow the money upon the credit of those ships.

Antonio and Bassanio went together to Shylock, and Antonio asked the Jew to lend him three thousand ducats upon an interest he should require to be paid out of the merchandise contained in his ships at sea. On this Shylock thought within himself, "If I can once catch him on the hip, I will feed fat the ancient grudge I bear him. He hates our Jewish nation; he lends out money gratis; and among the merchants he rails at me and my well-earned bargains, which he calls interest. Cursed be my tribe if I forgive him!" Antonio, finding he was musing within himself and did not answer, and being impatient for the money, said, "Shylock, do you hear—will you lend the money?" To this question the Jew replied: "Signior Antonio, on the Rialto many a time and often you have railed at me about my monies and my usuries, and I have borne it with a patient shrug, for sufferance is the badge of all our tribe; and then you have called me unbeliever, cut-throat dog, and spit upon my Jewish garments, and spurned at me with your foot, as if I was a cur. Well, then, it now appears you need my help; and you come to me and say, ' *Shylock, lend me monies.*' Has a dog money? Is it possible a cur should lend three thousand ducats? Shall I bend low and say, Fair sir, you spit upon me on Wednesday last, another time you called me dog, and for these courtesies I am to lend you monies?" Antonio replied: "I am as like to call you so again, to spit on you again, and spurn you too. If you will lend me this money, lend it not to me as to a friend, but rather lend it me as to an enemy, that if I break you may with better face exact the penalty." "Why, look you," said Shylock, "how you storm! I would be friends with you and have your love. I will forget the shames you have put upon me. I will supply your wants and take no interest for my money." This seemingly kind offer greatly surprised Antonio; and then Shylock, still pretending kindness, and that all he did was to gain Antonio's love, again said he would lend him the three thousand ducats, and take no interest for his money; only Antonio should go with him to a lawyer and there sign in merry sport a bond that if he did not repay the money by a certain day he would forfeit a pound of flesh, to be cut off from any part of his body that Shylock pleased.

"Content," said Antonio; "I will sign to this bond, and say there is much kindness in the Jew."

Bassanio said Antonio should not sign to such a bond for him; and still Antonio insisted that he would sign it, for that before the day of payment came his ships would return laden with many times the value of the money.

Shylock, hearing this debate, exclaimed: "O, Father Abraham, what suspicious people these Christians are! Their own hard dealings teach them to suspect the thoughts of others. I pray you tell me this, Bassanio: If he should break this day, what should I gain by the execution of the forfeiture? A pound of man's flesh, taken from a man, is not so estimable, nor profitable neither, as the flesh of mutton or of beef. I say, to buy his favour I offer this friendship. If he will take it, so; if not, adieu."

At last, against the advice of Bassanio, who, notwithstanding all the Jew had said of his kind intentions, did not like his friend should run the hazard of this shocking penalty for his sake, Antonio signed the bond, thinking it really was, as the Jew said, merely in sport.

The rich heiress that Bassanio wished to marry lived near Venice, at a place called Belmont; her name was Portia, and in the graces of her person and her mind she was nothing inferior to that Portia of whom we read, who was Cato's daughter, and the wife of Brutus.

Bassanio, being so kindly supplied with money by his friend Antonio, at the hazard of his life, set out for Belmont with a splendid train, and attended by a gentleman of the name of Gratiano.

Bassanio proving successful in his suit, Portia in a short time consented to accept of him for a husband.

Bassanio confessed to Portia that he had no fortune, and that his high birth and noble ancestry were all that he could boast of. She, who loved him for his worthy qualities, and had riches enough not to regard wealth in a husband, answered with a graceful modesty that she would wish herself a thousand times more fair, and ten thousand times more rich, to be more worthy of him; and then the accomplished Portia prettily dispraised herself, and said she was an unlessoned girl, unschooled, unpractised, yet not so old but that she could learn, and that she would commit her gentle spirit to be directed and governed by him in all things; and she said, "Myself and what is mine to you and yours is now converted. But yesterday, Bassanio, I was the lady of this fair mansion, queen of myself, and mistress over these servants; and now this house, these servants, and myself are yours, my lord; I give them with this ring," presenting a ring to Bassanio. Bassanio was so overpowered with gratitude and wonder at the gracious manner in which the rich and noble Portia accepted of a man of his humble fortunes, that he could not express his joy and reverence to the dear lady who so honoured him by anything but broken words of love and thankfulness; and taking the ring, he vowed never to part with it.

Gratiano and Nerissa, Portia's waiting-maid, were in attendance upon their lord and lady when Portia so gracefully promised to become the obedient wife of Bassanio; and Gratiano, wishing Bassanio and the generous lady joy, desired permission to be married at the same time.

"With all my heart, Gratiano," said Bassanio, "if you can get a wife."

Gratiano then said that he loved the Lady Portia's fair waiting-gentlewoman, Nerissa, and that she had promised to be his wife if her lady married Bassanio. Portia asked Nerissa if this was true. Nerissa replied, "Madam, it is so, if you approve of it," Portia willingly consenting, Bassanio pleasantly said, "Then our wedding-feast shall be much honoured by your marriage, Gratiano."

The happiness of these lovers was sadly crossed at this moment by the entrance of a messenger who brought a letter from Antonio containing fearful tidings. When Bassanio read Antonio's letter Portia feared it was to tell him of the death of some dear friend, he looked so pale; and inquiring what was the news which had so distressed him he said, "Oh, sweet Portia, here are a few of the unpleasantest words that ever blotted paper. Gentle lady, when I first imparted my love to you I freely told you all the wealth I had ran in my veins, but I should have told you that I had less than nothing, being in debt." Bassanio then told Portia what has been here related of his borrowing the money of Antonio, and of Antonio's procuring it of Shylock the Jew, and of the bond by which Antonio had engaged to forfeit a pound of flesh if it was not repaid by a certain day; and then Bassanio read Antonio's letter, the words of which were— "Sweet Bassanio, my ships are all lost, my bond to the Jew is forfeited, and since in paying it is impossible I should live, I could wish to see you at my death; notwithstanding, use your pleasure; if your love for me do not persuade you to come, let not my letter." "Oh, my dear love," said Portia, "despatch the business and be gone; you shall have gold to pay the money twenty times over before this kind friend shall lose a hair by my Bassanio's fault, and as you are so dearly bought I will dearly love you." Portia then said she would be married to Bassanio before he set out, to give him a legal right to her money; and that same day they were married, and Gratiano was also married to Nerissa, and Bassanio and Gratiano, the instant they were married, set out in great haste for Venice, where Bassanio found Antonio in prison.

The day of payment being past, the cruel Jew would not accept of the money which Bassanio offered him, but insisted upon having a pound of Antonio's flesh. A day was appointed to try this shocking cause before the Duke of Venice, and Bassanio awaited in dreadful suspense the event of the trial.

When Portia parted with her husband she spoke cheeringly to him and bade him bring his dear friend along with him when he returned; yet she feared it would go hard with Antonio, and when she was left alone, she began to think and consider within herself if she could by any means be instrumental in saving the life of her dear Bassanio's friend; and notwithstanding, when she wished to honour her Bassanio, she had said to him with such a meek and wife-like grace that she would submit in all things to be governed by his superior wisdom, yet, being now called forth into action by the peril of her honoured husband's friend, she did nothing doubt her own powers, and by the sole guidance of her own true and perfect judgment, at once resolved to go herself to Venice and speak in Antonio's defence.

Portia had a relation who was a counsellor in the law; to this gentleman, whose name was Bellario, she wrote, and stating the case to him desired his opinion, and that with his advice he would also send her the dress worn by a counsellor. When the messenger returned he brought letters from Bellario of advice how to proceed, and also everything necessary for her equipment.

Portia dressed herself and her maid Nerissa in men's apparel, and, putting on the robes of a counsellor, she took Nerissa along with her as her clerk; and setting out immediately, they arrived at Venice on the very day of the trial. The cause was just going to be heard before the duke and senators of Venice in the senate-house, when Portia entered this high court of justice and presented a letter from Bellario, in which that learned counsellor wrote to the duke, saying he would have come himself to plead for Antonio, but that he was prevented by sickness, and he requested that the learned young doctor Balthasar (so he called Portia) might be permitted to plead in his stead. This the duke granted, much wondering at the youthful appearance of the stranger, who was prettily disguised by her counsellor's robes and her large wig.

And now began this important trial. Portia looked around her, and she saw the merciless Jew; and she saw Bassanio, but he knew her not in her disguise. He was standing beside Antonio in an agony of distress and fear for his friend.

The importance of the arduous task Portia had engaged in gave this tender lady courage, and she boldly proceeded in the duty she had undertaken to perform; and first of all she addressed herself to Shylock; and allowing that he had a right by the Venetian law to have the forfeit expressed in the bond, she spoke so sweetly of the noble quality of mercy, as would have softened any heart but the unfeeling Shylock's; saying, that it dropped as the gentle rain from heaven upon the place beneath; and how mercy was a double blessing, it blessed him that gave, and him that received it; and how it became monarchs better than their crowns, being an attribute of God himself, and that earthly power came nearest to God's, in proportion as mercy tempered justice; and she bid Shylock remember that as we all pray for mercy, that same prayer should teach us to show mercy. Shylock only answered her by desiring to have the penalty forfeited in the bond. "Is he not able to pay the money?" asked Portia. Bassanio then offered the Jew the payment of the three thousand ducats as many times over as he should desire, which Shylock refusing, and still insisting upon having a pound of

Antonio's flesh, Bassanio begged the learned young counsellor would endeavour to wrest the law a little to save Antonio's life. But Portia gravely answered that laws once established must never be altered. Shylock hearing Portia say that the law might not be altered, it seemed to him that she was pleading in his favour, and he said, "A Daniel is come to judgment! O wise young judge, how I do honour you! How much older are you than your looks!"

Portia now desired Shylock to let her look at the bond, and when she had read it, she said, "This bond is forfeited, and by this the Jew may lawfully claim a pound of flesh, to be by him cut off nearest Antonio's heart." Then she said to Shylock, "Be merciful; take the money, and bid me tear the bond." But no mercy would the cruel Shylock show; and he said, "By my soul, I swear there is no power in the tongue of man to alter me." "Why then, Antonio," said Portia, "you must prepare your bosom for the knife"; and while Shylock was sharpening a long knife with great eagerness to cut off the pound of flesh, Portia said to Antonio, "Have you anything to say?" Antonio, with a calm resignation, replied that he had but little to say for that he had prepared his mind for death. Then he said to Bassanio, "Give me your hand, Bassanio,! Fare you well! Grieve not that I am fallen into this misfortune for you. Command me to your honourable wife, and tell her how I have loved you!" Bassanio, in the deepest affliction, replied, "Antonio, I am married to a wife, who is as dear to me as life itself; but life itself, my wife, and all the world, are not esteemed with me above your life: I would lose all, I would sacrifice all to this fiend here, to deliver you."

Portia hearing this, though the kind-hearted lady was not at all offended with her husband for expressing the love he owed to so true a friend as Antonio in these strong terms, yet could not help answering, "Your wife would give you little thanks if she were present to hear you make this offer." And then Gratiano, who loved to copy what his lord did, thought he must make a speech like Bassanio's, and he said, in Nerissa's hearing, who was writing in her clerk's dress by the side of Portia, "I have a wife, whom I protest I love; I wish she were in heaven, if she could but entreat some power there to change the cruel temper of this currish Jew." "It is well you wish this behind her back, else you would have but an unquiet house," said Nerissa.

Shylock now cried out impatiently, "We trifle time; I pray pronounce the sentence." And now all was awful expectation in the court, and every heart was full of grief for Antonio.

Portia asked if the scales were ready to weigh the flesh; and she said to the Jew, "Shylock, you must have some surgeon by, lest he bleed to death." Shylock, whose whole intent was that Antonio should bleed to death, said, "It is not so named in the bond." Portia replied, "It is not so named in the bond but what of that? It were good you did so much for charity." To this all the answer Shylock would make was, "I cannot find it; it is not in the bond." "Then," said Portia, "A pound of Antonio's flesh is thine. The law allows it, and the court awards it. And you may cut this flesh from off his breast. The law allows it, and the court awards it." Again Shylock exclaimed, "O wise and upright judge! A Daniel is come to judgment!" And then he sharpened his long knife again, and looking eagerly on Antonio, he said, "Come, prepare!"

"Tarry a little, Jew," said Portia; "there is something else. This bond here gives you no drop of blood; the words expressly are, 'a pound of flesh' . If in the cutting of the pound of flesh you shed one drop of Christian blood, your land and goods are by the law to be confiscated to the State of Venice." Now, as it was utterly impossible for Shylock to cut off the pound of flesh without shedding some of Antonio's blood, this wise discovery of Portia's, that it was flesh and not blood that was named in the bond, saved the life of Antonio; and all admiring the wonderful sagacity of the young counsellor who had so happily thought of this expedient, plaudits resounded from every part of the senate-house; and Gratiano exclaimed, in the words which Shylock had used, "O wise and upright Judge! mark, Jew, a Daniel is come to judgment!"

Shylock, finding himself defeated in his cruel intent said with a disappointed look, that he would take the money; and Bassanio, rejoiced beyond measure at Antonio's unexpected deliverance, cried out, "Here is the money!" But Portia stopped him, saying, "Softly, there is no haste; the Jew shall have nothing but the penalty; therefore prepare, Shylock, to cut off the flesh, but mind you shed no blood, nor do not cut off more nor less than just a pound; be it more or less by one poor scruple, nay, if the scale turn but by the weight of a single hair, you are condemned by the laws of Venice to die, and all your wealth is forfeited to the senate."

"Give me my money, and let me go," said Shylock. "I have it ready," said Bassanio; "here it is."

Shylock was going to take the money, when Portia again stopped him, saying, "Tarry, Jew; I have yet another hold upon you. By the laws of Venice your wealth is forfeited to the State for having conspired against the life of one of its citizens, and your life lies at the mercy of the duke; therefore down on your knees and ask him to pardon you."

The duke then said to Shylock, "That you may see the difference of our Christian spirit, I pardon you your life before you ask it; half your wealth belongs to Antonio, the other half comes to the State."

The generous Antonio then said that he would give up his share of Shylock's wealth if Shylock would sign a deed to make it over at his death to his daughter and her husband; for Antonio knew that the Jew had an only daughter, who had lately married against his consent to a young Christian, named Lorenzo, a friend of Antonio's, which had so offended Shylock that he had disinherited her.

The Jew agreed to this, and being thus disappointed in his revenge and despoiled of his riches, he said, "I am ill. Let me go home; send the deed after me and I will sign over half my riches to my daughter." "Get thee gone, then," said the duke, "and sign it; and if you repent your cruelty and turn Christian the State will forgive you the fine of the other half of your riches."

The duke now released Antonio and dismissed the court. He then highly praised the wisdom and ingenuity of the young counsellor, and invited him home to dinner. Portia, who meant to return to Belmont before her husband, replied, "I humbly thank your grace, but I must away directly." The duke said he was sorry he had not leisure to stay and dine with him, and turning to Antonio he added, "Reward this gentleman; for in my mind you are much indebted to him."

The duke and his senators left the court; and then Bassanio said to Portia, "Most worthy gentleman, I and my friend Antonio have by your wisdom been this day acquitted of grievous penalties, and I beg you will accept of three thousand ducats due unto the Jew." "And we shall stand indebted to you over and above," said Antonio, "in love and service evermore."

Portia could not be prevailed upon to accept the money, but upon Bassanio still pressing her to accept of some reward, she said, "Give me your gloves; I will wear them for your sake," and then Bassanio, taking off his gloves, she espied the ring which she had given him upon his finger; now it was the ring the wily lady wanted to get from him, to make a merry jest when she saw Bassanio again, that made her ask him for his gloves, and she said when she saw the ring, "And for your love, I will take this ring from you." Bassanio was sadly distressed that the counsellor should ask him for the only thing he could not part with, and he replied in great confusion that he could not give him that ring because it was his wife's gift, and he had vowed never to part with it; but that he would give him the most valuable ring in Venice, and find it out by proclamation. On this Portia affected to be affronted, and left the court saying, "You teach me, sir, how a beggar should be answered."

"Dear Bassanio," said Antonio, "let him have the ring; let my love and the great service he has done for me be valued against your wife's displeasure." Bassanio, ashamed to appear so ungrateful, yielded, and sent Gratiano after Portia with the ring; and then the *clerk* Nerissa, who had also given Gratiano a ring, she begged his ring, and Gratiano (not choosing to be outdone in generosity by his lord) gave it to her. And there was laughing among these ladies, to think, when they got home, how they would tax their husbands with giving away their rings, and swear that they had given them as a present to some woman.

Portia, when she returned, was in that happy temper of mind which never fails to attend the consciousness of having performed a good action; her cheerful spirits enjoyed everything she saw; the moon never seemed to shine so bright before, and when that pleasant moon was hid behind a cloud, then a light which she saw from her house at Belmont as well pleased her charmed fancy, and she said to Nerissa— "That light we see is burning in my hall; how far that little candle throws its beams, so shines a good deed in a naughty world"; and hearing the sound of music from her house, she said— "Methinks that music sounds much sweeter than by day."

And now Portia and Nerissa entered the house, and, dressing themselves in their own apparel, they awaited the arrival of their husbands, who soon followed them with Antonio; and Bassanio, presenting his dear friend to the Lady Portia, the congratulations and welcoming of that lady were hardly over when they perceived Nerissa and her husband quarrelling in a corner of the room. "A quarrel already?" said Portia. "What is the matter?" Gratiano replied— "Lady, it is about a paltry gilt ring that Nerissa gave me, with words upon it like the poetry on a cutler's knife: *Love me, and leave me not.*"

"What does the poetry or the value of the ring signify?" said Nerissa. "You swore to me, when I gave it to you, that you would keep it till the hour of death; and now you say you gave it to the lawyer's clerk. I know you gave it to a woman." "By this hand," replied Gratiano, "I gave it to a youth, a kind of boy, a little scrubbed boy no higher than yourself; he was clerk to the young counsellor, that by his wise pleading saved Antonio's life; this prating boy begged it for a fee, and I could not for my life deny him." Portia said— "You were to blame, Gratiano, to part with your wife's first gift. I gave my lord Bassanio a ring, and I am sure he would not part with it for all the world." Gratiano, in excuse for his fault, now said — "My lord Bassanio gave his ring away to the counsellor, and then the boy, his clerk, that took some pains in writing, he begged my ring."

Portia, hearing this, seemed very angry, and reproached Bassanio for giving away her ring; and she said Nerissa had taught her what to believe, and that she knew some woman had the ring. Bassanio was very unhappy to have so offended his dear lady, and he said with great earnestness— "No, by my honour, no woman had it, but a civil doctor, who refused three thousand ducats of me, and begged the ring, which when I denied him he went displeased away. What could I do, sweet Portia? I was so beset with shame for my seeming ingratitude that I was forced to send the ring after him. Pardon me, good lady; had you been there I think you would have begged the ring of me to give the worthy doctor."

"Ah!" said Antonio, "I am the unhappy cause of these quarrels."

Portia bid Antonio not to grieve at that, for that he was welcome notwithstanding; and then Antonio said, "I once did lend my body for Bassanio's sake; and but for him to whom your husband gave the ring I should have now been dead. I dare be bound again, my soul upon the forfeit, your lord will never more break his faith with you." "Then you shall be his surety," said Portia; "give him this ring and bid him keep it better than the other."

When Bassanio looked at this ring he was strangely surprised to find it was the same he gave away; and then Portia told him how she was the young counsellor, and Nerissa was her clerk; and Bassanio found, to his unspeakable wonder and delight, that it was by the noble courage and wisdom of his wife that Antonio's life was saved. And Portia again welcomed Antonio, and gave him letters which by some chance had fallen into her hands, which contained an account of Antonio's ships, that were supposed lost, being safely arrived in the harbour. So these tragical beginnings of this rich merchant's story were all forgotten in the unexpected good fortune which ensued; and there was leisure to laugh at the comical adventure of the rings, and the husbands that did not know their own wives; Gratiano merely vowing, in a sort of rhyming speech, that

—while he lived, he'd rear no other thing
So sore, as keeping safe Nerissa's ring.

The Comedy Of Errors

The States of Syracuse and Ephesus being at variance, there was a cruel law made at Ephesus, ordaining that if any merchant of Syracuse was seen in the city of Ephesus, he was to be put to death, unless he could pay a thousand marks for the ransom of his life.

Aegeon, an old merchant of Syracuse, was discovered in the streets of Ephesus, and brought before the duke, either to pay this heavy fine, or to receive sentence of death.

Aegeon had no money to pay the fine, and the duke, before he pronounced the sentence of death upon him, desired him to relate the history of his life, and to tell for what cause he had ventured to come to the city of Ephesus, which it was death for any Syracusan merchant to enter.

Aegeon said that he did not fear to die, for sorrow had made him weary of his life, but that a heavier task could not have been imposed upon him than to relate the events of his unfortunate life. He then began his own history in the following words:—

"I was born at Syracuse, and brought up to the profession of a merchant. I married a lady with whom I lived very happily, but being obliged to go to Epidamnium, I was detained there by my business six months, and then, finding I should be obliged to stay some time longer, I sent for my wife, who, as soon as she arrived, presented me with two sons, and what was very strange, they were both so exactly alike that it was impossible to distinguish the one from the other. At the same time that my wife became the mother of these twin boys, a poor woman in the inn where my wife lodged was likewise blessed with two sons, and these twins were as much like each other as my two sons were. The parents of these children being exceeding poor; I bought the two boys and brought them up to attend upon my sons.

"My sons were very fine children, and my wife was not a little

71

proud of two such boys; and she daily wishing to return home, I unwillingly agreed, and in an evil hour we got on shipboard; for we had not sailed above a league from Epidamnium before a dreadful storm arose, which continued with such violence, that the sailors, seeing no chance of saving the ship, crowded into the boat to save their own lives, leaving us alone in the ship, which we every moment expected would be destroyed by the fury of the storm.

"The incessant weeping of my wife and the piteous complaints of the pretty babes, who, not knowing what to fear, wept for fashion because they saw their mother weep, filled me with terror for them, though I did not for myself fear death; and all my thoughts were bent to contrive means for their safety. I tied my youngest son to the end of a small spare mast, such as seafaring men provide against storms; at the other end I bound the youngest of the twin slaves, and at the same time I directed my wife how to fasten the other children in like manner to another mast. She thus having the care of the two eldest children and I of the two younger, we bound ourselves separately to these masts with the children, and but for this contrivance we had all been lost, for the ship split on a mighty rock and was dashed in pieces, and we, clinging to these slender masts, were supported above the water, where I, having the care of two children, was unable to assist my wife, who with the other children was soon separated from me; but while they were yet in my sight they were taken up by a boat of fishermen from Corinth, as I supposed, and seeing them in safety I had no care but to struggle with the wild sea waves to preserve my dear son and the youngest slave. At length we in our turn were taken up by a ship, and the sailors knowing me, gave us kind welcome and assistance, and landed us in safety at Syracuse; but from that sad hour I have never known what became of my wife and eldest child.

"My youngest son, and now my only care, when he was eighteen years of age, began to be inquisitive after his mother and his brother, and often importuned me that he might take his attendant the young slave, who had also lost his brother, and go in search of them. At length I unwillingly gave consent, for though I anxiously desired to hear tidings of my wife and eldest son, yet in sending my younger one to find them I hazarded the loss of him also. It is now seven years since my son left me; five years have I passed in travelling through the world in search of him. I have been in farthest Greece, and through the bounds of Asia, and coasting homewards I landed here in Ephesus, being unwilling to leave any place unsought that harbours men; but this day must end the story of my life, and happy should I think myself in my death if I were sure my wife and sons were living."

Here the hapless Aegeon ended the account of his misfortunes; and the duke, pitying this unfortunate father, who had brought upon himself this great peril by his love for his lost son, said, if it were not against the laws, which his oath and dignity did not permit him to alter, he would freely pardon him; yet, instead of dooming him to instant death, as the strict letter of the law required, he would give him that day to try if he could beg or borrow the money to pay the fine.

This day of grace did seem no great favour to Aegeon, for not knowing any man in Ephesus, there seemed to him but little chance that any stranger would lend or give him a thousand marks to pay the fine; and helpless and hopeless of any relief, he retired from the presence of the duke in the custody of a jailer.

Aegeon supposed he knew no person in Ephesus; but at the very time he was in danger of losing his life through the careful search he was making after his youngest son, that son and his eldest son also were both in the city of Ephesus.

Aegeon's sons, besides being exactly alike in face and person, were both named alike, being both called Antipholis, and the two twin slaves were also both named Dromio. Aegeon's youngest son, Antipholis of Syracuse, he whom the old man had come to Ephesus to seek, happened to arrive at Ephesus with his slave Dromio that very same day that Aegeon did; and he being also a merchant of Syracuse, he would have been in the same danger that his father was, but by good fortune he met a friend who told him the peril an old merchant of Syracuse was in, and advised him to pass for a merchant of Epidamnium; this Antipholis agreed to do, and he was sorry to hear one of his own countrymen was in this danger, but he little thought this old merchant was his own father.

The oldest son of Aegeon (who must be called Antipholis of Ephesus, to distinguish him from his brother Antipholis of Syracuse) had lived at Ephesus twenty years, and being a rich man was well able to have paid the money for the ransom of his father's life; but Antipholis knew nothing of his father, being so young when he was taken out of the sea with his mother by the fishermen, that he only remembered he had been so preserved, but he had no recollection of either his father or his mother; the fishermen who took up this Antipholis and his mother and the young slave Dromio, having carried the two children away from her (to the great grief of that unhappy lady), intending to sell them.

Antipholis and Dromio were sold by them to Duke Menaphon, a famous warrior, who was uncle to the Duke of Ephesus, and he carried the boys to Ephesus, when he went to visit the duke his nephew.

The Duke of Ephesus taking a fancy to young Antipholis, when he grew up, made him an officer in his army, in which he distinguished himself by his great bravery in the wars, where he saved the life of his patron the duke, who rewarded his merit by marrying him to Adriana, a rich lady of Ephesus; with whom he was living (his slave Dromio still attending him) at the time his father came there.

Antipholis of Syracuse, when he parted with his friend, who advised him to say that he came from Epidamnium, gave his slave Dromio some money to carry to the inn where he intended to dine, and in the meantime he said he would walk about and view the city, and observe the manners of the people.

Dromio was a pleasant fellow, and when Antipholis was dull and melancholy, he used to divert himself with the odd humours and merry jests of his slave, so that the freedoms of speech he allowed in Dromio were greater than is usual between masters and their servants.

When Antipholis of Syracuse had sent Dromio away, he stood awhile thinking over his solitary wanderings in search of his mother and his brother, of whom in no place where he landed could he hear the least tidings; and he said sorrowfully to himself, "I am like a drop of water in the ocean, which, seeking to find his fellow drop, loseth itself in the wide sea. So I unhappily, to find a mother and a brother, do lose myself."

While he was thus meditating on his weary travels, which had hitherto been so useless, Dromio, as he thought, returned.

Antipholis, wondering that he came back so soon, asked him where he had left the money. Now it was not his own Dromio, but the twin brother that lived with Antipholis of Ephesus, that he spoke to. The two Dromios and the two Antipholises were still as much alike as Aegeon had said they were in their infancy; therefore no wonder Antipholis thought it was his own slave returned, and asked him why he came back so soon. Dromio replied, "My mistress sent me to bid you come to dinner. The capon burns, and the pig falls from the spit, and the meat will be all cold if you do not come home." "These jests are out of season," said Antipholis: "where did you leave the money?" Dromio still answering that his mistress had sent him to fetch Antipholis to dinner; "What mistress?" said Antipholis. "Why, your worship's wife, sir," replied Dromio. Antipholis having no wife, he was very angry with Dromio, and said, "Because I familiarly sometimes chat with you, you presume to jest with me in this free manner. I am not in a sportive humour now: where is the money? We being strangers here, how dare you trust so great a charge from your own custody?" Dromio hearing his master, as he thought him, talk of their being strangers, supposing Antipholis was jesting, replied merrily, "I pray you, sir, jest as you sit at dinner; I had no charge but to fetch you home to dine with my mistress and her sister." Now Antipholis lost all patience, and beat Dromio, who ran home, and told his mistress that his master had refused to come to dinner, and said that he had no wife.

Adriana, the wife of Antipholis of Ephesus, was very angry when she heard that her husband said he had no wife; for she was of a jealous temper, and she said her husband meant that he loved another lady better than herself; and she began to fret, and say unkind words of jealousy and reproach of her husband; and her sister Luciana, who lived with her, tried in vain to persuade her out of her groundless suspicions.

Antipholis of Syracuse went to the inn, and found Dromio with the money in safety there, and seeing his own Dromio, he was going again to chide him for his free jests, when Adriana came up to him, and not doubting but it was her husband she saw, she began to reproach him for looking strange upon her (as well he might, never having seen this angry lady before); and then she told him how well he loved her before they were married, and that now he loved some other lady instead of her. "How comes it now, my husband," said she, "oh how comes it that I have lost your love?" "Plead you to me, fair dame?" said the astonished Antipholis. It was in vain he told her he was not her husband, and that he had been in Ephesus but two hours; she insisted on his going home with her, and Antipholis at last, being unable to get away, went with her to his brother's house, and dined with Adriana and her sister, the one calling him husband, and the other brother, he, all amazed, thinking he must have been married to her in his sleep, or that he was sleeping now. And Dromio, who followed them, was no less surprised, for the cook-maid, who was his brother's wife, also claimed him for her husband.

While Antipholis of Syracuse was dining with his brother's wife, his brother, the real husband, returned home to dinner with his slave Dromio; but the servants would not open the door, because their mistress had ordered them not to admit any company; and when they repeatedly knocked, and said they were Antipholis and Dromio, the maids laughed at them, and said that Antipholis was at dinner with their mistress, and Dromio was in the kitchen; and though they almost knocked the door down, they could not gain admittance, and at last Antipholis went away very angry, and strangely surprised at hearing a gentleman was dining with his wife.

When Antipholis of Syracuse had finished his dinner, he was so perplexed at the lady still persisting in calling him husband, and at hearing that Dromio had also been claimed by the cook-maid, that he left the house as soon as he could find any pretence to get away; for though he was very much pleased with Luciana, the sister, yet the jealous-tempered Adriana he disliked very much; nor was Dromio at all better satisfied with his fair wife in the kitchen; therefore both master and man were glad to get away from their new wives as fast as they could.

The moment Antipholis of Syracuse had left the house he was met by a goldsmith, who mistaking him, as Adriana had done, for Antipholis of Ephesus, gave him a gold chain, calling him by his name; and when Antipholis would have refused the chain, saying it did not belong to him, the goldsmith replied he made it by his own orders; and went away, leaving the chain in the hand of Antipholis, who ordered his man Dromio to get his things on board a ship, not choosing to stay in a place any longer where he met with such strange adventures that he surely thought himself bewitched.

The goldsmith who had given the chain to the wrong Antipholis was arrested immediately after for a sum of money he owed; and Antipholis, the married brother, to whom the goldsmith thought he had given the chain, happened to come to the place where the officer was arresting the goldsmith, who, when he saw Antipholis, asked him to pay for the gold chain he had just delivered to him, the price amounting to nearly the same sum as that for which he had been arrested. Antipholis denying the having received the chain, and the goldsmith persisting to declare that he had but a few minutes before given it to him, they disputed the matter a long time, both thinking they were right, for Antipholis knew the goldsmith never gave him the chain, and, so like were the two brothers, the goldsmith was as certain he had delivered the chain into his hands, till at last the officer took the goldsmith away to prison for the debt he owed, and at the same time the goldsmith made the officer arrest Antipholis for the price of the chain; so that, at the conclusion of their dispute, Antipholis and the merchant were both taken away to prison together.

As Antipholis was going to prison he met Dromio of Syracuse, his brother's slave, and mistaking him for his own, he ordered him to go to Adriana, his wife, and tell her to send the money for which he was arrested. Dromio, wondering that his master should send him back to the strange house where he dined, and from which he had just before been in such haste to depart, did not dare to reply, though he came to tell his master the ship was ready to sail; for he saw Antipholis was in no humour to be jested with. Therefore he went away, grumbling within himself that he must return to Adriana's house, "where," said he, "Dowsabel claims me for a husband; but I must go, for servants must obey their master's commands."

Adriana gave him the money, and as Dromio was returning, he met Antipholis of Syracuse, who was still in amaze at the surprising adventures he met with; for his brother, being well known in Ephesus, there was hardly a man he met in the streets but saluted him as an old acquaintance: some offered him money which they said was owing to him, some invited him to come and see them, and some gave him thanks for kindnesses they said he had done them, all mistaking him for his brother. A tailor showed him some silks he had bought for him, and insisted upon taking measure of him for some clothes.

Antipholis began to think he was among a nation of sorcerers and witches, and Dromio did not at all relieve his master from his bewildered thoughts, by asking him how he got free from the officer who was carrying him to prison, and giving him the purse of gold which Adriana had sent to pay the debt with. This talk of Dromio's of the arrest and of a prison, and of the money he had brought from Adriana, perfectly confounded Antipholis, and he said, "This fellow Dromio is certainly distracted, and we wander here in illusions" ; and quite terrified at his own confused thoughts, he cried out, "Some blessed power deliver us from this strange place!"

And now another stranger came up to him, and she was a lady, and she too called him Antipholis, and told him he had dined with her that day, and asked him for a gold chain which she said he had promised to give her. Antipholis now lost all patience, and calling her a sorceress, he denied that he had ever promised her a chain or dined with her, or had ever seen her face before that moment. The lady persisted in affirming he had dined with her and had promised her a chain, which Antipholis still denying, she further said that she had given him a valuable ring, and if he would not give her the gold chain she insisted upon having her own ring again. On this Antipholis became quite frantic, and again calling her sorceress and witch, and denying all knowledge of her and her ring, ran away from her, leaving her astonished at his words and his wild looks, for nothing to her appeared more certain than that he had dined with her, and that she had given him a ring in consequence of his promising to make her a present of a gold chain. But this lady had fallen into the same mistake the others had done, for she had taken him for his brother; the married Antipholis had done all the things she taxed this Antipholis with.

When the married Antipholis was denied entrance into his own house (those within supposing him to be already there), he had gone away very angry, believing it to be one of his wife's jealous freaks, to which she was very subject, and remembering that she had often falsely accused him of visiting other ladies, he, to be revenged on her for shutting him out of his own house, determined to go and dine with this lady, and she receiving him with great civility, and his wife having so highly offended him, Antipholis promised to give her a gold chain, which he had intended as a present for his wife; it was the same chain which the goldsmith by mistake had given to his brother. The lady liked so well the thoughts of having a fine gold chain, that she gave the married Antipholis a ring, which when, as she supposed (taking his brother for him), he denied, and said he did not know her, and left her in such a wild passion, she began to think he was certainly out of his senses; and presently she resolved to go and tell Adriana that her husband was mad. And while she was telling it to Adriana he came, attended by the jailer (who allowed him to come home to get the money to pay the debt), for the purse of money, which Adriana had sent by Dromio, and he had delivered to the other Antipholis.

Adriana believed the story the lady told her of her husband's madness must be true, when he reproached her for shutting him out of his own house; and remembering how he had protested all dinner-time that he was not her husband, and had never been in Ephesus till that day, she had no doubt that he was mad; she therefore paid the jailer the money, and having discharged him, she ordered her servants to bind her husband with ropes, and had him conveyed into a dark room, and sent for a doctor to come and cure him of his madness; Antipholis all the while hotly exclaiming against this false accusation, which the exact likeness he bore to his brother had brought upon him. But his rage only the more confirmed them in the belief that he was mad: and Dromio persisting in the same story, they bound him also, and took him away along with his master.

Soon after Adriana had put her husband into confinement, a servant came to tell her that Antipholis and Dromio must have broken loose from their keepers, for that they were both walking at liberty in the next street. On hearing this, Adriana ran out to fetch him home, taking some people with her to secure her husband again, and her sister went along with her. When they came to the gates of a convent in the neighbourhood, there they saw Antipholis and Dromio, as they thought, being again deceived by the likeness of the twin brothers.

Antipholis of Syracuse was still beset with the perplexities this likeness had brought upon him. The chain which the goldsmith had given him was about his neck, and the goldsmith was reproaching him for denying that he had it, and refusing to pay for it, and Antipholis was protesting that the goldsmith freely gave him the chain in the morning and that from that hour he had never seen the goldsmith again.

And now Adriana came up to him, and claimed him as her lunatic husband, who had escaped from his keepers, and the men she brought with her were going to lay violent hands on Antipholis and Dromio; but they ran into the convent, and Antipholis begged the abbess to give him shelter in her house.

And now came out the lady abbess herself to inquire into the cause of this disturbance. She was a grave and venerable lady, and wise to judge of what she saw, and she would not too hastily give up the men who had sought protection in her house; so she strictly questioned the wife about the story she told of her husband's madness, and she said—"What is the cause of this sudden distemper of your husband's? Has he lost his wealth at sea? Or is it the death of some dear friend that has disturbed his mind?" Adriana replied that no such things as these had been the cause. "Perhaps," said the abbess, "he has fixed his affections on some other lady than you, his wife, and that has driven him into this state." Adriana said she had long thought the love of some other lady was the cause of his frequent absences from home. Now it was not his love for another but the teasing jealousy of his wife's temper that often obliged Antipholis to leave his home, and (the abbess suspecting this from the vehemence of Adriana's manner) to learn the truth, she said—

"You should have reprehended him for this." "Why, so I did," replied Adriana. "Ay," said the abbess, "but perhaps not enough." Adriana, willing to convince the abbess that she had said enough to Antipholis on this subject, replied— "It was the constant subject of our conversation; in bed I would not let him sleep for speaking of it. At table I would not let him eat for speaking of it. When I was alone with him I talked of, nothing else, and in company I gave him frequent hints of it. Still all my talk was how vile and bad it was in him to love any lady better than me."

The lady abbess, having drawn this full confession from the jealous Adriana, now said, "And therefore comes it that your husband is mad. The venomous clamour of a jealous woman is more deadly poisonous than a mad dog's tooth. It seems his sleep was hindered by your railing; no wonder that his head is light; and his meat was sauced with your upbraidings; unquiet meals make ill digestions, and that has thrown him into this fever. You say his sports were disturbed by your brawls; being debarred from the enjoyment of society and recreation, what could ensue but dull melancholy and comfortless despair? The consequence is, then, that your jealous fits have made your husband mad.

Luciana would have excused her sister, saying, she always reprehended her husband mildly, and she said to her sister, "Why do you hear these rebukes without answering them?" But the abbess had made her so plainly perceive her fault that she could only answer, "She has betrayed me to my own reproof."

Adriana, though ashamed of her own conduct, still insisted on having her husband delivered up to her; but the abbess would suffer no person to enter her house, nor would she deliver up this unhappy man to the care of the jealous wife, determining herself to use gentle means for his recovery, and she retired into her house again and ordered her gates to be shut against them.

During the course of this eventful day, in which so many errors had happened from the likeness the twin brothers bore to each other, old Aegeon's day of grace was passing away, it being now near sunset; and at sunset he was doomed to die if he could not pay the money.

The place of his execution was near this convent, and here he arrived just as the abbess retired into the convent, the duke attending in person, that if any offered to pay the money he might be present to pardon him.

Adriana stopped this melancholy procession and cried out to the duke for justice, telling him that the abbess had refused to deliver up her lunatic husband to her care. While she was speaking, her real husband and his servant Dromio, who had got loose, came before the duke to demand justice, complaining that his wife had confined him on a false charge of lunacy, and telling in what manner he had broken his bands and eluded the vigilance of his keepers. Adriana was strangely surprised to see her husband when she thought he had been within the convent.

Aegeon, seeing his son, concluded this was the son who had left him to go in search of his mother and his brother, and he felt secure that this dear son would readily pay the money demanded for his ransom. He therefore spoke to Antipholis in words of fatherly affection, with joyful hope that he should now be released. But to the utter astonishment of Aegeon, his son denied all knowledge of him, as well he might, for this Antipholis had never seen his father since they were separated in the storm in his infancy; but while the poor old Aegeon was in vain endeavouring to make his son acknowledge him, thinking surely that either his griefs and the anxieties he had suffered had so strangely altered him that his son did not know him, or else that he was ashamed to acknowledge his father in his misery—in the midst of this perplexity the lady abbess and the other Antipholis and Dromio came out, and the wondering Adriana saw two husbands and two Dromios standing before her.

And now these riddling errors, which had so perplexed them all, were clearly made out. When the duke saw the two Antipholises and the two Dromios both so exactly alike, he at once conjectured aright of these seeming mysteries, for he remembered the story Aegeon had told him in the morning; and, he said, these men must be the two sons of Aegeon and their twin slaves.

But now an unlooked-for joy indeed completed the history of Aegeon; and the tale he had in the morning told in sorrow and under sentence of death before the setting sun went down was brought to a happy conclusion, for the venerable lady abbess made herself known to be the long-lost wife of Aegeon and the fond mother of the two Antipholises.

When the fishermen took the eldest Antipholis and Dromio away from her, she entered a nunnery, and by her wise and virtuous conduct she was at length made lady abbess of this convent, and in discharging the rights of hospitality to an unhappy stranger she had unknowingly protected her own son.

Joyful congratulations and affectionate greetings between these long-separated parents and their children made them for a while forget that Aegeon was yet under sentence of death; but when they were become a little calm, Antipholis of Ephesus offered the duke the ransom money for his father's life; but the duke freely pardoned Aegeon, and would not take the money. And the duke went with the abbess and her newly found husband and children into the convent to hear this happy family discourse at leisure of the blessed ending of their adverse fortunes. And the two Dromios' humble joy must not be forgotten; they had their congratulations and greetings too, and each Dromio pleasantly complimented his brother on his good looks, being well pleased to see his own person (as in a glass) show so handsome in his brother.

Adriana had so well profited by the good counsel of her mother-in-law that she never after cherished unjust suspicions, or was jealous of her husband.

Antipholis of Syracuse married the fair Luciana, the sister of his brother's wife; and the good old Aegeon, with his wife and sons, lived at Ephesus many years. Nor did the unravelling of these perplexities so entirely remove every ground of mistake for the future, but that sometimes, to remind them of adventures past, comical blunders would happen, and the one Antipholis, and the one Dromio, be mistaken for the other, making altogether a pleasant and diverting Comedy of Errors.

Hamlet, Prince Of Denmark

Gertrude, Queen of Denmark, becoming a widow by the sudden death of King Hamlet, in less than two months after his death married his brother Claudius, which was noted by all people at the time for a strange act of indiscretion, or unfeelingness, or worse; for this Claudius did noways resemble her late husband in the qualities of his person or his mind, but was as contemptible in outward appearance as he was base and unworthy in disposition; and suspicions did not fail to arise in the minds of some that he had privately made away with his brother, the late king, with the view of marrying his widow, and ascending the throne of Denmark, to the exclusion of young Hamlet, the son of the buried king, and lawful successor to the throne.

But upon no one did this unadvised action of the queen make such impression as upon this young prince, who loved and venerated the memory of his dead father almost to idolatry, and being of a nice sense of honour, and a most exquisite practiser of propriety himself, did sorely take to heart this unworthy conduct of his mother Gertrude, insomuch that, between grief for his father's death and shame for his mother's marriage, this young prince was overclouded with a deep melancholy, and lost all his mirth and all his good looks; all his customary pleasure in books forsook him, his princely exercises and sports, proper to his youth, were no longer acceptable; he grew weary of the world, which seemed to him an unweeded garden, where all the wholesome flowers were choked up, and nothing but weeds could thrive. Not that the prospect of exclusion from the throne, his lawful inheritance, weighed so much upon his spirits, though that to a young and high-minded prince was a bitter wound and a sore indignity; but what so galled him, and took away all his cheerful spirits, was, that his mother had shown herself so forgetful to his father's memory; and such a father! who had been to her so loving and gentle a husband; and then she always appeared as loving and obedient a wife to him, and would hang upon him as if her affection grew to him; and now within two months, or, as it seemed to young Hamlet, less than two months, she had married again, married his uncle, her dead husband's brother; in itself a highly improper and unlawful marriage from the nearness of relationship, but made much more so by the indecent haste with which it was concluded, and the unkingly character of the man whom she had chosen to be the partner of her throne. This it was which, more than the loss of ten kingdoms, dashed the spirits, and brought a cloud over the mind of this honourable young prince.

In vain was all that his mother Gertrude or the king could do or contrive to divert him; he still appeared in court in a suit of deep black, as mourning for the king his father's death, which mode of dress he had never laid aside, not even in compliment to his mother upon the day she was married, nor could he be brought to join in any of the festivities or rejoicings of that (as appeared to him) disgraceful day.

What mostly troubled him was an uncertainty about the manner of his father's death. It was given out by Claudius that a serpent had stung him, but young Hamlet had shrewd suspicions that Claudius himself was the serpent; in plain English, that he had murdered him for his crown, and that the serpent who stung his father did now sit on his throne.

How far he was right in this conjecture, and what he ought to think of his mother—how far she was privy to this murder, and whether by her consent or knowledge, or without, it came to pass—were the doubts which continually harassed and distracted him.

A rumour had reached the ear of young Hamlet that an apparition, exactly resembling the dead king his father, had been seen by the soldiers upon watch on the platform before the palace at midnight for two or three nights successively. The figure came constantly clad in the same suit of armour, from head to foot, which the dead king was known to have worn, and they who saw it (Hamlet's bosom friend, Horatio, was one) agreed in their testimony as to the manner and time of its appearance; that it came just as the clock struck twelve, that it looked pale, with a face more of sorrow than of anger, that its beard was grisly, and the colour a *sable silvered*, as they had seen it in his lifetime, that it made no answer when they spoke to it, yet once they thought it lifted up its head and addressed itself to motion as if it were about to speak, but in that moment the morning cock crew, and it shrunk in haste away and vanished out of their sight.

The young prince, strangely amazed at their relation, which was too consistent and agreeing with itself to disbelieve, concluded that it was his father's ghost which they had seen, and determined to take his watch with the soldiers that night, that he might have a chance of seeing it; for he reasoned with himself that such an appearance did not come for nothing, but that the ghost had something to impart, and though it had been silent hitherto, yet it would speak to him. And he waited with impatience for the coming of night.

When night came he took his stand with Horatio and Marcellus, one of the guard, upon the platform where this apparition was accustomed to walk, and it being a cold night, and the air unusually raw and nipping, Hamlet and Horatio and their companion fell into some talk about the coldness of the night, which was suddenly broken off by Horatio announcing that the ghost was coming.

At the sight of his father's spirit Hamlet was struck with a sudden surprise and fear. He at first called upon the angels and heavenly ministers to defend them, for he knew not whether it were a good spirit or bad, whether it came for good or for evil; but he gradually assumed more courage, and his father (as it seemed to him) looked upon him so piteously, and as it were desiring to have conversation with him, and did in all respects appear so like himself as he was when he lived, that Hamlet could not help addressing him. He called him by his name Hamlet, king, father, and conjured him that he would tell the reason why he had left his grave, where they had seen him quietly bestowed, to come again and visit the earth and the moonlight, and besought him that he would let them know if there was anything which they could do to give peace to his spirit. And the ghost beckoned to Hamlet, that he should go with him to some more removed place, where they might be alone, and Horatio and Marcellus would have dissuaded the young prince from following it, for they feared lest it should be some evil spirit, who would tempt him to the neighbouring sea, or to the top of some dreadful cliff, and there put on some horrible shape which might deprive the prince of his reason. But their counsels and entreaties could not alter Hamlet's determination, who cared too little about life to fear the losing of it; and as to his soul, he said, what could the spirit do to that, being a thing immortal as itself? And he felt as hardy as a lion; and bursting from them, who did all they could to hold him, he followed whithersoever the spirit led him.

And when they were alone together, the spirit broke silence, and told him that he was the ghost of Hamlet, his father, who had been cruelly murdered, and he told the manner of it; that it was done by his own brother Claudius, Hamlet's uncle, as Hamlet had already but too much suspected, for the hope of succeeding to his wife and crown. That as he was sleeping in his garden, his custom always in the afternoon, this treasonous brother stole upon him in his sleep, and poured the juice of poisonous henbane into his ears, which has such an antipathy to the life of man, that swift as quicksilver it courses through all the veins of the body, baking up the blood, and spreading a crust-like leprosy all over the skin; thus sleeping, by a brother's hand he was cut off at once from his crown, his queen, and his life: and he adjured Hamlet, if he did ever his dear father love, that he would revenge his foul murder. And the ghost lamented to his son that his mother should so fall off from truth as to prove false to the wedded love of her first husband, and to marry his murderer; but he cautioned Hamlet, howsoever he proceeded in his revenge against his wicked uncle, by no means to act any violence against the person of his mother, but to leave her to Heaven, and to the stings and thorns of conscience. And Hamlet promised to observe the ghost's direction in all things, and the ghost vanished.

And when Hamlet was left alone, he took up a solemn resolution, that all he had in his memory, all that he had ever learned by books or observation, should be instantly forgotten by him, and nothing live in his brain but the memory of what the ghost had told him and enjoined him to do. And Hamlet related the particulars of the conversation which had passed to none but his dear friend Horatio; and he enjoined both to him and Marcellus the strictest secrecy as to what they had seen that night.

The terror which the sight of the ghost had left upon the senses of Hamlet, he being weak and dispirited before, almost unhinged his mind, and drove him beside his reason. And he, fearing that it would continue to have this effect, which might subject him to observation, and set his uncle upon his guard, if he suspected that he was meditating anything against him, or that Hamlet really knew more of his father's death than he professed, took up a strange resolution, from that time to counterfeit as if he were really and truly mad; thinking that he would be less an object of suspicion when his uncle should believe him incapable of any serious project, and that his real perturbation of mind would be best covered and pass concealed wider a disguise of pretended lunacy.

From this time Hamlet affected a certain wildness and strangeness in his apparel, his speech, and behaviour, and did so excellently counterfeit the madman, that the king and queen were both deceived, and not thinking his grief for his father's death a sufficient cause to produce such a distemper—for they knew not of the appearance of the ghost—they concluded that his malady was love, and they thought they had found out the object.

Before Hamlet fell into the melancholy way which has been related, he had dearly loved a fair maid called Ophelia, the daughter of Polonius, the king's chief councillor in affairs of state. He had sent her letters and rings, and made many tenders of his affection to her, and importuned her with love in honourable fashion; and she had given belief to his vows and importunities. But the melancholy which he fell into latterly had made him neglect her, and from the time he conceived the project of counterfeiting madness, he affected to treat her with unkindness, and a sort of rudeness; but she, good lady, rather than reproach him with being false to her, persuaded herself that it was nothing but the disease in his mind, and no settled unkindness, which had made him less observant of her than formerly; and she compared the faculties of his once noble mind and excellent understanding, impaired as they were with the deep melancholy that oppressed him, to sweet bells which in themselves are capable of most excellent music, but when jangled out of tune, or rudely handled, produce only a harsh and unpleasing sound.

Though the rough business which Hamlet had in hand, the revenging of his father's death upon his murderer, did not suit with the playful state of courtship, or admit of the society of so idle a passion as love now seemed to him, yet it could not hinder but that soft thoughts of his Ophelia would come between; and in one of these moments, when he thought that his treatment of this gentle lady had been unreasonably harsh, he wrote her a letter full of wild starts of passion, and extravagant terms, such as agreed with his supposed madness, but mixed with some gentle touches of affection, which could not but show to this honoured lady, that a deep love for her yet lay at the bottom of his heart. He bade her to doubt the stars were fire, and to doubt the sun did move, to doubt truth to be a liar, but never to doubt that he loved with more of such extravagant phrases. This letter Ophelia dutifully showed to her father, and the old man thought himself bound to communicate it to the king and queen, who from that time supposed that the true cause of Hamlet's madness was love. And the queen wished that the good beauties of Ophelia might be the happy cause of his wildness, for so she hoped that her virtues might happily restore him to his accustomed way again, to both their honours.

But Hamlet's malady lay deeper than she supposed or than could be so cured. His father's ghost, which he had seen, still haunted his imagination, and the sacred injunction to revenge his murder gave him no rest till it was accomplished. Every hour of delay seemed to him a sin, and a violation of his father's commands. Yet how to compass the death of the king, surrounded as he constantly was with his guards, was no easy matter. Or if it had been, the presence of the queen, Hamlet's mother, who was generally with the king, was a restraint upon his purpose, which he could not break through. Besides, the very circumstance that the usurper was his mother's husband filled him with some remorse, and still blunted the edge of his purpose. The mere act of putting a fellow-creature to death was in itself odious and terrible to a disposition naturally so gentle as Hamlet's was. His very melancholy, and the dejection of spirits he had so long been in, produced an irresoluteness and wavering of purpose which kept him from proceeding to extremities. Moreover, he could not help having some scruples upon his mind, whether the spirit which he had seen was indeed his father, or whether it might not be the evil one, who he had heard has power to take any form he pleases, and who might have assumed his father's shape only to take advantage of his weakness and his melancholy, to drive him to the doing of so desperate an act as murder. And he determined that he would have more certain grounds to go upon than a vision, or apparition, which might be a delusion.

While he was in this irresolute mind, there came to the court certain players, in whom Hamlet formerly used to take delight, and particularly to hear one of them speak a tragical speech, describing the death of old Priam, King of Troy, with the grief of Hecuba, his queen. Hamlet welcomed his old friends, the players, and remembering how that speech had formerly given him pleasure, requested the player to repeat it, which he did in so lively a manner, setting forth the cruel murder of the feeble old king, with the destruction of his people and city by fire, and the mad grief of the old queen, running barefoot up and down the palace, with a poor clout upon that head where a crown had been, and with nothing but a blanket upon her loins, snatched up in haste, where she had worn a royal robe; that not only it drew tears from all that stood by, who thought they saw the real scene, so lively was it represented, but even the player himself delivered it with a broken voice and real tears. This put Hamlet upon thinking, if that player could so work himself up to passion by a mere fictitious speech, to weep for one that he had never seen, for Hecuba, that had been dead so many hundred years; how dull was he, who, having a real motive and cue for passion, a real king and a dear father murdered, was yet so little moved, that his revenge all this while had seemed to have slept in dull and muddy forgetfulness! And while he meditated on actors and acting, and the powerful effects which a good play represented to the life has upon the spectator, he remembered the instance of some murderer, who, seeing a murder on the stage, was by the mere force of the scene and resemblance of circumstances so affected that on the spot he confessed the crime which he had committed. And he determined that these players should play something like the murder of his father before his uncle, and he would watch narrowly what effect it might have upon him, and from his looks he would be able to gather with more certainty if he were the murderer or not. To this effect he ordered a play to be prepared, to the representation of which he invited the king and queen.

The story of the play was of a murder done in Vienna upon a duke. The duke's name was Gonzago, his wife Baptista. The play showed how one Lucianus, a near relation to the duke, poisoned him in his garden for his estate, and how the murderer in a short time after got the love of Gonzago's wife.

At the representation of this play the king, who did not know the trap which was laid for him, was present with his queen and the whole court, Hamlet sitting attentively near him to observe his looks. The play began with a conversation between Gonzago and his wife, in which the lady made many protestations of love and of never marrying a second husband if she should outlive Gonzago, wishing she might be accursed if ever she took a second husband, and adding that no woman ever did so but those wicked women who kill their first husbands. Hamlet observed the king, his uncle, change colour at this expression, and that it was as bad as wormwood both to him and to the queen. But when Lucianus, according to the story, came to poison Gonzago sleeping in the garden, the strong resemblance which it bore to his own wicked act upon the late king, his brother, whom he had poisoned in his garden, so struck upon the conscience of this usurper that he was unable to sit out the rest of the play, but on a sudden calling for lights to his chamber, and affecting or partly feeling a sudden sickness, he abruptly left the theatre. The king being departed the play was given over. Now Hamlet had seen enough to feel satisfied that the words of the ghost were true and no illusion; and in a fit of gaiety, like that which comes over a man who suddenly has some great doubt or scruple resolved, he swore to Horatio that he would take the ghost's word for a thousand pounds. But before he could make up his resolution as to what measures of revenge he should take, now he was certainly informed that his uncle was his father's murderer, he was sent for by the queen, his mother, to a private conference in her closet.

It was by desire of the king that the queen sent for Hamlet, that she might signify to her son how much his late behaviour had displeased them both; and the king, wishing to know all that passed at that conference, and thinking that the too partial report of a mother might let slip some part of Hamlet's words, which it might much import the king to know, Polonius, the old councillor of state, was ordered to plant himself behind the hangings in the queen's closet, where he might unseen hear all that passed. This artifice was particularly adapted to the disposition of Polonius, who was a man grown old in crooked maxims and policies of state, and delighted to get at the knowledge of matters in an indirect and cunning way.

Hamlet being come to his mother, she began to tax him in the roundest way with his actions and behaviour, and she told him that he had given great offence to *his father*, meaning the king, his uncle, whom, because he had married her, she called Hamlet's father. Hamlet, sorely indignant that she should give so dear and honoured a name as father seemed to him to a wretch who was indeed no better than the murderer of his true father, with some sharpness replied, "Mother, *you* have much offended *my father*." The queen said that was but an idle answer. "As good as the question deserved," said Hamlet. The queen asked him if he had forgotten who it was he was speaking to? "Alas!" replied Hamlet, "I wish I could forget. You are the queen, your husband's brother's wife, and you are my mother; I wish you were not what you are." "Nay, then," said the queen, "if you show me so little respect, I will send those to you that can speak," and was going to send the king or Polonius to him. But Hamlet would not let her go, now he had her alone, till he had tried if his words could not bring her to some sense of her wicked life; and, taking her by the wrist, he held her fast, and made her sit down. She, affrighted at his earnest manner, and fearful lest in his lunacy he should do her a mischief, cried out; and a voice was heard from behind the hangings, "Help, help the queen!" which Hamlet hearing, and verily thinking it was the king himself there concealed, he drew his sword, and stabbed at the place where the voice came from, as he would have stabbed a rat that ran there, till the voice ceasing, he concluded the person to be dead. But when he dragged forth the body, it was not the king, but Polonius, the old officious councillor, that had planted himself as a spy behind the hangings. "O me!" exclaimed the queen, "what a rash and bloody deed you have done!" "A bloody deed, mother," replied Hamlet, "but not so bad as yours, who killed a king, and married his brother." Hamlet had gone too far to leave off here. He was now in the humour to speak plainly to his mother, and he pursued it. And though the faults of parents are to be tenderly treated by their children, yet in the case of great crimes the son may have leave to speak even to his own mother with some harshness, so as that harshness is meant for her good, and to turn her from her wicked ways, and not done for the purpose of upbraiding. And now this virtuous prince did in moving terms represent to the queen the heinousness of her offence, in being so forgetful of the dead king, his father, as in so short a space of time to marry with his brother and reputed murderer; such an act as, after the vows which she had sworn to her first husband, was enough to make all vows of women suspected, and all virtue to be accounted hypocrisy, wedding contracts to be less than gamesters' oaths, and religion to be a mockery and a mere form of words. He said she had done such a deed, that the heavens blushed at it, and the earth was sick of her because of it. And he showed her two pictures, the one of the late king, her first husband, and the other of the present king, her second husband, and he bade her mark the difference: what a grace was on the brow of his father, how like a god he looked! the curls of Apollo, the forehead of Jupiter, the eye of Mars, and a posture like to Mercury newly alighted on some heaven-kissing hill! this man *had been* her husband. And then he showed her whom she had got in his stead; how like a blight or a mildew he looked, for so he had blasted his wholesome brother. And the queen was sore ashamed that he should so turn her eyes inward upon her soul, which she now saw so black and deformed. And he asked her how she could continue to live with this man, and be a wife to him who had murdered her first husband, and got the crown by as false means as a thief. And just as he spoke, the ghost of his father, such as he was in his lifetime, and such as he had lately seen it, entered the room, and Hamlet, in great terror, asked what it would have; and the ghost said that it came to remind him of the revenge he had promised, which Hamlet seemed to have forgot; and the ghost bade him speak to his mother, for the grief and terror she was in would else kill her. It then vanished, and was seen by none but Hamlet, neither could he by pointing to where it stood, or by any description, make his mother perceive it, who was terribly frightened all this while to hear him conversing, as it seemed to her, with nothing; and she imputed it to the disorder of his mind. But Hamlet begged her not to flatter her wicked soul in such a manner as to think that it was his madness, and not her own offences, which had brought his father's spirit again on the earth. And he bade her feel his pulse, how temperately it beat, not like a madman's. And he begged of her with tears to confess herself to Heaven for what was past, and for the future to avoid the company of the king, and be no more as a wife to him; and when she should show herself a mother to him, by respecting his father's memory, he would ask a blessing of her as a son. And she promising to observe his directions, the conference ended.

And now Hamlet was at leisure to consider who it was that, in his unfortunate rashness, he had killed, and when he came to see that it was Polonius, the father of the lady Ophelia, whom he so dearly loved, he drew apart the dead body, and, his spirits being a little quieter, he wept for what he had done.

This unfortunate death of Polonius gave the king a pretence for sending Hamlet out of the kingdom. He would willingly have put him to death, fearing him as dangerous, but he dreaded the people, who loved Hamlet; and the queen, who, with all her faults, doted upon the prince, her son. So this subtle king, under pretence of providing for Hamlet's safety, that he might not be called to account for Polonius's death, caused him to be conveyed on board a ship bound for England, under the care of two courtiers, by whom he despatched letters to the English Court, which at that time was in subjection and paid tribute to Denmark, requiring, for special reasons there pretended, that Hamlet should be put to death as soon as he landed on English ground. Hamlet, suspecting some treachery, in the night time secretly got at the letters, and skilfully erasing his own name, he in the stead of it put in the names of those two courtiers who had the charge of him to be put to death; then sealing up the letters he put them into their place again. Soon after the ship was attacked by pirates, and a sea-fight commenced, in the course of which Hamlet, desirous to show his valour, with sword in hand singly boarded the enemy's vessel, while his own ship, in a cowardly manner, bore away, and, leaving him to his fate, the two courtiers made the best of their way to England, charged with those letters the sense of which Hamlet had altered to their own deserved destruction.

The pirates, who had the prince in their power, showed themselves gentle enemies; and knowing whom they had got prisoner, in the hope that the prince might do them a good turn at court in recompense for any favour they might show him, they set Hamlet on shore at the nearest port in Denmark. From that place Hamlet wrote to the king acquainting him with the strange chance which had brought him back to his own country, and saying that on the next day he should present himself before his majesty. When he got home a sad spectacle offered itself the first thing to his eyes.

This was the funeral of the young and beautiful Ophelia, his once dear mistress. The wits of this young lady had begun to turn ever since her poor father's death. That he should die a violent death, and by the hands of the prince whom she loved, so affected this tender young maid, that in a little time she grew perfectly distracted, and would go about giving flowers away to the ladies of the court, and saying that they were for her father's burial, singing songs about love and about death, and sometimes such as had no meaning at all, as if she had no memory of what happened to her. There was a willow which grew slanting over a brook, and reflected its leaves in the stream. To this brook she came one day when she was unwatched, with garlands she had been making, mixed up of daisies and nettles, flowers and weeds together, and clambering up to hang her garland upon the boughs of the willow, a bough broke and precipitated this fair young maid, garland and all that she had gathered, into the water, where her clothes bore her up for a while, during which she chanted scraps of old tunes, like one insensible to her own distress, or as if she were a creature natural to that element; but long it was not before her garments, heavy with the wet, pulled her in from her melodious singing to a muddy and miserable death. It was the funeral of this fair maid which her brother Laertes was celebrating, the king and queen and whole court being present, when Hamlet arrived. He knew not what all this show imported, but stood on one side, not inclining to interrupt the ceremony. He saw the flowers strewed upon her grave, as the custom was in maiden burials, which the queen herself threw in; and as she threw them, she said, "Sweets to the sweet! I thought to have decked thy bride-bed, sweet maid, not to have strewed thy grave. Thou shouldst have been my Hamlet's wife." And he heard her brother wish that violets might spring from her grave; and he saw him leap into the grave all frantic with grief, and bid the attendants pile mountains of earth upon him, that he might be buried with her. And Hamlet's love for this fair maid came back to him, and he could not bear that a brother should show so much transport of grief, for he thought that he loved

Ophelia better than forty thousand brothers. Then discovering himself, he leaped into the grave where Laertes was, all as frantic or more frantic than he, and Laertes, knowing him to be Hamlet, who had been the cause of his father's and his sister's death, grappled him by the throat as an enemy, till the attendants parted them; and Hamlet, after the funeral, excused his hasty act in throwing himself into the grave as if to brave Laertes, but he said he could not bear that any one should seem to outgo him in grief for the death of the fair Ophelia. And for the time these two noble youths seemed reconciled.

But out of the grief and anger of Laertes for the death of his father and Ophelia, the king, Hamlet's wicked uncle, contrived destruction for Hamlet. He set on Laertes, under cover of peace and reconciliation, to challenge Hamlet to a friendly trial of skill at fencing, which Hamlet accepting, a day was appointed to try the match. At this match all the court was present, and Laertes, by direction of the king, prepared a poisoned weapon. Upon this match great wagers were laid by the courtiers, as both Hamlet and Laertes were known to excel at this sword-play; and Hamlet, taking up the foils, chose one, not at all suspecting the treachery of Laertes, or being careful to examine Laertes' weapon, who, instead of a foil or blunted sword, which the laws of fencing require, made use of one with a point and poisoned. At first Laertes did but play with Hamlet, and suffered him to gain some advantages, which the dissembling king magnified and extolled beyond measure, drinking to Hamlet's success, and wagering rich bets upon the issue; but after a few passes, Laertes, growing warm, made a deadly thrust at Hamlet with his poisoned weapon, and gave him a mortal blow. Hamlet, incensed, but not knowing the whole of the treachery, in the scuffle exchanged his own innocent weapon for Laertes' deadly one, and with a thrust of Laertes' own sword repaid Laertes home, who was thus justly caught in his own treachery. In this instant the queen shrieked out that she was poisoned. She had inadvertently drunk out of a bowl which the king had prepared for Hamlet, in case that, being warm in fencing, he should call for drink, into this the treacherous king had infused a deadly poison, to make sure of Hamlet, if Laertes had failed. He had forgotten to warn the queen of the bowl, which she drank of, and immediately died, exclaiming with her last breath that she was poisoned. Hamlet, suspecting some treachery, ordered the doors to be shut, while he sought it out. Laertes told him to seek no further, for he was the traitor; and feeling his life go away with the wound which Hamlet had given him, he made confession of the treachery he had used, and how he had fallen a victim to it; and he told Hamlet of the envenomed point, and said that Hamlet had not half an hour to live, for no medicine could cure him; and begging forgiveness of Hamlet, he died, with his last words accusing the king of being the contriver of the mischief. When Hamlet saw his end draw near, there being yet some venom left upon the sword, he suddenly turned upon his false uncle, and thrust the point of it to his heart, fulfilling the promise which he had made to his father's spirit, whose injunction was now accomplished, and his foul murder revenged upon the murderer. Then Hamlet, feeling his breath fail and life departing, turned to his dear friend Horatio, who had been spectator of this fatal tragedy, and with his dying breath requested him that he would live to tell his story to the world (for Horatio had made a motion as if he would slay himself to accompany the prince in death); and Horatio promised that he would make a true report, as one that was privy to all the circumstances. And, thus satisfied, the noble heart of Hamlet cracked; and Horatio and the bystanders with many tears commended the spirit of their sweet prince to the guardianship of angels. For Hamlet was a loving and a gentle prince, and greatly beloved for his many noble and prince-like qualities; and if he had lived, would no doubt have proved a most royal and complete king to Denmark.

The Tempest

There was a certain island in the sea, the only inhabitants of which were an old man, whose name was Prospero, and his daughter Miranda, a very beautiful young lady. She came to this island so young that she had no memory of having seen any other human face than her father's.

They lived in a cave or cell made out of a rock; it was divided into several apartments, one of which Prospero called his study; there he kept his books, which chiefly treated of magic, a study at that time much affected by all learned men; and the knowledge of this art he found very useful to him, for being thrown by a strange chance upon this island, which had been enchanted by a witch called Sycorax, who died there a short time before his arrival, Prospero, by virtue of his art, released many good spirits, that Sycorax had imprisoned in the bodies of large trees, because they had refused to execute her wicked commands. These gentle spirits were ever after obedient to the will of Prospero. Of these Ariel was the chief.

The lively little sprite Ariel had nothing mischievous in his nature, except that he took rather too much pleasure in tormenting an ugly monster called Caliban, for he owed him a grudge because he was the son of his old enemy Sycorax. This Caliban Prospero found in the woods a strange misshapen thing, far less human in form than an ape; he took him home to his cell and taught him to speak, and Prospero would have been very kind to him, but the bad nature which Caliban inherited from his mother Sycorax would not let him learn anything good or useful; therefore he was employed like a slave to fetch wood, and do the most laborious offices; and Ariel had the charge of compelling him to these services.

When Caliban was lazy and neglected his work, Ariel (who was invisible to all eyes but Prospero's) would come slyly and pinch him, and sometimes tumble him down in the mire; and then Ariel, in the likeness of an ape, would make mouths at him. Then swiftly changing his shape, in the likeness of a hedgehog he would lie tumbling in Caliban's way, who feared the hedgehog's sharp quills would prick his bare feet. With a variety of such-like vexatious tricks Ariel would often torment him, whenever Caliban neglected the work which Prospero commanded him to do.

Having these powerful spirits obedient to his will, Prospero could by their means command the winds and the waves of the sea. By his orders they raised a violent storm, in the midst of which, and struggling with the wild sea-waves that every moment threatened to swallow it up, he showed his daughter a fine large ship, which he told her was full of living beings like themselves. "O my dear father," said she, "if by your art you have raised this dreadful storm, have pity on their sad distress. See! the vessel will be dashed to pieces. Pour souls! they will all perish. If I had power I would sink the sea beneath the earth rather than the good ship should be destroyed with all the precious souls within her."

"Be not so amazed, daughter Miranda," said Prospero; "there is no harm done. I have so ordered it that no person in the ship shall receive any hurt. What I have done has been in care of you, my dear child. You are ignorant who you are or where you came from, and you know no more of me but that I am your father, and live in this poor cave. Can you remember a time before you came to this cell? I think you cannot, for you were not then three years of age."

"Certainly I can, sir," replied Miranda.

"By what?" asked Prospero; "by any other house or person? Tell me what you can remember, my child.

Miranda said, "It seems to me like the recollection of a dream. But had I not once four or five women who attended upon me?"

Prospero answered, "You had, and more. How is it that this still lives in your mind? Do you remember how you came here?"

"No, sir," said Miranda, "I remember nothing more."

"Twelve years ago, Miranda," continued Prospero, "I was Duke of Milan, and you were a princess and my only heir. I had a younger brother whose name was Antonio, to whom I trusted everything; and as I was fond of retirement and deep study, I commonly left the management of my state affairs to your uncle, my false brother (for so indeed he proved). I, neglecting all worldly ends, buried among my books, did dedicate my whole time to the betterment of my mind. My brother Antonio, being thus in possession of my power, began to think himself the duke indeed. The opportunity I gave him of making himself popular among my subjects awakened in his bad nature a proud ambition to deprive me of my dukedom: this he soon effected with the aid of the King of Naples, a powerful prince, who was my enemy."

"Wherefore," said Miranda, "did they not that hour destroy us?"

"My child," answered her father, "they durst not, so dear was the love that my people bore me. Antonio carried us on board a ship, and when we were some leagues out at sea he forced us into a small boat, without either tackle, sail, or mast; there he left us, as he thought, to perish. But a kind lord of my court, one Gonzalo, who loved me, had privately placed in the boat water, provisions, apparel, and some books which I prize above my dukedom."

"O my father," said Miranda, "what a trouble must I have been to you then!"

"No, my love," said Prospero, "you were a little cherub that did preserve me. Your innocent smiles made me to bear up against my misfortunes. Our food lasted till we landed on this desert island, since when my chief delight has been in teaching you, Miranda, and well have you profited by my instructions."

"Heaven thank you, my dear father," said Miranda. "Now pray tell me, sir, your reason for raising this sea storm."

"Know then," said her father, "that by means of this storm my enemies, the King of Naples and my cruel brother, are cast ashore upon this island."

Having so said, Prospero gently touched his daughter with his magic wand, and she fell fast asleep; for the spirit Ariel just then presented himself before his master to give an account of the tempest, and how he had disposed of the ship's company; and though the spirits were always invisible to Miranda, Prospero did not choose she should hear him holding converse (as would seem to her) with the empty air.

"Well, my brave spirit," said Prospero to Ariel, "how have you performed your task?"

Ariel gave a lively description of the storm, and of the terror of the mariners, and how the king's son, Ferdinand, was the first who leaped into the sea, and his father thought he saw this dear son swallowed up by the waves and lost. "But he is safe," said Ariel, "in a corner of the isle, sitting with his arms folded, sadly lamenting the loss of the king, his father, whom he concludes drowned. Not a hair of his head is injured, and his princely garments, though drenched in the sea-waves, look fresher than before."

"That's my delicate Ariel," said Prospero. "Bring him hither; my daughter must see this young prince. Where is the king and my brother?"

"I left them," answered Ariel, "searching for Ferdinand, whom they have little hopes of finding, thinking they saw him perish. Of the ship's crew not one is missing, though each one thinks himself the only one saved; and the ship, though invisible to them, is safe in the harbour."

"Ariel," said Prospero, "thy charge is faithfully performed, but there is more work yet."

"Is there more work?" said Ariel. "Let me remind you, master, you have promised me my liberty. I pray, remember I have done you worthy service told you no lies, made no mistakes, served you without grudge or grumbling."

"How now?" said Prospero. "You do not recollect what a torment I freed you from. Have you forgotten the wicked witch Sycorax, who with age and envy was almost bent double? Where was she born? Speak; tell me."

"Sir, in Algiers," said Ariel.

"Oh, was she so?" said Prospero. "I must recount what you have been, which I find you do not remember. This bad witch Sycorax, for her witchcrafts, too terrible to enter human hearing, was banished from Algiers, and here left by the sailors, and because you were a spirit too delicate to execute her wicked commands, she shut you up in a tree, where I found you howling. This torment, remember, I did free you from."

"Pardon me, dear master," said Ariel, ashamed to seem ungrateful; "I will obey your commands."

"Do so," said Prospero, "and I will set you free." He then gave orders what further he would have him do, and away went Ariel, first to where he had left Ferdinand, and found him still sitting on the grass in the same melancholy posture.

"O, my young gentleman," said Ariel, when he saw him, "I will soon move you. You must be brought I find, for the Lady Miranda to have a sight of your pretty person. Come, sir, follow me." He then began singing,

> *"Full fathom five thy father lies:*
> *Of his bones are coral made;*
> *Those are pearls that were his eyes:*
> *Nothing of him that doth fade,*
> *But doth suffer a sea-change*
> *Into something rich and strange.*
> *Sea-nymphs hourly ring his knell:*
> *Hark, now I hear them, ding-dong bell."*

This strange news of his lost father soon roused the prince from the stupid fit into which he had fallen. He followed in amazement the sound of Ariel's voice till it led him to Prospero and Miranda, who were seated under the shade of a large tree. Now, Miranda had never seen a man before except her own father.

"Miranda," said Prospero, "tell me what you are looking at yonder."

"O, father," said Miranda, in a strange surprise, "surely that is a spirit. Lord! how it looks about! Believe me, sir, it is a beautiful creature. Is it not a spirit?"

"No, girl," answered her father; "it eats, and sleeps, and has senses such as we have. This young man you see was in the ship. He is somewhat altered by grief, or you might call him a handsome person. He has lost his companions, and is wandering about to find them."

Miranda, who thought all men had grave faces and grey beards like her father, was delighted with the appearance of this beautiful young prince; and Ferdinand, seeing such a lovely lady in this desert place, and from the strange sounds he had heard expected nothing but wonders, thought he was upon an enchanted island, and that Miranda was the goddess of the place, and as such he began to address her.

She timidly answered she was no goddess, but a simple maid, and was going to give an account of herself, when Prospero interrupted her. He was well pleased to find they admired each other, for he plainly perceived they had (as we say) fallen in love at first sight; but to try Ferdinand's constancy, he resolved to throw some difficulties in their way; therefore advancing forward, he addressed the prince with a stern air, telling him he came to the island as a spy, to take it from him who was the lord of it. "Follow me," said he, "I will tie you neck and feet together. You shall drink sea-water; shell-fish, withered roots, and husks of acorns shall be your food." "No," said Ferdinand, I will resist such entertainment till I see a more powerful enemy," and drew his sword, but Prospero, waving his magic wand, fixed him to the spot where he stood, so that he had no power to move.

Miranda hung upon her father, saying, "Why are you so ungentle? Have pity, sir, I will be his surety. This is the second man I ever saw, and to me he seems a true one."

"Silence," said her father, "one word more will make me chide you, girl! What! an advocate for an impostor! You think there are no more such fine men, having seen only him and Caliban. I tell you, foolish girl, most men as far excel this as he does Caliban. "This he said to prove his daughter's constancy; and she replied, "My affections are most humble. I have no wish to see a goodlier man."

"Come on, young man," said Prospero to the prince, "you have no power to disobey me."

"I have not indeed," answered Ferdinand; and not knowing it was by magic he was deprived of all power of resistance, he was astonished to find he was so strangely compelled to follow Prospero: looking back on Miranda as long as he could see her, he said, as he went after Prospero into the cave, "My spirits are all bound up, as if I were in a dream: but this man's threats, and the weakness which I feel, would seem light to me if from my prison I might once a day behold this fair maid."

Prospero kept Ferdinand not long confined within the cell: he soon brought out his prisoner, and set him a severe task to perform, taking care to let his daughter know the hard labour he had imposed on him, and then pretending to go into his study, he secretly watched them both.

Prospero had commanded Ferdinand to pile up some heavy-logs of wood. King's sons not being much used to laborious work,

Miranda soon after found her lover almost dying with fatigue. "Alas!" said she, "do not work so hard; my father is at his studies, he is safe for these three hours; pray rest yourself."

"O, my dear lady," said Ferdinand, "I dare not. I must finish my task before I take my rest."

"If you will sit down," said Miranda, "I will carry your logs the while." But this Ferdinand would by no means agree to. Instead of a help Miranda became a hindrance, for they began a long conversation, so that the business of log-carrying went on very slowly.

Prospero, who had enjoined Ferdinand this task merely as a trial of his love, was not at his books as his daughter supposed, but was standing by them invisible, to overhear what they said.

Ferdinand inquired her name, which she told him, saying it was against her father's express command she did so.

Prospero only smiled at this first instance of his daughter's disobedience, for having by his magic art caused his daughter to fall in love so suddenly, he was not angry that she showed her love by forgetting to obey his commands. And he listened well pleased to a long speech of Ferdinand's, in which he professed to love her above all the ladies he ever saw.

In answer to his praises of her beauty, which he said exceeded all the women in the world, she replied, "I do not remember the face of any woman, nor have I see any more men than you, my good friend, and my dear father. How features are abroad, I know not: but believe me, sir, I would not wish any companion in the world but you, nor can my imagination form any shape but yours that I could like. But, sir, I fear I talk to you too freely, and my father's precepts I forget."

At this Prospero smiled and nodded his head, as much as to say, "This goes on exactly as I could wish; my girl will be Queen of Naples."

And then Ferdinand, in another fine long speech (for young princes speak in courtly phrases), told the innocent Miranda he was heir to the crown of Naples, and that she should be his queen.

"Ah! sir," said she, "I am a fool to weep at what I am glad of. I will answer you in plain and holy innocence. I am your wife if you will marry me."

Prospero prevented Ferdinand's thanks by appearing visible before them.

"Fear nothing, my child," said he, "I have overheard and approve of all you have said. And, Ferdinand, if I have too severely used you, I will make you rich amends by giving you my daughter. All your vexations were but my trials of your love, and you have nobly stood the test. Then as my gift, which your true love has worthily purchased, take my daughter, and do not smile that I boast she is above all praise." He then, telling them that he had business which required his presence, desired they would sit down and talk together till he returned; and this command Miranda seemed not at all disposed to disobey.

When Prospero left them, he called his spirit Ariel, who quickly appeared before him, eager to relate what he had done with Prospero's brother and the King of Naples. Ariel said he had left them almost out of their senses with fear at the strange things he had caused them to see and hear. When fatigued with wandering about and famished for want of food, he had suddenly set before them a delicious banquet, and then, just as they were going to eat, he appeared visible before them, in the shape of a harpy, a voracious monster with wings, and the feast vanished away. Then, to their utter amazement, this seeming harpy spoke to them, reminding them of their cruelty in driving Prospero from his dukedom, and leaving him and his infant daughter to perish in the sea, saying that for this cause these terrors were suffered to afflict them.

The King of Naples and Antonio, the false brother, repented the injustice they had done to Prospero; and Ariel told his master he was certain their penitence was sincere, and that he, though a spirit, could not but pity them.

"Then bring them hither, Ariel," said Prospero; "if you, who are but a spirit, feel for their distress, shall not I, who am a human being like themselves, have compassion on them? Bring them quickly, my dainty Ariel."

Ariel soon returned with the king, Antonio, and old Gonzalo in their train, who had followed him wondering at the wild music he played in the air to draw them on to his master's presence. This Gonzalo was the same who had so kindly provided Prospero formerly with books and provisions, when his wicked brother left him, as he thought, to perish in an open boat in the sea.

Grief and terror had so stupefied their senses that they did not know Prospero. He first discovered himself to the good old Gonzalo, calling him the preserver of his life, and then his brother and the king knew that he was the injured Prospero.

Antonio, with tears and sad words of sorrow and true repentance, implored his brother's forgiveness; and the king expressed his sincere remorse for having assisted Antonio to depose his brother; and Prospero forgave them, and upon their engaging to restore his dukedom, he said to the King of Naples, "I have a gift in store for you too," and opening a door, showed him his son Ferdinand playing at chess with Miranda

Nothing could exceed the joy of the father and the son at this unexpected meeting, for they each thought the other drowned in the storm.

"O wonder!" said Miranda, "what noble creatures these are! it must surely be a brave world that has such people in it."

The King of Naples was almost as much astonished at the beauty and excellent graces of the young Miranda as his son had been. "Who is this maid?" said he; "she seems the goddess that has parted us and brought us thus together." "No, sir," answered Ferdinand, smiling to find his father had fallen into the same mistake that he had done when he first saw Miranda, "she is a mortal, but by immortal Providence she is mine; I chose her when I could not ask you, my father, for your consent, not thinking you were alive. She is the daughter of this Prospero, who is the famous Duke of Milan, of whose renown I have heard so much, but never saw him till now; of him I have received a new life; he has made himself to me a second father, giving me this dear lady."

"Then I must be her father," said the king "but oh! how oddly will it sound, that I must ask my child's forgiveness."

"No more of that," said Prospero; "let us not remember our troubles past, since they so happily have ended." And then Prospero embraced his brother, and again assured him of his forgiveness, and said that a wise, overruling Providence had permitted that he should be driven from his poor dukedom of Milan, that his daughter might inherit the crown of Naples, for that by their meeting in this desert island it had happened that the king's son had loved Miranda.

These kind words which Prospero spoke, meaning to comfort his brother, so filled Antonio with shame and remorse that he wept and was unable to speak, and the kind old Gonzalo wept to see this joyful reconciliation, and prayed for blessings on the young couple.

Prospero now told them that their ship was safe in the harbour, and the sailors all on board her, and that he and his daughter would accompany them home the next morning. "In the meantime," said he, "partake of such refreshments as my poor cave affords, and for your evening's entertainment I will relate the history of my life from my first landing in this desert island." He then called for Caliban to prepare some food and set the cave in order, and the company were astonished at the uncouth form and savage appearance of this ugly monster, who, Prospero said, was the only attendant he had to wait upon him.

Before Prospero left the island he dismissed Ariel from his service, to the great joy of that lively little spirit, who, though he had been a faithful servant to his master, was always longing to enjoy his free liberty, to wander uncontrolled in the air like a wild bird, under green trees, among pleasant fruits and sweet-smelling flowers. "My quaint Ariel," said Prospero to the little sprite when he made him free, "I shall miss you; yet you shall have your freedom." "Thank you, my dear master," said Ariel; "but give me leave to attend your ship home with prosperous gales before you bid farewell to the assistance of your faithful spirit, and then, master, when I am free how merrily I shall live!" Here Ariel sung this pretty song—

> *"Where the bee sucks, there suck I;*
> *In a cowslips bell I lie:*
> *There I couch when owls do fly*
> *After summer merrily.*
> *Merrily, merrily, shall I live now*
> *Under the blossom that hangs on the bow."*

Prospero then buried deep in the earth his magical books and wand, for he was resolved never more to make use of the magic art. And having thus overcome his enemies, and being reconciled to his brother and the King of Naples, nothing now remained to complete his happiness but to revisit his native land, to take possession of his dukedom, and to witness the happy nuptials of his daughter Miranda and Prince Ferdinand, which the king said should be instantly celebrated with great splendour on their return to Naples, at which place, under the safe convoy of the spirit Ariel, they after a pleasant voyage soon arrived.

As You Like It

During the time that France was divided into provinces (or duke-doms as they were called) there reigned in one of these provinces an usurper, who had deposed and banished his elder brother, the lawful duke.

The duke, who was thus driven from his dominions, retired with a few faithful followers to the forest of Arden; and here the good duke lived with his loving friends, who had put themselves into a voluntary exile for his sake, while their lands and revenues en-riched the false usurper; and custom soon made the life of careless ease they led here more sweet to them than the pomp and uneasy splendour of a courtier's life. Here they lived like the old Robin Hood of England, and to this forest many noble youths daily re-sorted from the court, and did fleet the time carelessly, as they did who lived in the golden age. In the summer they lay along under the fine shade of the large forest trees, marking the playful sports of the wild deer; and so fond were they of these poor dappled fools, who seemed to be the native inhabitants of the forest, that it grieved them to be forced to kill them to supply themselves with venison for their food. When the cold winds of winter made the duke feel the change of his adverse fortune, he would endure it patiently and say, "These chilling winds which blow upon my body are true counsellors; they do not flatter, but represent truly to me my condi-tion; and though they bite sharply, their tooth is nothing like so keen as that of unkindness and ingratitude. I find that, howsoever man speak against adversity, yet some sweet uses are to be ex-tracted from it; like the jewel, precious for medicine, which is taken from the head of the venomous and despised toad." In this manner did the patient duke draw a useful moral from everything that he saw, and by the help of this moralising turn, in that life of his, re-mote from public haunts, he could find tongues in trees, books in the running brooks, sermons in stones, and good in everything.

The banished duke had an only daughter, named Rosalind, whom the usurper, Duke Frederick, when he banished her father, still retained in his court as a companion for his own daughter Celia. A strict friendship subsisted between these ladies, which the disagreement between their fathers did not in the least interrupt, Celia striving by every kindness in her power to make amends to Rosalind for the injustice of her own father in deposing the father of Rosalind, and whenever the thoughts of her father's banishment, and her own dependence on the false usurper, made Rosalind melancholy, Celia's whole care was to comfort and console her.

One day, when Celia was talking in her usual kind manner to Rosalind, saying, "I pray you, Rosalind, my sweet cousin, be merry," a messenger entered from the duke, to tell them that if they wished to see a wrestling match, which was just going to begin, they must come instantly to the court before the palace; and Celia, thinking it would amuse Rosalind, agreed to go and see it.

In those times wrestling, which is only practised now by country clowns, was a favourite sport even in the courts of princes, and before fair ladies and princesses. To this wrestling match, therefore, Celia and Rosalind went. They found that it was likely to prove a very tragical sight, for a large and powerful man, who had long been practised in the art of wrestling, and had slain many men in contests of this kind, was just going to wrestle with a very young man, who, from his extreme youth and inexperience in the art, the beholders all thought would certainly be killed.

When the duke saw Celia and Rosalind, he said "How now, daughter and niece, are you crept hither to see the wrestling? You will take little delight in it; there is such odds in the men. In pity to this young man, I would wish to persuade him from wrestling. Speak to him, ladies, and see if you can move him."

The ladies were well pleased to perform this humane office, and first Celia entreated the young stranger that he would desist from the attempt, and then Rosalind spoke so kindly to him, and with such feeling consideration for the danger he was about to undergo, that, instead of being persuaded by her gentle words to forego his purpose, all his thoughts were bent to distinguish himself by his courage in this lovely lady's eyes. He refused the request of Celia and Rosalind in such graceful and modest words that they felt still more concern for him. He concluded his refusal with saying "I am sorry to deny such fair and excellent ladies anything. But let your fair eyes and gentle wishes go with me to my trial, wherein, if I be conquered, there is one shamed that was never gracious; if I am killed, there is one dead that is willing to die. I shall do my friends no wrong, for I have none to lament me; the world no injury, for in it I have nothing; for I only fill up a place in the world which may be better supplied when I have made it empty."

And now the wrestling match began. Celia wished the young stranger might not be hurt, but Rosalind felt most for him. The friendless state which he said he was in, and that he wished to die, made Rosalind think that he was, like herself, unfortunate, and she pitied him so much, and so deep an interest she took in his danger while he was wrestling, that she might almost be said at that moment to have fallen in love with him.

The kindness shown this unknown youth by these fair and noble ladies gave him courage and strength, so that he performed wonders, and in the end completely conquered his antagonist, who was so much hurt that for a while he was unable to speak or move.

The Duke Frederick was much pleased with the courage and skill shown by this young stranger, and desired to know his name and parentage, meaning to take him under his protection.

The stranger said his name was Orlando, and that he was the youngest son of Sir Rowland de Bois.

Sir Rowland de Bois, the father of Orlando, had been dead some years; but when he was living he had been a true subject and dear friend of the banished duke; therefore, when Frederick heard Orlando was the son of his banished brother's friend, all his liking for this brave young man was changed into displeasure, and he left the place in very ill humour. Hating to hear the very name of any of his brother's friends, and yet still admiring the valour of the youth, he said as he went out that he wished Orlando had been the son of any other man.

Rosalind was delighted to hear that her new favourite was the son of her father's old friend, and she said to Celia, "My father loved Sir Rowland de Bois, and if I had known this young man was his son I would have added tears to my entreaties before he should have ventured."

The ladies then went up to him, and seeing him abashed by the sudden displeasure shown by the duke, they spoke kind and encouraging words to him; and Rosalind, when they were going away, turned back to speak some more civil things to the brave young son of her father's old friend; and taking a chain from off her neck, she said, "Gentleman, wear this for me. I am out of suits with fortune, or I would give you a more valuable present."

When the ladies were alone, Rosalind's talk being still of Orlando, Celia began to perceive her cousin had fallen in love with the handsome young wrestler, and she said to Rosalind, "Is it possible you should fall in love so suddenly?" Rosalind replied, "The duke, my father, loved his father dearly." "But" said Celia, "does it therefore follow that you should love his son dearly? for then I ought to hate him, for my father hated his father; yet I do not hate Orlando."

Frederick being enraged at the sight of Sir Rowland de Bois' son, which reminded him of the many friends the banished duke had among the nobility, and having been for some time displeased with his niece, because the people praised her for her virtues, and pitied her for her good father's sake, his malice suddenly broke out against her; and while Celia and Rosalind were talking of Orlando, Frederick entered the room, and with looks full of anger ordered Rosalind instantly to leave the palace, and follow her father into banishment, telling Celia, who in vain pleaded for her, that he had only suffered Rosalind to stay upon her account. "I did not then," said Celia, "entreat you to let her stay, for I was too young at that time to value her; but now that I know her worth, and that we so long have slept together, rose at the same instant, learned, played, and eat together, I cannot live out of her company." Frederick replied, "She is too subtle for you; her smoothness, her very silence and her patience speak to the people, and they pity her. You are a fool to plead for her, for you will seem more bright and virtuous when she is gone; therefore open not your lips in her favour, for the doom which I have passed upon her is irrevocable."

When Celia found she could not prevail upon her father to let Rosalind remain with her, she generously resolved to accompany her; and, leaving her father's palace that night, she went along with her friend to seek Rosalind's father, the banished duke, in the forest of Arden.

Before they set out, Celia considered that it would be unsafe for two young ladies to travel in the rich clothes they then wore; she therefore proposed that they should disguise their rank by dressing themselves like country maids. Rosalind said it would be a still greater protection if one of them was to be dressed like a man; and so it was quickly agreed on between them, that as Rosalind was the taller, she should wear the dress of a young countryman, and Celia should be habited like a country lass, and that they should say they were brother and sister; and Rosalind said she would be called Ganymede, and Celia chose the name of Aliena.

In this disguise, and taking their money and jewels to defray their expenses, these fair princesses set out on their long travel, for the forest of Arden was a long way off, beyond the boundaries of the duke's dominions.

The Lady Rosalind (or Ganymede, as she must now be called) with her manly garb seemed to have put on a manly courage. The faithful friendship Celia had shown in accompanying Rosalind so many weary miles made the new brother, in recompense for this true love, exert a cheerful spirit, as if he were indeed Ganymede, the rustic and stout-hearted brother of the gentle village maiden, Aliena.

When at last they came to the forest of Arden, they no longer found the convenient inns and good accommodations they had met with on the road, and being in want of food and rest, Ganymede, who had so merrily cheered his sister with pleasant speeches and happy remarks all the way, now owned to Aliena that he was so weary he could find in his heart to disgrace his man's apparel and cry like a woman, and Aliena declared she could go no farther, and then again Ganymede tried to recollect that it was a man's duty to comfort and console a woman as the weaker vessel, and, to seem courageous to his new sister, he said—"Come, have a good heart, my sister Aliena; we are now at the end of our travel in the forest of Arden." But feigned manliness and forced courage would no longer support them, for though they were in the forest of Arden they knew not where to find the duke, and here the travel of these weary ladies might have come to a sad conclusion, for they might have lost themselves and have perished for want of food; but, providentially, as they were sitting on the grass, almost dying with fatigue and hopeless of any relief, a countryman chanced to pass that way, and Ganymede once more tried to speak with a manly boldness, saying, "Shepherd, if love or gold can in this desert place procure us entertainment, I pray you bring us where we may rest ourselves, for this young maid, my sister, is much fatigued with travelling, and faints for want of food."

The man replied that he was only servant to a shepherd, and that his master's house was just going to be sold, and therefore they would find but poor entertainment, but that if they would go with him they should be welcome to what there was. They followed the man, the near prospect of relief giving them fresh strength, and bought the house and sheep of the shepherd, and took the man who conducted them to the shepherd's house to wait on them, and being by this means so fortunately provided with a neat cottage, and well supplied with provisions, they agreed to stay here till they could learn in what part of the forest the duke dwelt.

When they were rested after the fatigue of their journey, they began to like their new way of life, and almost fancied themselves the shepherd and shepherdess they feigned to be; yet sometimes Ganymede remembered he had once been the same Lady Rosalind who had so dearly loved the brave Orlando, because he was the son of old Sir Rowland, her father's friend, and though Ganymede thought that Orlando was many miles distant, even so many weary miles as they had travelled, yet it soon appeared that Orlando was also in the forest of Arden, and in this manner this strange event came to pass.

Orlando was the youngest son of Sir Rowland de Bois, who, when he died, left him (Orlando being then very young) to the care of his eldest brother Oliver, charging Oliver, on his blessing, to give his brother a good education, and provide for him as became the dignity of their ancient house. Oliver proved an unworthy brother, and, disregarding the commands of his dying father, he never put his brother to school, but kept him at home untaught and entirely neglected. But in his nature and in the noble qualities of his mind Orlando so much resembled his excellent father that, without any advantages of education, he seemed like a youth who had been bred with the utmost care; and Oliver so envied the fine person and dignified manners of his untutored brother, that at last he wished to destroy him; and to effect this he set on people to persuade him to wrestle with the famous wrestler, who, as has been before related, had killed so many men. Now it was this cruel brother's neglect of him which made Orlando say he wished to die, being so friendless.

When, contrary to the wicked hopes he had formed, his brother proved victorious, his envy and malice knew no bounds, and he swore he would burn the chamber where Orlando slept. He was overheard making his vow by one that had been an old and faithful friend to their father, and that loved Orlando because he resembled Sir Rowland. This old man went out to meet him when he returned from the duke's palace, and when he saw Orlando, the peril his dear young master was in made him break out into these passionate exclamations: "O, my gentle master, my sweet master; O, you memory of old Sir Rowland! why are you virtuous, why are you gentle, strong, and valiant, and why would you be so fond to overcome the famous wrestler? Your praise is come too swiftly home before you." Orlando, wondering what all this meant, asked him what was the matter.

And then the old man told him how his wicked brother, envying the love all people bore him, and now hearing the fame he had gained by his victory in the duke's palace, intended to destroy him by setting fire to his chamber that night; and, in conclusion, advised him to escape the danger he was in by instant flight; and knowing Orlando had no money, Adam (for that was the good old man's name) had brought out with him his own little hoard, and he said, "I have five hundred crowns, the thrifty hire I saved under your father, and laid by to be provision for me when my old limbs should become unfit for service; take that, and He that doth the ravens feed be comfort to my age! Here is the gold; all this I give to you; let me be your servant; though I look old, I will do the service of a younger man in all your business and necessities."

O good old man!" said Orlando, "how well appears in you the constant service of the old world! You are not for the fashion of these times. We will go along together, and before your youthful wages are spent I shall light upon some means for both our maintenance."

Together, then, this faithful servant and his loved master set out; and Orlando and Adam travelled on uncertain what course to pursue, till they came to the forest of Arden, and there they found themselves in the same distress for want of food that Ganymede and Aliena had been. They wandered on, seeking some human habitation, till they were almost spent with hunger and fatigue. Adam at last said, "O my dear master, I die for want of food, I can go no farther!" He then laid himself down, thinking to make that place his grave, and bade his dear master farewell. Orlando, seeing him in this weak state, took his old servant up in his arms, and carried him under the shelter of some pleasant trees; and he said to him, "Cheerily, old Adam, rest your weary limbs here a while, and do not talk of dying!" Orlando then searched about to find some food, and he happened to arrive at that part of the forest where the duke was, and he and his friends were just going to eat their dinner, this royal duke being seated on the grass, under no other canopy than the shady cover of some large trees.

Orlando, whom hunger had made desperate, drew his sword, intending to take their meat by force, and said, "Forbear, and eat no more; I must have your food!" The duke asked him if distress had made him so bold, or if he were a rude despiser of good manners? On this Orlando said he was dying with hunger, and then the duke told him he was welcome to sit down and eat with them. Orlando, hearing him speak so gently, put up his sword, and blushed with shame at the rude manner in which he had demanded their food. "Pardon me, I pray you," said he; "I thought that all things had been savage here, and therefore I put on the countenance of stern command; but whatever men you are that in this desert, under the shade of melancholy boughs, lose and neglect the creeping hours of time; if ever you have looked on better days; if ever you have been where bells have knolled to church; if you have ever sat at any good man's feast; if ever from your eyelids you have wiped a tear, and know what it is to pity or be pitied, may gentle speeches now move you to do me human courtesy!" The duke replied, "True it is that we are men (as you say) who have seen better days, and though we have now our habitation in this wild forest, we have lived in towns and cities, and have with holy bell been knolled to church, have sat at good men's feasts, and from our eyes have wiped the drops which sacred pity has engendered: therefore sit you down, and take of our refreshment as much as will minister to your wants." "There is a poor old man," answered Orlando, "who has limped after me many a weary step in pure love, oppressed at once with two sad infirmities, age and hunger; till he be satisfied I must not touch a bit." "Go, find him out, and bring him hither," said the duke; "we will forbear to eat till you return." Then Orlando went like a doe to find its fawn and give it food, and presently returned bringing Adam in his arms; and the duke said, "Set down your venerable burden; you are both welcome": and they fed the old man and cheered his heart, and he revived, and recovered his health and strength again.

The duke inquired who Orlando was, and when he found that he was the son of his old friend, Sir Rowland de Bois, he took him under his protection, and Orlando and his old servant lived with the duke in the forest.

Orlando arrived in the forest not many days after Ganymede and Aliena came there, and (as has been before related) bought the shepherd's cottage.

Ganymede and Aliena were strangely surprised to find the name of Rosalind carved on the trees, and love sonnets fastened to them, all addressed to Rosalind; and while they were wondering how this could be, they met Orlando, and they perceived the chain which Rosalind had given him about his neck.

Orlando little thought that Ganymede was the fair princess Rosalind, who, by her noble condescension and favour, had so won his heart that he passed his whole time in carving her name upon the trees, and writing sonnets in praise of her beauty; but being much pleased with the graceful air of this pretty shepherd youth, he entered into conversation with him, and he thought he saw a likeness in Ganymede to his beloved Rosalind, but that he had none of the dignified deportment of that noble lady; for Ganymede assumed the forward manners often seen in youths when they are between boys and men, and with much archness and humour talked to Orlando of a certain lover, "who," said he, "haunts our forest, and spoils our young trees with carving Rosalind upon their barks; and he hangs odes upon hawthorns, and elegies on brambles, all praising this same Rosalind. If I could find this lover, I would give him some good counsel that would soon cure him of his love."

Orlando confessed that he was the fond lover of whom he spoke, and asked Ganymede to give him the good counsel he talked of. The remedy Ganymede proposed, and the counsel he gave him, was that Orlando should come every day to the cottage where he and his sister Aliena dwelt: "And then," said Ganymede, "I will feign myself to be Rosalind, and you shall feign to court me in the same manner as you would do if I was Rosalind, and then I will imitate the fantastic ways of whimsical ladies to their lovers, till I make you ashamed of your love; and this is the way I propose to cure you." Orlando had no great faith in the remedy, yet he agreed to come every day to Ganymede's cottage, and feign a playful courtship; and every day Orlando visited Ganymede and Aliena, and Orlando called the shepherd Ganymede his Rosalind, and every day talked over all the fine words and flattering compliments, which young men delight to use when they court their mistresses. It does not appear, however, that Ganymede made any progress in curing Orlando of his love for Rosalind.

Though Orlando thought all this was but a sportive play (not dreaming that Ganymede was his very Rosalind), yet the opportunity it gave him of saying all the fond things he had in his heart pleased his fancy almost as well as it did Ganymede's, who enjoyed the secret jest in knowing these fine love speeches were all addressed to the right person.

In this manner many days passed pleasantly on with these young people; and the good-natured Aliena, seeing it made Ganymede happy, let him have his own way, and was diverted at the mock courtship, and did not care to remind Ganymede that the Lady Rosalind had not yet made herself known to the duke her father, whose place of resort in the forest they had learnt from Orlando. Ganymede met the duke one day, and had some talk with him, and the duke asked of what parentage he came. Ganymede answered that he came of as good a parentage as he did, which made the duke smile, for he did not suspect the pretty shepherd boy came of royal lineage. Then seeing the duke look well and happy, Ganymede was content to put off all further explanation for a few days longer.

One morning, as Orlando was going to visit Ganymede, he saw a man lying asleep on the ground, and a large green snake had twisted itself about his neck. The snake, seeing Orlando approach, glided away among the bushes. Orlando went nearer, and then he discovered a lioness lie couching, with her head on the ground, with a cat-like watch, waiting till the sleeping man awaked (for it is said that lions will prey on nothing that is dead or sleeping). It seemed as if Orlando was sent by Providence to free the man from the danger of the snake and lioness; but when Orlando looked in the man's face, he perceived that the sleeper, who was exposed to this double peril was his own brother Oliver, who had so cruelly used him, and had threatened to destroy him by fire, and he was almost tempted to leave him a prey to the hungry lioness; but brotherly affection and the gentleness of his nature soon overcame his first anger against his brother, and he drew his sword and attacked the lioness, and slew her, and thus preserved his brother's life both from the venomous snake and from the furious lioness; but before Orlando could conquer the lioness, she had torn one of his arms with her sharp claws.

While Orlando was engaged with the lioness, Oliver awaked, and perceiving that his brother Orlando, whom he had so cruelly treated, was saving him from the fury of a wild beast at the risk of his own life, shame and remorse at once seized him, and he repented of his unworthy conduct, and besought with many tears his brother's pardon for the injuries he had done him. Orlando rejoiced to see him so penitent, and readily forgave him; they embraced each other, and from that hour Oliver loved Orlando with a true brotherly affection, though he had come to the forest bent on his destruction.

The wound in Orlando's arm having bled very much, he found himself too weak to go to visit Ganymede, and therefore he desired his brother to go and tell Ganymede, "whom," said Orlando, "I in sport do call my Rosalind," the accident which had befallen him.

Thither then Oliver went, and told to Ganymede and Aliena how Orlando had saved his life; and when he had finished the story of Orlando's bravery, and his own providential escape, he owned to them that he was Orlando's brother, who had so cruelly used him; and then he told them of their reconciliation.

The sincere sorrow that Oliver expressed for his offences made such a lively impression on the kind heart of Aliena, that she instantly fell in love with him; and Oliver observing how much she pitied the distress he told her he felt for his fault, he as suddenly fell in love with her. But while love was thus stealing into the hearts of Aliena and Oliver, he was no less busy with Ganymede, who hearing of the danger Orlando had been in, and that he was wounded by the lioness, fainted; and when he recovered, he pretended that he had counterfeited the swoon in the imaginary character of Rosalind, and Ganymede said to Oliver, "Tell your brother Orlando how well I counterfeited a swoon." But Oliver saw by the paleness of his complexion that he did really faint, and, much wondering at the weakness of the young man, he said, "Well, if you did counterfeit, take a good heart, and counterfeit to be a man." "So I do," replied Ganymede, truly, "but I should have been a woman by right."

Oliver made this visit a very long one, and when at last he returned back to his brother, he had much news to tell him; for, besides the account of Ganymede's fainting at the hearing that Orlando was wounded, Oliver told him how he had fallen in love with the fair shepherdess Aliena, and that she had lent a favourable ear to his suit, even in this their first interview; and he talked to his brother, as of a thing almost settled, that he should marry Aliena, saying that he so well loved her that he would live here as a shepherd, and settle his estate and house at home upon Orlando.

"You have my consent," said Orlando. "Let your wedding be tomorrow, and I will invite the duke and his friends. Go and persuade your shepherdess to agree to this: she is now alone, for look, here comes her brother." Oliver went to Aliena; and Ganymede, whom Orlando had perceived approaching, came to inquire after the health of his wounded friend.

When Orlando and Ganymede began to talk over the sudden love which had taken place between Oliver and Aliena, Orlando said he had advised his brother to persuade his fair shepherdess to be married on the morrow, and then he added how much he could wish to be married on the same day to his Rosalind.

Ganymede, who well approved of this arrangement said, that if Orlando really loved Rosalind as well as he professed to do, he should have his wish; for on the morrow he would engage to make Rosalind appear in her own person, and also that Rosalind should be willing to marry Orlando.

This seemingly wonderful event, which, as Ganymede was the Lady Rosalind, he could so easily perform, he pretended he would bring to pass by the aid of magic, which he said he had learnt of an uncle who was a famous magician.

The fond lover Orlando, half believing and half doubting what he heard, asked Ganymede if he spoke in sober meaning. "By my life I do," said Ganymede; "therefore put on your best clothes, and bid the duke and your friends to your wedding; for if you desire to be married tomorrow to Rosalind, she shall be here."

The next morning, Oliver having obtained the consent of Aliena, they came into the presence of the duke, and with them also came Orlando.

They being all assembled to celebrate this double marriage, and as yet only one of the brides appearing, there was much of wondering and conjecture, but they mostly thought that Ganymede was making a jest of Orlando.

The duke, hearing that it was his own daughter that was to be brought in this strange way, asked Orlando if he believed the shepherd boy could really do what he had promised; and while Orlando was answering that he knew not what to think, Ganymede entered and asked the duke, if he brought his daughter, whether he would consent to her marriage with Orlando. "That I would," said the duke, "if I had kingdoms to give with her." Ganymede then said to Orlando, "And you say you will marry her if I bring her here?" "That I would," said Orlando, "if I were king of many kingdoms."

Ganymede and Aliena then went out together, and Ganymede throwing off his male attire and being once more dressed in woman's apparel, quickly became Rosalind without the power of magic; and Aliena, changing her country garb for her own rich clothes, was with as little trouble transformed into the Lady Celia.

While they were gone, the duke said to Orlando that he thought the shepherd Ganymede very like his daughter Rosalind; and Orlando said he also had observed the resemblance.

They had no time to wonder how all this would end, for Rosalind and Celia in their own clothes entered; and, no longer pretending that it was by the power of magic that she came there, Rosalind threw herself on her knees before her father and begged his blessing. It seemed so wonderful to all present that she should so suddenly appear, that it might well have passed for magic; but Rosalind would no longer trifle with her father, but told him the story of her banishment, and of her dwelling in the forest as a shepherd boy, her cousin Celia passing as her sister.

The duke ratified the consent he had already given to the marriage; and Orlando and Rosalind, Oliver and Celia, were married at the same time. And though their wedding could not be celebrated in this wild forest with any of the parade or splendour usual on such occasions, yet a happier wedding-day was never passed: and while they were eating their venison under the cool shade of the trees, as if nothing should be wanting to complete the felicity of this good duke and the true lovers, an unexpected messenger arrived to tell the duke the joyful news that his dukedom was restored to him.

The usurper, enraged at the flight of his daughter Celia, and hearing that every day men of great worth resorted to the forest of Arden to join the lawful duke in his exile, much envying that his brother should be so highly respected in his adversity, put himself at the head of a large force and advanced to the forest, intending to seize his brother and put him, with all his faithful followers, to the sword; but, by a wonderful interposition of Providence, this bad brother was converted from his evil intention: for, just as he entered the skirts of the wild forest, he was met by an old religious man, a hermit, with whom he had much talk, and who in the end completely turned his heart from his wicked design. Thenceforward he became a true penitent, and resolved, relinquishing his unjust dominion, to spend the remainder of his days in a religious house. The first act of his newly-conceived penitence was to send a messenger to his brother (as has been related) to offer to restore to him his dukedom, which he had usurped so long, and with it the lands and revenues of his friends, the faithful followers of his adversity.

This joyful news, as unexpected as it was welcome, came opportunely to heighten the festivity and rejoicings at the wedding of the princesses. Celia complimented her cousin on this good fortune which had happened to the duke, Rosalind's father, and wished her joy very sincerely, though she herself was no longer heir to the dukedom, but by this restoration which her father had made Rosalind was now the heir: so completely was the love of these two cousins unmixed with anything of jealousy or envy.

The duke had now an opportunity of rewarding those true friends who had stayed with him in his banishment, and these worthy followers, though they had patiently shared his adverse fortune, were very well pleased to return in peace and prosperity to the palace of their lawful duke.

Much Ado About Nothing

There lived in the palace at Messina two ladies, whose names were Hero and Beatrice. Hero was the daughter, and Beatrice the niece, of Leonato, the governor of Messina.

Beatrice was of a lively temper, and loved to divert her cousin Hero, who was of a more serious disposition, with her sprightly sallies. Whatever was going forward was sure to make matter of mirth for the light-hearted Beatrice.

At the time the history of these ladies commences, some young men of high rank in the army, as they were passing through Messina on their return from a war that was just ended, in which they had distinguished themselves by their great bravery, came to visit Leonato. Among these were Don Pedro, the Prince of Arragon, and his friend Claudio, who was a lord of Florence; and with them came the wild and witty Benedick, and he was a lord of Padua.

These strangers had been at Messina before, and the hospitable governor introduced them to his daughter and his niece as their old friends and acquaintance.

Benedick, the moment he entered the room, began a lively conversation with Leonato and the prince. Beatrice, who liked not to be left out of any discourse, interrupted Benedick with saying, "I wonder that you will still be talking, Signior Benedick; nobody marks you." Benedick was just such another rattle-brain as Beatrice, yet he was not pleased at this free salutation; he thought it did not become a well-bred lady to be so flippant with her tongue; and he remembered, when he was last at Messina, that Beatrice used to select him to make her merry jests upon. And as there is no one who so little likes to be made a jest of as those who are apt to take the same liberty themselves, so it was with Benedick and Beatrice; these two sharp wits never met in former times but a perfect war of raillery was kept up between them, and they always parted mutually displeased with each other. Therefore when Beatrice stopped him in the middle of his discourse with telling him nobody marked what he was saying, Benedick, affecting not to have observed before that she was present, said, "What, my dear Lady Disdain, are you yet living?" And now war broke out afresh between them, and a long jangling argument ensued, during which Beatrice, although she knew he had so well approved his valour in the late war, said that she would eat all he had killed there; and observing the prince take delight in Benedick's conversation, she called him "the prince's jester". This sarcasm sunk deeper into the mind of Benedick than all Beatrice had said before. The hint she gave him that he was a coward, by saying she would eat all he had killed, he did not regard, knowing himself to be a brave man; but there is nothing that great wits so much dread as the imputation of buffoonery, because the charge comes sometimes a little too near the truth; therefore Benedick perfectly hated Beatrice when she called him "the prince's jester ".

The modest Lady Hero was silent before the noble guests, and while Claudio was attentively observing the improvement which time had made in her beauty, and was contemplating the exquisite graces of her fine figure (for she was an admirable young lady), the prince was highly amused with listening to the humorous dialogue between Benedick and Beatrice, and he said in a whisper to Leonato, "This is a pleasant-spirited young lady. She were an excellent wife for Benedick." Leonato replied to this suggestion, "O my lord, my lord, if they were but a week married, they would talk themselves mad." But though Leonato thought they would make a discordant pair, the prince did not give up the idea of matching these two keen wits together.

When the prince returned with Claudio from the palace, he found that the marriage he had devised between Benedick and Beatrice was not the only one projected in that good company, for Claudio spoke in such terms of Hero as made the prince guess at what was passing in his heart; and he liked it well, and he said to Claudio, "Do you affect Hero?" To this question Claudio replied, "O my lord, when I was last at Messina, I looked upon her with a soldier's eye that liked, but had no leisure for loving; but now, in this happy time of peace, thoughts of war have left their places vacant in my mind, and in their room come thronging soft and delicate thoughts, all prompting me how fair young Hero is, reminding me that I liked her before I went to the wars." Claudio's confession of his love for Hero so wrought upon the prince that he lost no time in soliciting the consent of Leonato to accept of Claudio for a son-in-law. Leonato agreed to this proposal, and the prince found no great difficulty in persuading the gentle Hero herself to listen to the suit of the noble Claudio, who was a lord of rare endowments and highly accomplished; and Claudio assisted by his kind prince, soon prevailed upon Leonato to fix an early day for the celebration of his marriage with Hero.

Claudio was to wait but a few days before he was to be married to his fair lady; yet he complained of the interval being tedious, as indeed most young men are impatient when they are waiting for the accomplishment of any event they have set their hearts upon; the prince, therefore, to make the time seem short to him, proposed, as a kind of merry pastime, that they should invent some artful scheme to make Benedick and Beatrice fall in love with each other. Claudio entered with great satisfaction into this whim of the prince, and Leonato promised them his assistance, and even Hero said she would do any modest office to help her cousin to a good husband.

The device the prince invented was, that the gentlemen should make Benedick believe that Beatrice was in love with him, and that Hero should make Beatrice believe that Benedick was in love with her.

The prince, Leonato, and Claudio began their operations first; and, watching an opportunity when Benedick was quietly seated reading in an arbour, the prince and his assistants took their station among the trees behind the arbour, so near that Benedick could not choose but hear all they said; and after some careless talk, the prince said, "Come hither, Leonato. What was it you told me the other day—that your niece Beatrice was in love with Signior Benedick? I did never think that lady would have loved any man." "No, nor I neither, my lord," answered Leonato. "It is most wonderful that she should so dote on Benedick, whom she in all outward behaviour seemed ever to dislike." Claudio confirmed all this with saying, that Hero had told him Beatrice was so in love with

Benedick that she would certainly die of grief if he could not be brought to love her; which Leonato and Claudio seemed to agree was impossible, he having always been such a railer against all fair ladies, and in particular against Beatrice.

The prince affected to hearken to all this with great compassion for Beatrice, and he said, "It were good that Benedick were told of this." "To what end?" said Claudio; "he would but make sport of it, and torment the poor lady worse." "And if he should," said the prince, "it were a good deed to hang him, for Beatrice is an excellent sweet lady, and exceeding wise in everything but in loving Benedick." Then the prince motioned to his companions that they should walk on, and leave Benedick to meditate upon what he had overheard.

Benedick had been listening with great eagerness to this conversation, and he said to himself when he heard Beatrice loved him, "Is it possible? Sits the wind in that corner?" And when they were gone he began to reason in this manner with himself. "This can be no trick! they were very serious, and they have the truth from Hero, and seem to pity the lady. Love me! Why, it must be requited! I did never think to marry. But when I said I should die a bachelor I did not think I should live to be married. They say the lady is virtuous and fair. She is so. And wise in everything but in loving me. Why, that is no great argument of her folly. But here comes Beatrice. By this day, she is a fair lady. I do spy some marks of love in her." Beatrice now approached him, and said with her usual tartness, "Against my will I am sent to bid you come in to dinner." Benedick, who never felt himself disposed to speak so politely to her before, replied, "Fair Beatrice, I thank you for your pains." And when Beatrice, after two or three more rude speeches, left him, Benedick thought he observed a concealed meaning of kindness under the uncivil words she uttered, and he said aloud, "If I do not take pity on her, I am a villain. If I do not love her, I am a Jew. I will go get her picture."

The gentleman being thus caught in the net they had spread for him, it was now Hero's turn to play her part with Beatrice; and for this purpose she sent for Ursula and Margaret, two gentlewomen who attended upon her, and she said to Margaret, "Good Margaret, run to the parlour; there you will find my cousin Beatrice talking with the prince and Claudio. Whisper in her ear that I and Ursula are walking in the orchard, and that our discourse is all of her. Bid her steal into that pleasant arbour, where honeysuckles, ripened by the sun, like ungrateful minions, forbid the sun to enter." This arbour into which Hero desired Margaret to entice Beatrice was the very same pleasant arbour where Benedick had so lately been an attentive listener. "I will make her come, I warrant, presently," said Margaret.

"Hero then, taking Ursula with her into the orchard, said to her, "Now, Ursula, when Beatrice comes we will walk up and down this alley, and our talk must be only of Benedick, and when I name him let it be your part to praise him more than ever man did merit. My talk to you must be how Benedick is in love with Beatrice. Now begin, for look where Beatrice, like a lapwing, runs close by the ground, to hear our conference." They then began, Hero saying, as if in answer to something which Ursula had said, "No, truly, Ursula, she is too disdainful, her spirits are as coy as wild birds of the rock." "But are you sure," said Ursula, "that Benedick loves Beatrice so entirely?" Hero replied, "So says the prince and my Lord Claudio, and they entreated me to acquaint her with it, but I persuaded them, if they loved Benedick, never to let Beatrice know of it." "Certainly," replied Ursula, "it were not good she knew his love, lest she made sport of it." "Why, to say truth," said Hero, "I never yet saw a man, how wise soever, or noble, young or rarely featured, but she would dispraise him." "Sure, sure, such carping is not commendable," said Ursula. "No," replied Hero, "but who dare tell her so? If I should speak, she would mock me into air." "O you wrong your cousin," said Ursula; "she cannot be so much without true judgment as to refuse so rare a gentleman as Signior Benedick." "He hath an excellent good name," said Hero; "indeed he is the first man in Italy, always excepting my dear Claudio." And now, Hero giving her attendant a hint that it was time to change the discourse, Ursula said, "And when are you to be married, madam?" Hero then told her that she was to be married to Claudio the next day, and desired she would go in with her and look at some new attire, as she wished to consult with her on what she would wear on the morrow. Beatrice, who had been listening with breathless eagerness to this dialogue, when they went away, exclaimed, "What fire is in my ears? Can this be true? Farewell, contempt and scorn, and maiden pride, adieu! Benedick, love on; I will requite you, taming my wild heart to your loving hand."

It must have been a pleasant sight to see these old enemies converted into new and loving friends, and to behold their first meeting after being cheated into mutual liking by the merry artifice of the good-humoured prince. But a sad reverse in the fortunes of Hero must now be thought of. The morrow, which was to have been her wedding day, brought sorrow on the heart of Hero and her good father Leonato.

The prince had a half-brother, who came from the wars along with him to Messina. This brother (his name was Don John), was a melancholy, discontented man, whose spirits seemed to labour in the contriving of villainies. He hated the prince his brother, and he hated Claudio because he was the prince's friend, and determined to prevent Claudio's marriage with Hero only for the malicious pleasure of making Claudio and the prince unhappy; for he knew the prince had set his heart upon this marriage almost as much as Claudio himself, and to effect this wicked purpose he employed one Borachio, a man as bad as himself, whom he encouraged with the offer of a great reward. This Borachio paid his court to Margaret, Hero's attendant; and Don John knowing this, prevailed upon him to make Margaret promise to talk with him from her lady's chamber window that night, after Hero was asleep, and also to dress herself in Hero's clothes, the better to deceive Claudio into the belief that it was Hero, for that was the end he meant to compass by this wicked plot.

Don John then went to the prince and Claudio, and told them that Hero was an imprudent lady, and that she talked with men from her chamber window at midnight. Now this was the evening before the wedding, and he offered to take them that night where they should themselves hear Hero discoursing with a man from her window; and they consented to go along with him, and Claudio said, "If I see anything tonight why I should not marry her, tomorrow in the congregation, where I intended to wed her, there will I shame her." The prince also said, "And as I assisted you to obtain her, I will join with you to disgrace her."

When Don John brought them near Hero's chamber that night,

they saw Borachio standing under the window, and they saw Margaret looking out of Hero's window, and heard her talking with Borachio; and Margaret being dressed in the same clothes they had seen Hero wear, the prince and Claudio believed it was the Lady Hero herself.

Nothing could equal the anger of Claudio when he had made, as he thought, this discovery. All his love for the innocent Hero was at once converted into hatred, and he resolved to expose her in the church, as he had said he would, the next day; and the prince agreed to this, thinking that no punishment could be too severe for the naughty lady who talked with a man from her window the very night before she was going to be married to the noble Claudio.

The next day they were all met to celebrate the marriage, and Claudio and Hero were standing before the priest, and the priest, or friar, as he was called, was proceeding to pronounce the marriage ceremony, when Claudio, in the most passionate language, proclaimed the guilt of the blameless Hero, who, amazed at the strange words he uttered, said meekly:

"Is my lord well that he does speak so wide?"

Leonato, in the utmost horror, said to the prince:

"My lord, why speak not you?" "What should I speak?" said the prince; "I stand dishonoured, that have gone about to link my dear friend to an unworthy woman. Leonato, upon my honour, myself, my brother, and this grieved Claudio did see and hear her last night at midnight talk with a man at her chamber window."

Benedick, in astonishment at what he had heard, said, "This looks not like a nuptial."

"True, O God!" replied the heart-struck Hero; and then this hapless lady sunk down in a fainting fit to all appearance dead. The prince and Claudio left the church without staying to see if Hero would recover, or at all regarding the distress into which they had thrown Leonato. So hard-hearted had their anger made them.

Benedick remained, and assisted Beatrice to recover Hero from her swoon, saying, "How does the lady?" "Dead, I think," replied Beatrice in great agony, for she loved her cousin; and, knowing her virtuous principles, she believed nothing of what she had heard spoken against her. Not so the poor old father; he believed the story of his child's fault, and it was piteous to hear him lamenting over her as she lay like one dead before him, wishing she might never more open her eyes.

But the ancient friar was a wise man and full of observation on human nature, and he had attentively marked the lady's countenance when she heard herself accused, and noted a thousand blushing shames to start into her face, and then he saw an angel-like whiteness bear away those blushes, and in her eye he saw a fire that did belie the error that the prince did speak against her maiden truth, and he said to the sorrowing father, "Call me a fool; trust not my reading, nor my observation; trust not my age, my reverence, nor my calling, if this sweet lady lie not guiltless here under some biting error."

When Hero recovered from the swoon into which she had fallen the friar said to her, "Lady, what man is he you are accused of?" Hero replied, "They know that do accuse me; I know of none"; then turning to Leonato she said, "O my father, if you can prove that any man has ever conversed with me at hours unmeet, or that I yesternight exchanged words with any creature, refuse me, hate me, torture me to death."

"There is," said the friar, "some strange misunderstanding in the prince and Claudio"; and then he counselled Leonato that he should report that Hero was dead; and he said that the death-like swoon in which they had left Hero would make this easy of belief; and he also advised him that he should put on mourning, and erect a monument for her, and do all rites that appertain to a burial. "What will this do?" The friar replied, "This report of her death shall change slander into pity; that is some good, but that is not all the good I hope for. When Claudio shall hear she died upon hearing his words, the idea of her life shall sweetly creep into his imagination. Then shall he mourn, if ever love had interest in his heart, and wish he had not so accused her; yea, though he thought his accusation true."

Benedick now said, "Leonato, let the friar advise you; and though you know how well I love the prince and Claudio, yet on my honour I will not reveal this secret to them."

Leonato, thus persuaded, yielded; and he said, sorrowfully, "I am so grieved that the smallest twine may lead me." The kind friar then led Leonato and Hero away to comfort and console them, and Beatrice and Benedick remained alone; and this was the meeting from which their friends, who contrived the merry plot against them, expected so much diversion; those friends who were now overwhelmed with affliction, and from whose minds all thoughts of merriment seemed for ever banished.

Benedick was the first who spoke, and he said, "Lady Beatrice, have you wept all this while?" "Yea, and I will weep a while longer," said Beatrice. "Surely," said Benedick, "I do believe your fair cousin is wronged." "Ah!" said Beatrice, "how much might that man deserve of me who would right her!" Benedick then said, "Is there any way to show such friendship? I do love nothing in the world so well as you; is not that strange?" "It were as possible," said Beatrice, "for me to say I loved nothing in the world so well as you; but believe me not, and yet I lie not. I confess nothing, nor I deny nothing. I am sorry for my cousin." "By my sword," said Benedick, "you love me, and I protest I love you. Come, bid me do anything for you." "Kill Claudio," said Beatrice.

"Ha! not for the wide world," said Benedick; for he loved his friend Claudio, and he believed he had been imposed upon. "Is not Claudio a villain, that has slandered, scorned, and dishonoured my cousin?" said Beatrice; "O that I were a man!" "Hear me Beatrice!" said Benedick. But Beatrice would hear nothing in Claudio's defence; and she continued to urge on Benedick to revenge her cousin's wrongs; and she said, "Talk with a man out of the window; a proper saying! Sweet Hero! she is wronged; she is slandered; she is undone. O that I were a man for Claudio's sake, or that I had any friend who would be a man for my sake! but valour is melted into courtesies and compliments. I cannot be a man with wishing, therefore I will die a woman with grieving." "Tarry, good Beatrice," said Benedick; "by this hand I love you." "Use it for my love some other way than by swearing by it," said Beatrice. "Think you, on your soul, that Claudio has wronged Hero?" asked Benedick. "Yea," answered Beatrice, "as sure as I have a thought, or a soul." "Enough," said Benedick; "I am engaged; I will challenge him. I will kiss your hand, and so leave you. By this hand Claudio shall render me a dear account! As you hear from me, so think of me. Go, comfort your cousin."

While Beatrice was thus powerfully pleading with Benedick, and working his gallant temper, by the spirit of her angry words, to engage in the cause of Hero, and fight even with his dear friend Claudio, Leonato was challenging the prince and Claudio to answer with their swords the injury they had done his child who, he affirmed, had died for grief. But they respected his age and his sorrow, and they said, "Nay, do not quarrel with us, good old man." And now came Benedick, and he also challenged Claudio to answer with his sword the injury he had done to Hero; and Claudio and the prince said to each other, "Beatrice has set him on to do this." Claudio nevertheless must have accepted this challenge of Benedick had not the justice of Heaven at the moment brought to pass a better proof of the innocence of Hero than the uncertain fortune of a duel.

While the prince and Claudio were yet talking of the challenge of Benedick, a magistrate brought Borachio as a prisoner before the prince. Borachio had been overheard talking with one of his companions of the mischief he had been employed by Don John to do.

Borachio made a full confession to the prince, in Claudio's hearing, that it was Margaret dressed in her lady's clothes that he had talked with from the window, whom they had mistaken for the Lady Hero herself, and no doubt continued on the minds of Claudio and the prince of the innocence of Hero. If a suspicion had remained it must have been removed by the flight of Don John, who, finding his villainies were detected, fled from Messina to avoid the just anger of his brother.

The heart of Claudio was sorely grieved when he found he had falsely accused Hero, who, he thought, died upon hearing his cruel words; and the memory of his beloved Hero's image came over him, in the rare semblance that he loved it first; and the prince asking him if what he heard did not run like iron through his soul, he answered, that he felt as if he had taken poison while Borachio was speaking.

And the repentant Claudio implored forgiveness of the old man Leonato for the injury he had done his child, and promised that whatever penance Leonato would lay upon him for his fault in believing the false accusation against his betrothed wife, for her dear sake he would endure it.

The penance Leonato enjoined him was to marry the next morning a cousin of Hero's, who, he said, was now his heir, and in person very like Hero. Claudio, regarding the solemn promise he made to Leonato, said he would marry this unknown lady, even though she were an Ethiop; but his heart was very sorrowful, and he passed that night in tears, and in remorseful grief, at the tomb which Leonato had erected for Hero.

When the morning came, the prince accompanied Claudio to the church, where the good friar, and Leonato and his niece, were already assembled, to celebrate a second nuptial; and Leonato presented to Claudio his promised bride; and she wore a mask, that Claudio might not discover her face. And Claudio said to the lady in the mask, "Give me your hand before this holy friar; I am your husband, if you will marry me." "And when I lived I was your other wife," said this unknown lady; and, taking off her mask, she proved to be no niece (as was pretended), but Leonato's very daughter, the Lady Hero herself. We may be sure that this proved a most agreeable surprise to Claudio, who thought her dead, so that he could scarcely for joy believe his eyes; and the prince, who was equally amazed at what he saw, exclaimed, "Is not this Hero, Hero that was dead?" Leonato replied, "She died, my lord, but while her slander lived." The friar promised them an explanation of this seeming miracle after the ceremony was ended; and was proceeding to marry them, when he was interrupted by Benedick, who desired to be married at the same time to Beatrice. Beatrice making some demur to this match, and Benedick challenging her with her love for him, which he had learned from Hero, a pleasant explanation took place; and they found they had both been tricked into a belief of love which had never existed, and had become lovers in truth by the power of a false jest; but the affection, which a merry invention had cheated them into, was grown too powerful to be shaken by a serious explanation; and since Benedick proposed to marry, he was resolved to think nothing to the purpose that the world could say against it; and he merrily kept up the jest, and swore to Beatrice that he took her but for pity, and because he heard she was dying of love for him; and Beatrice protested that she yielded but upon great persuasion, and partly to save his life, for she heard he was in a consumption. So these two mad wits were reconciled, and made a match of it, after Claudio and Hero were married; and to complete the history Don John, the contriver of the villainy, was taken in his flight and brought back to Messina; and a brave punishment it was to this gloomy and discontented man to see the joy and feastings which, by the disappointment of his plots, took place in the palace in Messina.

A Midsummer Night's Dream

There was a law in the city of Athens which gave to its citizens the power of compelling their daughters to marry whomsoever they pleased; for upon a daughter's refusing to marry the man her father had chosen to be her husband, the father was empowered by this law to cause her to be put to death; but, as fathers do not often desire the death of their own daughters, even though they do happen to prove a little refractory, this law was seldom or never put into execution, though perhaps the young ladies of that city were not unfrequently threatened by their parents with the terrors of it.

There was one instance, however, of an old man, whose name was Egeus, who actually did come before Theseus (at that time the reigning duke of Athens) to complain that his daughter Hermia, whom he had commanded to marry Demetrius, a young man of a noble Athenian family, refused to obey him, because she loved another young Athenian, named Lysander. Egeus demanded justice of Theseus, and desired that this cruel law might be put in force against his daughter.

Hermia pleaded in excuse for her disobedience that Demetrius had formerly professed love for her dear friend Helena, and that Helena loved Demetrius to distraction; but this honourable reason which Hermia gave for not obeying her father's command moved not the stern Egeus.

Theseus, though a great and merciful prince, had no power to alter the laws of his country; therefore he could only give Hermia four days to consider of it, and at the end of that time, if she still refused to marry Demetrius, she was to be put to death.

When Hermia was dismissed from the presence of the duke she went to her lover Lysander, and told him the peril she was in, and that she must either give up him and marry Demetrius or lose her life in four days.

Lysander was in great affliction at hearing these evil tidings; but recollecting that he had an aunt who lived at some distance from Athens, and that at the place where she lived the cruel law could not be put in force against Hermia (this law not extending beyond the boundaries of the city), he proposed to Hermia that she should steal out of her father's house that night and go with him to his aunt's house, where he would marry her. "I will meet you," said Lysander "in the wood a few miles without the city; in that delightful wood where we have so often walked with Helena in the pleasant month of May."

To this proposal Hermia joyfully agreed, and she told no one of her intended flight but her friend Helena. Helena (as maidens will do foolish things for love) very ungenerously resolved to go and tell this to Demetrius, though she could hope no benefit from betraying her friend's secret but the poor pleasure of following her faithless lover to the wood; for she well knew that Demetrius would go thither in pursuit of Hermia.

The wood in which Lysander and Hermia proposed to meet was the favourite haunt of those little beings known by the name of *Fairies*.

Oberon the king, and Titania the queen, of the fairies, with all their tiny train of followers, in this wood held their midnight revels.

Between this little king and queen of sprites there happened at this time a sad disagreement; they never met by moonlight in the shady walks of this pleasant wood but they were quarrelling, till all their fairy elves would creep into acorn-cups and hide themselves for fear.

The cause of this unhappy disagreement was Titania's refusing to give Oberon a little changeling boy, whose mother had been Titania's friend; and upon her death the fairy queen stole the child from its nurse, and brought him up in the woods.

The night on which the lovers were to meet in this wood, as Titania was walking with some of her maids of honour she met Oberon, attended by his train of fairy courtiers.

"Ill met by moonlight, proud Titania," said the fairy king. The queen replied, "What, jealous Oberon, is it you? Fairies, skip hence; I have forsworn his company." "Tarry, rash fairy," said Oberon; "am not I thy lord? Why does Titania cross her Oberon? Give me your little changeling boy to be my page."

"Set your heart at rest," answered the queen; "your whole fairy kingdom buys not the boy of me." She then left her lord in great anger. "Well, go your way," said Oberon; "before the morning dawns I will torment you for this injury."

Oberon then sent for Puck, his chief favourite and privy councillor.

Puck (or, as he was sometimes called, Robin Goodfellow) was a shrewd and knavish sprite, and used to play comical pranks in the neighbouring villages, sometimes getting into the dairies and skimming the milk, sometimes plunging his light and airy form into the butter-churn, and while he was dancing his fantastic shape in the churn, in vain the dairymaid would labour to change her cream into butter. Nor had the village swains any better success; whenever Puck chose to play his freaks in the brewing copper the ale was sure to be spoiled. When a few good neighbours were met to drink some comfortable ale together, Puck would jump into the bowl of ale in the likeness of a roasted crab, and when some old goody was going to drink he would bob against her lips, and spill the ale over her withered chin; and presently after, when the same old dame was gravely seating herself to tell her neighbours a sad and melancholy story, Puck would slip her three-legged stool from under her, and down toppled the poor old woman, and then the old gossips would hold their sides and laugh at her, and vow they never wasted a merrier hour.

"Come hither, Puck," said Oberon to this little merry wanderer of the night; "fetch me the flower which maids call *Love in Idleness*; the juice of that little purple flower laid on the eyelids of those who sleep will make them, when they awake, dote on the first thing they see. Some of the juice of that flower I will drop on the eyelids of my Titania when she is asleep, and the first thing she looks upon when she opens her eyes she will fall in love with, even though it be a lion, or a bear, a meddling monkey, or a busy ape; and before I will take this charm from off her sight, which I can do with another charm I know of, I will make her give me that boy to be my page.

Puck, who loved mischief to his heart, was highly diverted with this intended frolic of his master, and ran to seek the flower; and while Oberon was waiting the return of Puck, he observed Demetrius and Helena enter the wood; he overheard Demetrius reproaching Helena for following him, and after many unkind words on his part, and gentle expostulations from Helena, reminding him of his former love and professions of true faith to her, he left her, as he said, to the mercy of the wild beasts, and she ran after him as swiftly as she could.

The fairy king, who was always friendly to true lovers, felt great compassion for Helena; and perhaps, as Lysander said they used to walk by moonlight in this pleasant wood, Oberon might have seen Helena in those happy times when she was beloved by Demetrius. However that might be, when Puck returned with the little purple flower, Oberon said to his favourite, "Take a part of this flower; there has been a sweet Athenian lady here, who is in love with a disdainful youth; if you find him sleeping, drop some of the love-Juice in his eyes, but contrive to do it when she is near him, that the first thing he sees when he awakes may be this despised lady. You will know the man by the Athenian garments which he wears." Puck promised to manage this matter very dexterously; and then Oberon went, unperceived by Titania, to her bower, where she was preparing to go to rest. Her fairy bower was a bank where grew wild thyme, cowslips, and sweet violets under a canopy of woodbine, musk-roses, and eglantine. There Titania always slept some part of the night; her coverlet the enamelled skin of a snake, which, though a small mantle, was wide enough to wrap a fairy in.

He found Titania giving orders to her fairies how they were to employ themselves while she slept. "Some of you," said her majesty, "must kill cankers in the musk-rose buds, and some wage war with the bats for their leathern wings, to make my small elves coats; and some of you keep watch that the clamorous owl that nightly hoots come not near me; but first sing me to sleep." Then they began to sing this song:

> "*You spotted snakes with double tongue,*
> *Thorny hedgehogs, be not seen;*
> *Newts and blind-worms, do no wrong,*
> *Come not near our Fairy Queen.*
> *Philomel, with melody,*
> *Sing in your sweet lullaby,*
> *Lulla, lulla, lullaby; lulla, lulla, lullaby;*
> *Never harm, nor spell, nor charm,*
> *Come our lovely lady nigh;*
> *So good night with lullaby.*"

When the fairies had sung their queen asleep with this pretty lullaby, they left her to perform the important services she had enjoined them. Oberon then softly drew near his Titania, and dropped some of the love-juice on her eyelids, saying:

> "What thou seest, when thou dost wake,
> Do it for thy true love take."

But to return to Hermia, who made her escape out of her father's house that night, to avoid the death she was doomed to for refusing to marry Demetrius. When she entered the wood she found her dear Lysander waiting for her to conduct her to his aunt's house; but before they had passed half through the wood, Hermia was so much fatigued that Lysander, who was very careful of this dear lady, who had proved her affection for him even by hazarding her life for his sake, persuaded her to rest till morning on a bank of soft moss, and lying down himself on the ground at some little distance, they soon fell fast asleep. Here they were found by Puck, who, seeing a handsome young man asleep, and perceiving that his clothes were made in the Athenian fashion, and that a pretty lady was sleeping near him, concluded that this must be the Athenian maid and her disdainful lover whom Oberon had sent him to seek; and he naturally enough conjectured that, as they were alone together, she must be the first thing he would see when he awoke; so, without more ado, he proceeded to pour some of the juice of the little purple flower into his eyes. But it so fell out that Helena came that way, and, instead of Hermia, was the first object Lysander beheld when he opened his eyes; and, strange to relate, so powerful was the love-charm, all his love for Hermia vanished away, and Lysander fell in love with Helena.

Had he first seen Hermia when he awoke, the blunder Puck committed would have been of no consequence, for he could not love that faithful lady too well; but for poor Lysander to be forced by a fairy love-charm to forget his own true Hermia, and to run after another lady, and leave Hermia asleep quite alone in a wood at midnight, was a sad chance indeed.

Thus this misfortune happened. Helena, as has been before related, endeavoured to keep pace with Demetrius when he ran away so rudely from her; but she could not continue this unequal race long, men being always better runners in a long race than ladies. Helena soon lost sight of Demetrius; and as she was wandering about dejected and forlorn, she arrived at the place where Lysander was sleeping. "Ah!" said she, "this is Lysander lying on the ground: is he dead or asleep?" Then, gently touching him, she said, "Good sir, if you are alive, awake." Upon this Lysander opened his eyes, and (the love-charm beginning to work) immediately addressed her in terms of extravagant love and admiration, telling her she as much excelled Hermia in beauty as a dove does a raven, and that he would run through fire for her sweet sake, and many more such lover-like speeches. Helena, knowing Lysander was her friend Hermia's lover, and that he was solemnly engaged to marry her, was in the utmost rage when she heard herself addressed in this manner; for she thought (as well she might) that Lysander was making a jest of her. "Oh!" said she, "why was I born to be mocked and scorned by every one? Is it not enough, is it not enough, young man, that I can never get a sweet look or a kind word from Demetrius, but you, sir, must pretend in this disdainful manner to court me? I thought, Lysander, you were a lord of more true gentleness." Saying these words in great anger, she ran away; and Lysander followed her, quite forgetful of his own Hermia, who was still asleep.

When Hermia awoke, she was in a sad fright at finding herself alone. She wandered about the wood, not knowing what was become of Lysander, or which way to go to seek for him. In the meantime Demetrius, not being able to find Hermia and his rival Lysander, and fatigued with his fruitless search, was observed by Oberon fast asleep. Oberon had learnt, by some questions he had asked of Puck, that he had applied the love-charm to the wrong person's eyes; and now, having found the person first intended, he touched the eyelids of the sleeping Demetrius with the love-juice, and he instantly awoke; and the first thing he saw being Helena, he, as Lysander had done before, began to address love-speeches to her; and just at that moment Lysander, followed by Hermia (for through Puck's unlucky mistake it was now become Hermia's turn to run after her lover), made his appearance; and then Lysander and Demetrius, both speaking together, made love to Helena, they being each one under the influence of the same potent charm.

The astonished Helena thought that Demetrius, Lysander, and her once dear friend Hermia, were all in a plot together to make a jest of her.

Hermia was as much surprised as Helena; she knew not why Lysander and Demetrius, who both before loved her, were now become the lovers of Helena, and to Hermia the matter seemed to be no jest.

The ladies, who before had always been the dearest of friends, now fell to high words together.

"Unkind Hermia," said Helena, "it is you have set Lysander on to vex me with mock praises, and your other lover Demetrius, who used almost to spurn me with his foot, have you not bid him call me goddess, nymph, rare, precious, and celestial? He would not speak thus to me, whom he hates, if you did not set him on to make a jest of me. Unkind Hermia, to join with men in scorning your poor friend. Have you forgot our schoolday friendship? How often, Hermia, have we two, sitting on one cushion, both singing one song, with our needles working the same flower, both on the same sampler wrought, growing up together in fashion of a double cherry, scarcely seeming parted? Hermia, it is not friendly in you, it is not maidenly, to join with men in scorning your poor friend." "I am amazed at your passionate words," said Hermia. "I scorn you not; it seems you scorn me." "Ay, do," returned Helena; "persevere, counterfeit serious looks, and make mouths at me when I turn my back; then wink at each other, and hold the sweet jest up. If you had any pity, grace, or manners you would not use me thus."

While Helena, and Hermia were speaking these angry words to each other, Demetrius and Lysander left them to fight together in the wood for the love of Helena.

When they found the gentlemen had left them, they departed and once more wandered weary in the wood in search of their lovers.

As soon as they were gone the fairy king, who, with little Puck, had been listening to their quarrels, said to him, "This is your negligence, Puck; or did you do this wilfully?" "Believe me, king of shadows," answered Puck, "it was a mistake; did not you tell me I should know the man by his Athenian garments? However, I am not sorry this has happened, for I think their jangling makes me excellent sport." "You heard," said Oberon, "that Demetrius and

Lysander are gone to seek a convenient place to fight in. I command you to overhang the night with a thick fog, and lead these quarrelsome lovers so astray in the dark that they shall not be able to find each other. Counterfeit each of their voices to the other, and with bitter taunts provoke them to follow you, while they think it is their rival's tongue they hear. See you do this till they are so weary that they can go no farther, and when you find they are asleep drop the juice of this other flower into Lysander's eyes, and when he awakes he will forget his new love for Helena, and return to his old passion for Hermia, and then the two fair ladies may each one be happy with the man she loves, and they will think all that has passed a vexatious dream. About this quickly, Puck, and I will go and see what sweet love my Titania has found."

Titania was still sleeping, and Oberon, seeing a clown near her who had lost his way in the wood, and was likewise asleep: "This fellow," said he, "shall be my Titania's true love," and, clapping an ass's head over the clown's, it seemed to fit him as well as if it had grown upon his own shoulders. Though Oberon fixed the ass's head on very gently, it awakened him, and rising up unconscious of what Oberon had done to him, he went towards the bower where the fairy queen slept.

"Ah! what angel is that I see?" said Titania, opening her eyes, and the juice of the little purple flower beginning to take effect: "Are you as wise as you are beautiful ?"

"Why, mistress," said the clown, "if I have wit enough to find my way out of this wood, I have enough to serve my turn."

"Out of the wood do not desire to go," said the enamoured queen. "I am a spirit of no common rate. I love you. Go with me and I will give you fairies to attend upon you."

She then called four of her fairies. Their names were Pease-blossom, Cobweb, Moth, and Mustard-seed.

"Attend," said the queen, "upon this sweet gentleman: hop in his walks and gambol in his sight; feed him with grapes and apricots, and steal for him the honey-bags from the bees. Come, sit with me," said she to the clown, "and let me play with your amiable hairy cheeks, my beautiful ass! and kiss your fair large ears, my gentle joy!"

"Where is Pease-blossom?" said the ass-headed clown, not much regarding the fairy queen's courtship, but very proud of his new attendants.

"Here, sir," said little Pease-blossom.

"Scratch my head," said the clown. "Where is Cobweb?"

"Here, sir," said Cobweb.

"Good Mr. Cobweb," said the foolish clown, "kill me the red humble-bee on the top of that thistle yonder; and, good Mr. Cobweb, bring me the honey-bag. Do not fret yourself too much in the action, Mr. Cobweb, and take care the honey-bag break not; I should be sorry to have you overflown with a honey-bag. Where is Mustard-seed?"

"Here, sir," said Mustard-seed; "what is your will?"

"Nothing," said the clown, "good Mr. Mustard-seed, but to help Mr. Pease-blossom to scratch. I must go to a barber's, Mr. Mustard-seed, for methinks I am marvellous hairy about the face."

"My sweet love," said the queen, "what will you have to eat? I have a venturous fairy shall seek the squirrel's hoard and fetch you some new nuts."

"I had rather have a handful of dried peas," said the clown, who with his ass's head had got an ass's appetite. "But, I pray, let none of your people disturb me, for I have a mind to sleep."

"Sleep then," said the queen, "and I will wind you in my arms. O how I love you! How I dote upon you!

When the fairy king saw the clown sleeping in the arms of his queen, he advanced within her sight, and reproached her with having lavished her favours upon an ass.

This she could not deny, as the clown was then sleeping within her arms, with his ass's head crowned by her with flowers.

When Oberon had teased her for some time, he again demanded the changeling-boy, which she, ashamed of being discovered by her lord with her new favourite, did not dare to refuse him.

Oberon, having thus obtained the little boy he had so long wished for to be his page, took pity on the absurd situation into which, by his merry contrivance, he had brought his Titania, and threw some of the juice of the other flower into her eyes; and the fairy queen immediately recovered her senses, and wondered at her late dotage, saying how she now loathed the sight of the strange monster.

Oberon likewise took the ass's head from off the clown, and left him to finish his nap with his own fool's head upon his shoulders.

Oberon and his Titania being now perfectly reconciled, he related to her the history of the lovers, and their midnight quarrels; and she agreed to go with him and see the end of their adventures.

The fairy king and queen found the lovers and their fair ladies at no great distance from each other, sleeping on a grass plot; for Puck, to make amends for his former mistake, had contrived, with the utmost diligence, to bring them all to the same spot, unknown to each other; and he had carefully removed the charm from off the eyes of Lysander with the antidote the fairy king gave to him.

Hermia first awoke, and, finding her lost Lysander asleep so near her, was looking at him and wondering at his strange inconstancy. Lysander presently opening his eyes, and seeing his dear Hermia, recovered his reason which the fairy charm had before clouded, and with his reason, his love for Hermia; and they began to talk over the adventures of the night, doubting if these things had really happened, or if they had both been dreaming the same bewildering dream.

Helena and Demetrius were by this time awake; and a sweet sleep having quieted Helena's disturbed and angry spirits, she listened with delight to the professions of love which Demetrius still made to her, and which, to her surprise as well as pleasure, she began to perceive were sincere.

These fair night-wandering ladies, now no longer rivals, became once more true friends; all the unkind words which had passed were forgiven, and they calmly consulted together what was best to be done in their present situation. It was soon agreed that, as Demetrius had given up his pretensions to Hermia, he should endeavour to prevail upon her father to revoke the cruel sentence of death which had been passed against her. Demetrius was preparing to return to Athens for this friendly purpose when they were surprised with the sight of Egeus, Hermia's father, who came to the wood in pursuit of his runaway daughter.

When Egeus understood that Demetrius would not now marry his daughter, he no longer opposed her marriage with Lysander, but gave his consent that they should be wedded on the fourth day from that time, being the same day on which Hermia had been condemned to lose her life; and on that same day Helena joyfully agreed to marry her beloved and now faithful Demetrius.

The fairy king and queen, who were invisible spectators of this reconciliation, and now saw the happy ending of the lovers' history brought about through the good offices of Oberon, received so much pleasure, that these kind spirits resolved to celebrate the approaching nuptials with sports and revels throughout their fairy kingdom.

And now, if any are offended with this story of fairies and their pranks, as judging it incredible and strange, they have only to think that they have been asleep and dreaming, and that all these adventures were visions which they saw in their sleep; and I hope none of my readers will be so unreasonable as to be offended with a pretty, harmless Midsummer Night's Dream.

Twelfth Night Or, What You Will

Sebastian and his sister Viola, a young gentleman and lady of
Messaline, were twins, and (which was accounted a great wonder)
from their birth they so much resembled each other, that, but for the
difference in their dress, they could not be known apart. They were
both born in one hour, and in one hour they were both in danger of
perishing, for they were shipwrecked on the coast of Illyria as they
were making a sea voyage together. The ship on board of which
they were split on a rock in a violent storm, and a very small
number of the ship's company escaped with their lives. The captain
of the vessel, with a few of the sailors that were saved, got to land
in a small boat, and with them they brought Viola safe on shore,
where she, poor lady, instead of rejoicing at her own deliverance,
began to lament her brother's loss; but the captain comforted her
with the assurance that he had seen her brother, when the ship split,
fasten himself to a strong mast, on which, as long as he could see
anything of him for the distance, he perceived him borne up above
the waves. Viola was much consoled by the hope this account gave
her, and now considered how she was to dispose of herself in a
strange country, so far from home; and she asked the captain if he
knew anything of Illyria. "Ay, very well, madam," replied the captain, "for I was born not three hours' travel from this place." "Who
governs here?" said Viola. The Captain told her Illyria was governed by Orsino, a duke noble in nature as well as dignity. Viola
said she had heard her father speak of Orsino, and that he was un-
married then. "And he is so now," said the captain; "or was so very
lately, for but a month ago I went from here, and then it was the
general talk (as you know what great ones do the people will prattle
of) that Orsino sought the love of fair Olivia, a virtuous maid, the

daughter of a count who died twelve months ago, leaving Olivia to the protection of her brother, who shortly after died also; and for the love of this dear brother, they say, she has abjured the sight and company of men." Viola, who was herself in such a sad affliction for her brother's loss, wished she could live with this lady, who so tenderly mourned a brother's death. She asked the captain if he could introduce her to Olivia, saying she would willingly serve this lady. But he replied, this would be a hard thing to accomplish, because the Lady Olivia would admit no person into her house since her brother's death, not even the duke himself. Then Viola formed another project in her mind, which was, in a man's habit to serve the Duke Orsino as a page. It was a strange fancy in a young lady to put on male attire, and pass for a boy; but the forlorn and unprotected state of Viola, who was young and of uncommon beauty, alone, and in a foreign land, must plead her excuse.

She having observed a fair behaviour in the captain, and that he showed a friendly concern for her welfare, entrusted him with her design, and he readily engaged to assist her. Viola gave him money, and directed him to furnish her with suitable apparel, ordering her clothes to be made of the same colour and in the same fashion her brother Sebastian used to wear, and when she was dressed in her manly garb she looked so exactly like her brother, that some strange errors happened by means of their being mistaken for each other; for, as will afterwards appear, Sebastian was also saved.

Viola's good friend, the captain, when he had transformed this pretty lady into a gentleman, having some interest at court, got her presented to Orsino under the feigned name of Cesario. The duke was wonderfully pleased with the address and graceful deportment of this handsome youth, and made Cesario one of his pages, that being the office Viola wished to obtain; and she so well fulfilled the duties of her new station and showed such a ready observance and faithful attachment to her lord, that she soon became his most favoured attendant. To Cesario, Orsino confided the whole story of his love for the Lady Olivia. To Cesario he told the long and unsuccessful suit he had made to one who, rejecting his long services, and despising his person, refused to admit him to her presence; and for the love of this lady, who had so unkindly treated him the noble Orsino, forsaking the sports of the field, and all manly exercises in which he used to delight, passed his hours in ignoble sloth, listening to the effeminate sounds of soft music, gentle airs, and passionate love songs; and, neglecting the company of the wise and learned lords with whom he used to associate, he was now all day long conversing with young Cesario. Unmeet companion, no doubt, his grave courtiers thought Cesario was for their once noble master, the great Duke Orsino.

It is a dangerous matter for young maidens to be the confidants of handsome young dukes; which Viola too soon found to her sorrow, for all that Orsino told her he endured for Olivia she presently perceived she suffered for the love of him; and much it moved her wonder that Olivia could be so regardless of this her peerless lord and master, whom she thought no one should behold without the deepest admiration, and she ventured gently to hint to Orsino that it was pity he should affect a lady who was so blind to his worthy qualities; and she said; "If a lady were to love you, my lord, as you love Olivia (and perhaps there may be one who does), if you could not love her in return, would you not tell her that you could not love, and must not she be content with this answer?" But Orsino would not admit of this reasoning, for he denied that it was possible for any woman to love as he did. He said, no woman's heart was big enough to hold so much love, and therefore it was unfair to compare the love of any lady for him to his love for Olivia. Now, though Viola had the utmost deference for the duke's opinions, she could not help thinking this was not true, for she thought her heart had full as much love in it as Orsino's had; and she said, "Ah, but I know, my lord."— "What do you know, Cesario?" said Orsino. "Too well I know," replied Viola, "what love woman may owe to men. They are as true of heart as we are. My father had a daughter loved a man as I, perhaps, were I a woman, should love your lordship." "And what is her history?" said Orsino. "A blank, my lord," replied Viola; "she never told her love, but let concealment, like a worm in the bud, prey on her damask cheek. She pined in thought, and with a green and yellow melancholy, she sat like Patience on a monument, smiling at grief." The duke inquired if this lady died of her love, but to this question Viola returned an evasive answer, as probably she had feigned the story, to speak words expressive of the secret love and silent grief she suffered for Orsino.

While they were talking a gentleman entered, whom the duke had sent to Olivia, and he said, "So please you, my lord, I might not be admitted to the lady, but by her handmaid she returned you this answer: Until seven years hence the element itself shall not behold her face; but like a cloistress she will walk veiled, watering her chamber with her tears for the sad remembrance of her dead brother." On hearing this the duke exclaimed, "O, she that has a heart of this fine frame to pay this debt of love to a dead brother, how will she love when the rich golden shaft has touched her heart?" And then he said to Viola, "You know, Cesario, I have told you all the secrets of my heart; therefore, good youth, go to Olivia's house. Be not denied access; stand at the doors, and tell her there your fixed foot shall grow till you have audience." "And if I do speak to her, my lord, what then?" said Viola. "O, then," replied Orsino, "unfold to her the passion of my love. Make a long discourse to her of my dear faith. It will well become you to act my woes, for she will attend more to you than to one of graver aspect."

Away then went Viola, but not willingly did she undertake this courtship, for she was to woo a lady to become a wife to him she wished to marry; but having undertaken the affair, she performed it with fidelity, and Olivia soon heard that a youth was at her door who insisted upon being admitted to her presence. "I told him," said the servant, "that you were sick; he said he knew you were, and, therefore, he came to speak with you. I told him that you were asleep; he seemed to have a foreknowledge of that too, and said that therefore, he must speak with you. What is to be said to him, lady, for he seems fortified against all denial, and will speak with you whether you will or no?" Olivia, curious to see who this peremptory messenger might be, desired he might be admitted, and throwing her veil over her face, she said she would once more hear Orsino's embassy, not doubting but that he came from the duke, by his importunity. Viola, entering, put on the most manly air she could assume, and affecting the fine courtier's language of great men's pages, she said to the veiled lady, "Most radiant, exquisite, and matchless beauty, I pray you tell me if you are the lady of the house, for I should be sorry to cast away my speech upon another, for, besides that it is excellently well penned, I have taken great pains to learn it." "Whence come you, sir?" said Olivia. "I can say little more than I have studied," replied Viola, "and that question is out of my part." "Are you a comedian?" said Olivia. "No," replied Viola, "and yet I am not that which I play," meaning that she, being a woman, feigned herself to be a man. And again she asked Olivia if she were the lady of the house. Olivia said she was, and then Viola, having more curiosity to see her rival's features than haste to deliver her master's message, said, "Good madam, let me see your face." With this bold request Olivia was not averse to comply, for this haughty beauty, whom the Duke Orsino had loved so long in vain, at first sight conceived a passion for the supposed page, the humble Cesario.

When Viola asked to see her face Olivia said, "Have you any commission from your lord and master to negotiate with my face?" And then, forgetting her determination to go veiled for seven long years, she drew aside her veil, saying, "But I will draw the curtain and show the picture. Is it not well done?" Viola replied, "It is beauty truly mixed; the red and white upon your cheeks is by Nature's own cunning hand laid on. You are the most cruel lady living if you will lead these graces to the grave and leave the world no copy." "Oh, sir," replied Olivia, "I will not be so cruel. The world may have an inventory of my beauty. As, *item*, two lips, indifferent red; *item*, two grey eyes, with lids to them; one neck, one chin, and so forth. Were you sent here to praise me?" Viola replied, "I see what you are; you are too proud, but you are fair. My lord and master loves you. O, such a love could but be recompensed though you were crowned the queen of beauty; for Orsino loves you with adoration and with tears, with groans that thunder love, and sighs of fire." "Your lord," said Olivia, "knows well my mind. I cannot love him, yet I doubt not he is virtuous; I know him to be noble and of high estate, of fresh and spotless youth. All voices proclaim him learned, courteous, and valiant; yet I cannot love him; he might have taken his answer long ago." "If I did love you as my master does," said Viola, "I would make me a willow cabin at your gates and call upon your name. I would write complaining sonnets on Olivia, and sing them in the dead of the night; your name should sound among the hills, and I would make Echo, the babbling gossip of the air, cry out *Olivia*. O you should not rest between the elements of earth and air but you should pity me." "You might do much," said Olivia; "what is your parentage?" Viola replied,

"Above my fortunes, yet my state is well. I am a gentleman." Olivia now reluctantly dismissed Viola, saying, "Go to your master and tell him I cannot love him. Let him send no more, unless perchance you come again to tell me how he takes it." And Viola departed, bidding the lady farewell by the name of Fair Cruelty. When she was gone Olivia repeated the words, *Above my fortunes, yet my state is well. I am a gentleman.* And she said aloud, "I will be sworn he is; his tongue, his face, his limbs, action, and spirit plainly show he is a gentleman." And then she wished Cesario was the duke, and, perceiving the fast hold he had taken on her affections, she blamed herself for her sudden love; but the gentle blame which people lay upon their own faults has no deep root: and presently the noble Lady Olivia so far forgot the inequality between her fortunes and those of this seeming page, as well as the maidenly reserve (which is the chief ornament of a lady's character), that she resolved to court the love of young Cesario, and sent a servant after him with a diamond ring under the pretence that he had left it with her as a present from Orsino. She hoped, by thus artfully making Cesario a present of the ring, she should give him some intimation of her design; and truly it did make Viola suspect, for, knowing that Orsino had sent no ring by her, she began to recollect that Olivia's looks and manner were expressive of admiration, and she presently guessed her master's mistress had fallen in love with her. "Alas!" said she, "the poor lady might as well love a dream. Disguise I see is wicked, for it has caused Olivia to breathe as fruitless sighs for me as I do for Orsino."

Viola returned to Orsino's palace and related to her lord the ill success of the negotiation, repeating the command of Olivia, that the duke should trouble her no more. Yet still the duke persisted in hoping that the gentle Cesario would in time be able to persuade her to show some pity, and therefore he bade him he should go to her again the next day. In the meantime, to pass away the tedious intervals, he commanded a song which he loved to be sung, and he said, "My good Cesario, when I heard that song last night, methought it did relieve my passion much. Mark it, Cesario, it is old and plain. The spinsters and the knitters, when they sit in the sun, and the young maids that weave their thread with bone, chant this song. It is silly, yet I love it, for it tells of the innocence of love in the old times."

SONG

Come away, come away, Death,
    And in sad cypress let me be laid;
Fly away, fly away, breath,
    I am slain by a fair cruel maid.
My shroud of white stuck all with yew, O prepare it,
My part of death no one so true did share it.

Not a flower, not a flower sweet,
    On my black coffin let there be strown!
Not a friend, not a friend greet
    My poor corpse where my bones shall be thrown.
A thousand thousand sighs to save, lay me O where
Sad true lover never find my grave, to weep there.

Viola did not fail to mark the words of the old song, which in such true simplicity described the pangs of unrequited love, and she bore testimony in her countenance of feeling what the song expressed. Her sad looks were observed by Orsino, who said to her, "My life upon it, Cesario, though you are so young, your eye hath looked upon some face that it loves; has it not, boy?" "A little, with your leave," replied Viola. "And what kind of woman, and of what age is she?" said Orsino. "Of your age, and of your complexion, my lord," said Viola, which made the duke smile to hear this fair young boy loved a woman so much older than himself, and of a man's dark complexion; but Viola secretly meant Orsino, and not a woman like him.

When Viola made her second visit to Olivia she found no difficulty in gaining access to her. Servants soon discover when their ladies delight to converse with handsome young messengers; and the instant Viola arrived the gates were thrown wide open, and the duke's page was shown into Olivia's apartment with great respect; and when Viola told Olivia that she was come once more to plead in her lord's behalf, this lady said, "I desire you never to speak of him again; but if you would undertake another suit, I had rather hear you solicit than music from the spheres." This was pretty plain speaking; but Olivia soon explained herself still more plainly, and openly confessed her love; and when she saw displeasure with perplexity expressed on Viola's face, she said, "O what a deal of scorn looks beautiful in the contempt and anger of his lip! Cesario, by the roses of the spring, by maidhood honour, and by truth, I love you so, that, in spite of your pride, I have neither wit nor reason to conceal my passion." But in vain the lady wooed. Viola hastened from her presence, threatening never more to come to plead Orsino's love; and all the reply she made to Olivia's fond solicitations was a declaration of a resolution *Never to love any woman.*

No sooner had Viola left the lady than a claim was made upon her valour. A gentleman, a rejected suitor of Olivia, who had learned how that lady had favoured the duke's messenger, challenged him to fight a duel. What should poor Viola do, who, though she carried a manlike outside, had a true woman's heart, and feared to look on her own sword!

When she saw her formidable rival advancing towards her with his sword drawn, she began to think of confessing that she was a woman; but she was relieved at once from her terror, and the shame of such a discovery, by a stranger that was passing by, who made up to them, and as if he had been long known to her, and were her dearest friend, said to her opponent, "If this young gentleman has done offence, I will take the fault on me; and if you offend him, I will for his sake defy you." Before Viola had time to thank him for his protection, or to inquire the reason of his kind interference, her new friend met with an enemy where his bravery was of no use to him; for the officers of justice coming up in that instant, apprehended the stranger in the duke's name to answer for an offence he had committed some years before; and he said to Viola, "This comes with seeking you." And then he asked her for a purse, saying, "Now my necessity makes me ask for my purse, and it grieves me much more for what I cannot do for you than for what befalls myself. You stand amazed, but be of comfort." His words did indeed amaze Viola, and she protested she knew him not, nor had ever received a purse from him; but for the kindness he had just shown her, she offered him a small sum of money, being nearly the whole she possessed. And now the stranger spoke severe things, charging her with ingratitude and unkindness. He said, "This youth, whom you see here, I snatched from the jaws of death, and for his sake alone I came to Illyria, and have fallen into this danger." But the officers cared little for hearkening to the complaints of their prisoner, and they hurried him off, saying, "What is that to us?" And as he was carried away, he called Viola by the name of Sebastian, reproaching the supposed Sebastian for disowning his friend, as long as he was within hearing. When Viola heard herself called Sebastian, though the stranger was taken away too hastily for her to ask an explanation, she conjectured that this seeming mystery might arise from her being mistaken for her brother; and she began to cherish hopes that it was her brother whose life this man said he had preserved. And so indeed it was. The stranger whose name was Antonio, was a sea captain. He had taken Sebastian up into his ship, when, almost exhausted with fatigue, he was floating on the mast to which he had fastened himself in the storm. Antonio conceived such a friendship for Sebastian that he resolved to accompany him whithersoever he went; and when the youth expressed a curiosity to visit Orsino's court, Antonio, rather than part from him, came to Illyria, though he knew, if his person should be known there, his life would be in danger, because in a sea fight he had once dangerously wounded the Duke Orsino's nephew. This was the offence for which he was now made a prisoner.

Antonio and Sebastian had landed together but a few hours before Antonio met Viola. He had given his purse to Sebastian, desiring him to use it freely if he saw anything he wished to purchase, telling him he would wait at the inn, while Sebastian went to view the town; but Sebastian not returning at the time appointed, Antonio had ventured out to look for him, and Viola being dressed the same, and in face so exactly resembling her brother, Antonio drew his sword, as he thought, in defence of the youth he had saved, and when Sebastian, as he supposed, disowned him, and denied him his own purse, no wonder he accused him of ingratitude.

Viola, when Antonio was gone, fearing a second invitation to fight, slunk home as fast as she could. She had not been long gone when her adversary thought he saw her return, but it was her brother Sebastian who happened to arrive at this place, and he said, "Now, sir, have I met with you again? There's for you," and struck him a blow. Sebastian was no coward; he returned the blow with interest, and drew his sword.

A lady now put a stop to this duel, for Olivia came out of the house, and she, too, mistaking Sebastian for Cesario, invited him to come into her house, expressing much sorrow at the rude attack he had met with. Though Sebastian was as much surprised at the courtesy of this lady as at the rudeness of his unknown foe, yet he went very willingly into the house, and Olivia was delighted to find Cesario (as she thought him) become more sensible of her attentions; for though their features were exactly the same, there was none of the contempt and anger to be seen in his face, which she had complained of when she told her love to Cesario.

Sebastian did not at all object to the fondness the lady lavished on him. He seemed to take it in very good part, yet he wondered how it had come to pass, and he was rather inclined to think Olivia was not in her right senses; but perceiving that she was mistress of a fine house, and that she ordered her affairs and seemed to govern her family discreetly, and that in all but her sudden love for him she appeared in the full possession of her reason, he well approved of the courtship; and Olivia finding Cesario in this good humour, and fearing he might change his mind, proposed that, as she had a priest in the house, they should be instantly married. Sebastian assented to this proposal, and when the marriage ceremony was over, he left his lady for a short time, intending to go and tell his friend Antonio the good fortune he had met with. In the meantime Orsino came to visit Olivia, and at the moment he arrived before Olivia's house, the officers of justice brought their prisoner, Antonio, before the duke. Viola was with Orsino, her master and when Antonio saw Viola, whom he still imagined to be Sebastian, he told the duke in what manner he had rescued this youth from the perils of the sea; and after fully relating all the kindness he had really shown to Sebastian, he ended his complaint with saying that for three months, both day and night, this ungrateful youth had been with him. But now the lady Olivia coming forth from her house, the duke could no longer attend to Antonio's story; and he said, "Here comes the countess: now Heaven walks on earth but for thee, fellow, thy words are madness. Three months has this youth attended on me"; and then he ordered Antonio to be taken aside. But Orsino's heavenly countess soon gave the duke cause to accuse Cesario as much of ingratitude as Antonio had done, for all the words he could hear Olivia speak were words of kindness to Cesario; and when he found his page had obtained this high place in Olivia's favour he threatened him with all the terrors of his just revenge; and as he was going to depart he called Viola to follow him, saying, "Come, boy, with me. My thoughts are ripe for mischief." Though it seemed, in his jealous rage, he was going to doom Viola to instant death, yet her love made her no longer a coward, and she said she would most joyfully suffer death to give her master ease. But Olivia would not so lose her husband, and she cried, "Where goes my Cesario?" Viola replied, "After him I love more than my life." Olivia, however, prevented their departure by loudly proclaiming that Cesario was her husband, and sent for the priest, who declared that not two hours had passed since he had married the lady Olivia to this young man. In vain Viola protested she was not married to Olivia; the evidence of that lady and the priest made Orsino believe that his page had robbed him of the treasure he prized above his life. But, thinking that it was past recall, he was bidding farewell to his faithless mistress, and the *young dissembler*, her husband, as he called Viola, warning her never to come in his sight again, when, as it seemed to them, a miracle appeared, for another Cesario entered and addressed Olivia as his wife. This new Cesario was Sebastian, the real husband of Olivia; and when their wonder had a little ceased at seeing two persons with the same face, the same voice, and the same habit, the brother and sister began to question each other, for Viola could scarce be persuaded that her brother was living, and Sebastian knew not how to account for the sister he supposed drowned being found in the habit of a young man. But Viola presently acknowledged that she was indeed Viola and his sister under that disguise.

When all the errors were cleared up which the extreme likeness between this twin brother and sister had occasioned, they laughed at the Lady Olivia for the pleasant mistake she had made in falling in love with a woman, and Olivia showed no dislike to her exchange when she found she had wedded the brother instead of the sister.

The hopes of Orsino were for ever at an end by this marriage of Olivia, and with his hopes, all his fruitless love seemed to vanish away, and all his thoughts were fixed on the event of his favourite, young Cesario, being changed into a fair lady. He viewed Viola with great attention, and he remembered how very handsome he had always thought Cesario was, and he concluded she would look very beautiful in a woman's attire; and then he remembered how often she had said *she loved him*, which at the time seemed only the dutiful expressions of a faithful page, but now he guessed that something more was meant, for many of her pretty sayings, which were like riddles to him, came now into his mind, and he no sooner remembered these things than he resolved to make Viola his wife. And he said to her (he still could not help calling her *Cesario* and *boy*), "Boy, you have said to me a thousand times that you should never love a woman like to me, and for the faithful service you have done for me so much beneath your soft and tender breeding, and since you have called me master so long, you shall now be your master's mistress, and Orsino's true duchess."

Olivia, perceiving Orsino was making over that heart which she had so ungraciously rejected to Viola, invited them to enter her house, and offered the assistance of the good priest, who had married her to Sebastian in the morning, to perform the same ceremony in the remaining part of the day for Orsino and Viola. Thus the twin brother and sister were both wedded on the same day; the storm and shipwreck which had separated them being the means of bringing to pass their high and mighty fortunes. Viola was the wife of Orsino, the Duke of Illyria, and Sebastian the husband of the rich and noble countess, the Lady Olivia.

The Winter's Tale

Leontes, King of Sicily, and his queen, the beautiful and virtuous Hermione, once lived in the greatest harmony together. So happy was Leontes in the love of this excellent lady, that he had no wish ungratified, except that he sometimes desired to see again, and to present to his queen, his old companion and schoolfellow, Polixenes, King of Bohemia. Leontes and Polixenes were brought up together from their infancy, but being by the death of their fathers called to reign over their respective kingdoms, they had not met for many years, though they frequently interchanged gifts, letters, and loving embassies.

At length, after repeated invitations, Polixenes came from Bohemia to the Sicilian court, to make his friend Leontes a visit.

At first this visit gave nothing but pleasure to Leontes. He recommended the friend of his youth to the queen's particular attention, and seemed, in the presence of his dear friend and old companion, to have his felicity quite completed. They talked over old times; their schooldays and their youthful pranks were remembered, and recounted to Hermione, who always took a cheerful part in these conversations.

When, after a long stay, Polixenes was preparing to depart, Hermione, at the desire of her husband, joined her entreaties to his that Polixenes would prolong his visit.

And now began this good queen's sorrow; for Polixenes, refusing to stay at the request of Leontes, was won over by Hermione's gentle and persuasive words to put off his departure for some weeks longer. Upon this, although Leontes had so long known the integrity and honourable principles of his friend Polixenes, as well as the excellent disposition of his virtuous queen, he was seized with an ungovernable jealousy. Every attention Hermione showed to Polixenes, though by her husband's particular desire, and merely to

159

please him, increased the unfortunate king's jealousy, and from being a loving and true friend, and the best and fondest of husbands, Leontes became suddenly a savage and inhuman monster. Sending for Camillo, one of the lords of his court, and telling him of the suspicion he entertained, he commanded him to poison Polixenes.

Camillo was a good man; and he, well knowing that the jealousy of Leontes had not the slightest foundation in truth, instead of poisoning Polixenes, acquainted him with the king his master's orders, and agreed to escape with him out of the Sicilian dominions; and Polixenes, with the assistance of Camillo, arrived safe in his own kingdom of Bohemia, where Camillo lived from that time in the king's court, and became the chief friend and favourite of Polixenes.

The flight of Polixenes enraged the jealous Leontes still more; he went to the queen's apartment, where the good lady was sitting with her little son Mamillus, who was just beginning to tell one of his best stories to amuse his mother, when the king entered, and, taking the child away, sent Hermione to prison.

Mamillus, though but a very young child, loved his mother tenderly; and when he saw her so dishonoured, and found she was taken from him to be put into a prison, he took it deeply to heart, and drooped and pined away by slow degrees, losing his appetite and his sleep, till it was thought his grief would kill him.

The king, when he had sent his queen to prison, commanded Cleomenes and Dion, two Sicilian lords, to go to Delphos, there to inquire of the oracle at the temple of Apollo if his queen had been unfaithful to him.

When Hermione had been a short time in prison, she was presented with a daughter; and the poor lady received much comfort from the sight of her pretty baby, and she said to it, "My poor little prisoner, I am as innocent as you are."

Hermione had a kind friend in the noble-spirited Paulina, who was the wife of Antigonus, a Sicilian lord; and when the Lady Paulina heard her royal mistress was ill, she went to the prison where Hermione was confined; and she said to Emilia, a lady who attended upon Hermione, "I pray you, Emilia, tell the good queen, if her majesty dare trust me with her little babe, I will carry it to the king its father; we do not know how he may soften at the sight of his innocent child." "Most worthy madam," replied Emilia, "I will acquaint the queen with your noble offer; she was wishing today that she had any friend who would venture to present the child to the king." "And tell her," said Paulina, "that I will speak boldly to Leontes in her defence." "May you be for ever blessed," said Emilia, "for your kindness to our gracious queen!" Emilia then went to Hermione, who joyfully gave up her baby to the care of Paulina, for she had feared that no one would dare venture to present the child to its father.

Paulina took the new-born infant, and forcing herself into the king's presence, notwithstanding her husband, fearing the king's anger, endeavoured to prevent her, she laid the babe at its father's feet, and Paulina made a noble speech to the king in defence of Hermione, and she reproached him severely for his inhumanity, and implored him to have mercy on his innocent wife and child. But Paulina's spirited remonstrances only aggravated Leontes's displeasure, and he ordered her husband Antigonus to take her from his presence.

When Paulina went away, she left the little baby at its father's feet, thinking, when he was alone with it, he would look upon it, and have pity upon its helpless innocence.

The good Paulina was mistaken; for no sooner was she gone than the merciless father ordered Antigonus, Paulina's husband, to take the child, and carry it out to sea, and leave it upon some desert shore to perish.

Antigonus, unlike the good Camillo, too well obeyed the orders of Leontes; for he immediately carried the child on shipboard, and put out to sea, intending to leave it on the first desert coast he could find.

So firmly was the king persuaded of the guilt of Hermione, that he would not wait for the return of Cleomenes and Dion, whom he had sent to consult the oracle of Apollo at Delphos; but before the queen was recovered from her illness, and from the grief for the loss of her precious baby, he had her brought to a public trial before all the lords and nobles of his court. And when all the great lords, the judges, and all the nobility of the land were assembled together to try Hermione, and that unhappy queen was standing as a prisoner before her subjects to receive their judgment, Cleomenes and Dion entered the assembly, and presented to the king the answer of the oracle sealed up; and Leontes commanded the seal to be broken, and the words of the oracle to be read aloud; and these were the words:— "Hermione is innocent, Polixenes blameless, Camillo a true subject, Leontes a jealous tyrant, and the king shall live without an heir if that which is lost be not found." The king would give no credit to the words of the oracle; he said it was a falsehood invented by the queen's friends, and he desired the judge to proceed in the trial of the queen; but while Leontes was speaking a man entered and told him that the Prince Mamillus, hearing his mother was to be tried for her life, struck with grief and shame, had suddenly died.

Hermione, upon hearing of the death of this dear affectionate child, who had lost his life in sorrowing for her misfortune, fainted, and Leontes, pierced to the heart by the news, began to feel pity for his unhappy queen, and he ordered Paulina, and the ladies who were her attendants, to take her away, and use means for her recovery. Paulina soon returned, and told the king that Hermione was dead.

When Leontes heard that the queen was dead, he repented of his cruelty to her; and now that he thought that his ill usage had broken Hermione's heart, he believed her innocent; and he now thought the words of the oracle were true, as he knew "if that which was lost was not found," which he concluded was his young daughter, he should be without an heir, the young Prince Mamillus being dead; and he would give his kingdom now to recover his lost daughter; and Leontes gave himself up to remorse, and passed many years in mournful thoughts and repentant grief.

The ship in which Antigonus carried the infant princess out to sea was driven by a storm upon the coast of Bohemia, the very kingdom of the good King Polixenes. Here Antigonus landed, and here he left the little baby.

Antigonus never returned to Sicily to tell Leontes where he had left his daughter, for as he was going back to the ship, a bear came out of the woods, and tore him to pieces, a just punishment on him for obeying the wicked order of Leontes.

The child was dressed in rich clothes and jewels; for Hermione had made it very fine when she sent it to Leontes, and Antigonus had pinned a paper to its mantle, with the name of *Perdita* written thereon, and words obscurely intimating its high birth and untoward fate.

This poor deserted baby was found by a shepherd. He was a humane man, and so he carried the little Perdita home to his wife, who nursed it tenderly; but poverty tempted the shepherd to conceal the rich prize he had found; therefore he left that part of the country, that no one might know where he got his riches, and with part of Pedita's jewels he bought herds of sheep, and became a wealthy shepherd. He brought up Perdita as his own child, and she knew not she was any other than a shepherd's daughter.

The little Perdita grew up a lovely maiden; and though she had no better education than that of a shepherd's daughter, yet so did the natural graces she inherited from her royal mother shine forth in her untutored mind that no one from her behaviour would have known she had not been brought up in her father's court.

Polixenes, the King of Bohemia, had an only son, whose name was Florizel. As this young prince was hunting near the shepherd's dwelling he saw the old man's supposed daughter, and the beauty, modesty, and queen-like deportment of Perdita caused him instantly to fall in love with her. He soon, under the name of Doricles, and in the disguise of a private gentleman, became a constant visitor at the old shepherd's house.

Florizel's frequent absence from court alarmed Polixenes, and, setting people to watch his son, he discovered his love for the shepherd's fair daughter.

Polixenes then called for Camillo, the faithful Camillo, who had preserved his life from the fury of Leontes, and desired that he would accompany him to the house of the shepherd, the supposed father of Perdita.

Polixenes and Camillo, both in disguise, arrived at the old shepherd's dwelling while they were celebrating the feast of sheepshearing, and though they were strangers, yet, at the sheep-shearing every guest being made welcome, they were invited to walk in and join in the general festivity.

Nothing but mirth and jollity was going forward. Tables were spread, and great preparations were making for the rustic feast. Some lads and lasses were dancing on the green before the house, while others of the young men were buying ribands, gloves, and such toys of a pedlar at the door.

While this busy scene was going forward, Florizel and Perdita sat quietly in a retired corner, seemingly more pleased with the conversation of each other than desirous of engaging in the sports and silly amusements of those around them.

The king was so disguised that it was impossible his son could know him; he therefore advanced near enough to hear the conversation. The simple yet elegant manner in which Perdita conversed with his son did not a little surprise Polixenes. He said to Camillo, "This is the prettiest low-born lass I ever saw; nothing she does or says but looks like something greater than herself, too noble for this place."

Camillo replied, "Indeed she is the very queen of curds and cream."

"Pray, my good friend," said the king to the old shepherd, "what fair swain is that talking with your daughter?" "They call him Doricles," replied the shepherd. "He says he loves my daughter, and to speak the truth there is not a kiss to choose which loves the other best. If young Doricles can get her she shall bring him that he little dreams of," meaning the remainder of Perdita's jewels, which, after he had bought herds of sheep with part of them, he had carefully hoarded up for her marriage portion.

Polixenes then addressed his son. "How, now, young man!" said he; "your heart seems full of something that takes off your mind from feasting. When I was young, I used to load my love with presents; but you have let the pedlar go, and have bought your lass no toy."

The young prince, who little thought he was talking to the king his father, replied, "Old sir, she prizes not such trifles; the gifts which Perdita expects from me are locked up in my heart." Then, turning to Perdita, he said to her, "Oh, hear me, Perdita, before this ancient gentleman, who, it seems, was once himself a lover; he shall hear what I profess." Florizel then called upon the old stranger to be a witness to a solemn promise of marriage which he made to Perdita, saying to Polixenes, "I pray you mark our contract."

"Mark your divorce, young sir," said the king, discovering himself. Polixenes then reproached his son for daring to contract himself to this low-born maiden, calling Perdita "shepherd's brat, sheephook," and other disrespectful names; and threatening, if ever she suffered his son to see her again, he would put her and the old shepherd her father to a cruel death.

The king then left them in great wrath, and ordered Camillo to follow him with Prince Florizel.

When the king had departed, Perdita, whose royal nature was roused by Polixenes' reproaches, said, "Though we are all undone, I was not much afraid; and once or twice I was about to speak, and tell him plainly that the selfsame sun which shines upon his palace hides not his face from our cottage, but looks on both alike." Then sorrowfully she said, "But now I am awakened from this dream, I will queen it no further. Leave me, sir; I will go milk my ewes and weep."

The kind-hearted Camillo was charmed with the spirit and propriety of Perdita's behaviour; and perceiving that the young prince was too deeply in love to give up his mistress at the command of his royal father, he thought of a way to befriend the lovers, and, at the same time, to execute a favourable scheme he had in his mind.

Camillo had long known that Leontes, the King of Sicily, was become a true penitent, and though Camillo was now the favoured friend of King Polixenes, he could not help wishing once more to see his late royal master and his native home. He therefore proposed to Florizel and Perdita that they should accompany him to the Sicilian court, where he would engage Leontes should protect them, till, through his mediation, they could obtain pardon from Polixenes, and his consent to their marriage.

To this proposal they joyfully agreed; and Camillo, who conducted everything relative to their flight, allowed the old shepherd to go along with them.

The shepherd took with him the remainder of Perdita's jewels, her baby clothes, and the paper which he had found pinned to her mantle.

After a prosperous voyage, Florizel and Perdita, Camillo and the old shepherd, arrived in safety at the court of Leontes. Leontes, who still mourned his dead Hermione and his lost child, received Camillo with great kindness, and gave a cordial welcome to Prince Florizel. But Perdita, whom Florizel introduced as his princess, seemed to engross all Leontes' attention: perceiving a resemblance between her and his dead Queen Hermione, his grief broke out afresh, and he said, such a lovely creature might his own daughter have been if he had not so cruelly destroyed her "And then, too," said he to Florizel, "I lost the society and friendship of your brave father, whom I now desire more than my life once again to look upon."

When the old shepherd heard how much notice the king had taken of Perdita, and that he had lost a daughter who was exposed in infancy, he fell to comparing the time when he found the little Perdita, with the manner of its exposure, the jewels and other tokens of its high birth, from all which it was impossible for him not to conclude that Perdita and the king's lost daughter were the same.

Florizel and Perdita, Camillo and the faithful Paulina were present when the old shepherd related to the king the manner in which he had found the child, and also the circumstances of Antigonus' death, he having seen the bear seize upon him. He showed the rich mantle in which Paulina remembered Hermione had wrapped the child, and he produced a jewel which she remembered Hermione had tied about Perdita's neck; and he gave up the paper which Paulina knew to be the writing of her husband; it could not be doubted that Perdita was Leontes' own daughter; but oh, the noble struggles of Paulina between sorrow for her husband's death and joy that the oracle was fulfilled in the king's heir, his long-lost daughter, being found! When Leontes heard that Perdita was his daughter, the great sorrow that he felt that Hermione was not living to behold her child made him that he could say nothing for a long time, but "O thy mother, thy mother!"

Paulina interrupted this joyful yet distressful scene, with saying to Leontes that she had a statue newly finished by that rare Italian master, Julio Romano, which was such a perfect resemblance of the queen, that would his majesty be pleased to go to her house and look upon it, he would almost be ready to think it was Hermione herself. Thither then they all went; the king anxious to see the semblance of his Hermione, and Perdita longing to behold what the mother she never saw did look like.

When Paulina drew back the curtain which concealed this famous statue, so perfectly did it resemble Hermione that all the king's sorrow was renewed at the sight; for a long time he had no power to speak or move.

"I like your silence, my liege," said Paulina: "it the more shows your wonder. Is not this statue very like your queen?"

At length the king said, "O thus she stood, even with such majesty, when I first wooed her. But yet, Paulina, Hermione was not so aged as this statue looks." Paulina replied, "So much the more the carver's excellence, who has made the statue as Hermione would have looked had she been living now. But let me draw the curtain, sire, lest presently you think it moves."

The king then said, "Do not draw the curtain. Would I were dead. See, Camillo, would you no think it breathed? Her eye seems to have motion in it." "I must draw the curtain, my liege," said Paulina "You are so transported you are persuaded the statue lives." "O sweet Paulina," said Leontes, "make me think so twenty years together. Still methinks there is an air comes from her. What fine chisel could ever yet cut breath? Let no man mock me, for I will kiss her." "Good, my lord, forbear!" said Paulina. "The ruddiness upon her lips is wet; you will stain your own with oily painting. Shall I draw the curtain?" "No not these twenty years," said Leontes.

Perdita, who all this time had been kneeling and beholding in silent admiration the statue of her matchless mother, said now, "And so long could I stay here, looking upon my dead mother."

"Either forbear this transport," said Paulina to Leontes, "and let me draw the curtain, or prepare yourself for more amazement. I can make the statue move indeed, ay, and descend from off the pedestal and take you by the hand. But then you will think (which I protest I am not) that I am assisted by some wicked powers."

"What you can make her do," said the astonished king, "I am content to look upon. What you can make her speak I am content to hear; for it is as easy to make her speak as move."

Paulina then ordered some slow and solemn music, which she had prepared for the purpose, to strike up, and to the amazement of all the beholders the statue came down from off the pedestal, and threw its arms around Leontes' neck. The statue then began to speak, praying for blessings on her husband, and on her child, the newly-found Perdita.

No wonder that the statue hung upon Leontes' neck, and blessed her husband and her child. No wonder; for the statue was indeed Hermione herself, the real and living queen.

Paulina had falsely reported to the king the death of Hermione, thinking that the only means to preserve her royal mistress's life; and with the good Paulina, Hermione had lived ever since, never choosing Leontes should know she was living till she heard Perdita was found; for though she had long forgiven the injuries which Leontes had done to herself, she could not pardon his cruelty to his infant daughter.

His dead queen thus restored to life, his lost daughter found, the long-sorrowing Leontes could scarcely support the excess of his own happiness.

Nothing but congratulations and affectionate speeches were heard on all sides. Now the delighted parents thanked Prince Florizel for loving their lowly-seeming daughter; and now they blessed the good old shepherd for preserving their child. Greatly did Camillo and Paulina rejoice that they had lived to see so good an end of all their faithful services.

And as if nothing should be wanting to complete this strange and unlooked-for joy, King Polixenes himself now entered the palace.

When Polixenes first missed his son and Camillo, knowing that Camillo had long wished to return to Sicily, he conjectured he should find the fugitives here; and following them with all speed, he happened to arrive just at this the happiest moment of Leontes' life.

Polixenes took a part in the general joy; he forgave his friend Leontes the unjust jealousy he had conceived against him, and they once more loved each other with all the warmth of their first boyish friendship. And there was no fear that Polixenes would now oppose his son's marriage with Perdita. She was no "sheephook" now, but the heiress of the crown of Sicily.

Thus have we seen the patient virtues of the long-suffering Hermione rewarded. That excellent lady lived many years with her Leontes and her Perdita, the happiest of mothers and of queens.

The Two Gentlemen Of Verona

There lived in the city of Verona two young gentlemen, whose names were Valentine and Protheus between whom a firm and un-interrupted friendship had long subsisted. They pursued their studies together and their hours of leisure were always passed in each other's company, except when Protheus visited a lady he was in love with; and these visits to his mistress, and this passion of Protheus for the fair Julia, were the only topics on which these two friends disagreed; for Valentine, not being himself a lover, was sometimes a little weary of hearing his friend for ever talking of his Julia, and then he would laugh at Protheus, and in pleasant terms ridicule the passion of love, and declare that no such idle fancies should ever enter his head, greatly preferring, as he said, the free and happy life he led to the anxious hopes and fears of the lover Protheus.

One morning Valentine came to Protheus to tell him that they must for a time be separated, for that he was going to Milan. Protheus, unwilling to part with his friend, used many arguments to prevail upon Valentine not to leave him; but Valentine said, "Cease to persuade me, my loving Protheus. I will not, like a sluggard, wear out my youth in idleness at home. Home-keeping youths have ever homely wits. If your affection were not chained to the sweet glances of your honoured Julia, I would entreat you to accompany me to see the wonders of the world abroad; but since you are a lover, love on still, and may your love be prosperous!"

They parted with mutual expressions of unalterable friendship. "Sweet Valentine, adieu," said Protheus; "think on me when you see some rare object worthy of notice in your travels, and wish me partaker of your happiness."

Valentine began his journey that same day towards Milan; and when his friend had left him, Protheus sat down to write a letter to

Julia, which he gave to her maid Lucetta to deliver to her mistress.

Julia loved Protheus as well as he did her, but she was a lady of a noble spirit, and she thought it did not become her maiden dignity too easily to be won; therefore she affected to be insensible of his passion, and gave him much uneasiness in the prosecution of his suit.

And when Lucetta offered the letter to Julia, she would not receive it, and chid her maid for taking letters from Protheus, and ordered her to leave the room. But she so much wished to see what was written in the letter, that she soon called in her maid again, and when Lucetta returned, she said, "What o'clock is it?" Lucetta, who knew her mistress more desired to see the letter than to know the time of day, without answering her question, again offered the rejected letter. Julia, angry that her maid should thus take the liberty of seeming to know what she really wanted, tore the letter in pieces, and threw it on the floor, ordering her maid once more out of the room. As Lucetta was retiring, she stopped to pick up the fragments of the torn letter; but Julia, who meant not so to part with them, said, in pretended anger, "Go, get you gone, and let the papers lie; you would be fingering them to anger me."

Julia then began to piece together as well as she could the torn fragments. She first made out these words, "love-wounded Protheus "; and lamenting over these and such like loving words, which she made out though they were all torn asunder, or, she said, wounded (the expression, "love-wounded Protheus," giving her that idea), she talked to these kind words, telling them she would lodge them in her bosom as in a bed till their wounds were healed, and that she would kiss each several piece to make amends.

In this manner she went on talking with a pretty lady-like childishness, till, finding herself unable to make out the whole, and vexed at her own ingratitude in destroying such sweet and loving words, as she called them, she wrote a much kinder letter to Protheus than she had ever done before.

Protheus was greatly delighted at receiving this favourable answer to his letter; and while he was reading it, he exclaimed, "Sweet love, sweet lines, sweet life!" In the midst of his raptures he was interrupted by his father. "How now!" said the old gentleman; what letter are you reading there?"

"My lord," replied Protheus, "it is a letter from my friend Valentine, at Milan."

"Lend me the letter," said his father; "let me see what news."

"There are no news, my lord," said Protheus, greatly alarmed, "but he writes how well beloved he is of the Duke of Milan, who daily graces him with favours, and how he wishes me with him, the partner of his fortune.

"And how stand you affected to his wish?" asked the father.

"As one relying on your lordship's will, and not depending on his friendly wish," said Protheus.

Now it so happened that Protheus' father had just been talking with a friend on this very subject: his friend had said he wondered his lordship suffered his son to spend his youth at home, while most men were sending their sons to seek preferment abroad; "some," said he, "to the wars, to try their fortunes there, and some to discover islands far away, and some to study in foreign universities: and there is his companion Valentine, he is gone to the Duke of Milan's court. Your son is fit for any of these things, and it will be a great disadvantage to him in his riper age not to have travelled in his youth."

Protheus' father thought the advice of his friend was very good, and upon Protheus telling him that Valentine "wished him with him, the partner of his fortune," he at once determined to send his son to Milan; and without giving Protheus any reason for this sudden resolution, it being the usual habit of this positive old gentleman to command his son, not reason with him, he said, "My will is the same as Valentine's wish"; and seeing his son look astonished, he added, "Look not amazed that I so suddenly resolve you shall spend some time in the Duke of Milan's court; for what I will I will, and there is an end. Tomorrow be in readiness to go. Make no excuses, for I am peremptory."

Protheus knew it was of no use to make objections to his father, who never suffered him to dispute his will; and he blamed himself for telling his father an untruth about Julia's letter, which had brought upon him the sad necessity of leaving her.

Now that Julia found she was going to lose Protheus for so long a time, she no longer pretended indifference; and they bade each other a mournful farewell, with many vows of love and constancy. Protheus and Julia exchanged rings, which they both promised to keep for ever in remembrance of each other; and thus, taking a sorrowful leave, Protheus set out on his journey to Milan, the abode of his friend Valentine.

Valentine was in reality what Protheus had feigned to his father, in high favour with the Duke of Milan; and another event had happened to him of which Protheus did not even dream, for Valentine had given up the freedom of which he used to boast so much, and was become as passionate a lover as Protheus.

She who had wrought this wondrous change in Valentine was the Lady Silvia, daughter of the Duke of Milan, and she also loved him; but they concealed their love from the duke, because, although he showed much kindness for Valentine, and invited him every day to his palace, yet he designed to marry his daughter to a young courtier whose name was Thurio. Silvia despised this Thurio, for he had none of the fine sense and excellent qualities of Valentine.

These two rivals, Thurio and Valentine, were one day on a visit to Silvia, and Valentine was entertaining Silvia with turning everything Thurio said into ridicule, when the duke himself entered the room, and told Valentine the welcome news of his friend Protheus' arrival. Valentine said, "If I had wished a thing, it would have been to have seen him here"; and then he highly praised Protheus to the duke, saying, "My lord, though I have been a truant of my time, yet hath my friend made use and fair advantage of his days, and is complete in person and in mind, in all good grace to grace a gentleman."

"Welcome him, then, according to his worth," said the duke; "Silvia, I speak to you, and you, Sir Thurio; for Valentine, I need not bid him do so." They were here interrupted by the entrance of Protheus, and Valentine introduced him to Silvia, saying, "Sweet lady, entertain him to be my fellow-servant to your ladyship."

When Valentine and Protheus had ended their visit, and were alone together, Valentine said, "Now tell me how all does from whence you came? How does your lady, and how thrives your love?" Protheus replied, "My tales of love used to weary you. I know you joy not in a love discourse."

"Ay, Protheus," returned Valentine, "but that life is altered now. I have done penance for condemning love. For in revenge of my contempt of love, Love has chased sleep from my enthralled eyes. O gentle Protheus, Love is a mighty lord, and hath so humbled me, that I confess there is no woe like his correction nor no such joy on earth as in his service. I now like no discourse except it be of love. Now I can break my fast, dine, sup, and sleep upon the very name of love."

This acknowledgment of the change which love had made in the disposition of Valentine was a great triumph to his friend Protheus. But "friend" Protheus must he be called no longer, for the same all-powerful deity Love, of whom they were speaking (yea, even while they were talking of the change he had made in Valentine), was working in the heart of Protheus; and he, who had till this time been a pattern of true love and perfect friendship, was now, in one short interview with Silvia, become a false friend and a faithless lover; for at the first sight of Silvia all his love for Julia vanished away like a dream, nor did his long friendship for Valentine deter him from endeavouring to supplant him in her affections; and although, as it will always be, when people of dispositions naturally good become unjust, he had many scruples before he determined to forsake Julia, and become the rival of Valentine; yet he at length overcame his sense of duty, and yielded himself up almost without remorse to his new, unhappy passion.

Valentine imparted to him in confidence the whole history of his love, and how carefully they had concealed it from the duke her father, and told him that, despairing of ever being able to obtain his consent he had prevailed upon Silvia to leave her father's palace that night and go with him to Mantua. Then he showed Protheus a ladder of ropes, by help of which he meant to assist Silvia to get out of one of the windows of the palace after it was dark.

Upon hearing this faithful recital of his friend's dearest secrets, it is hardly possible to be believed, but so it was, that Protheus resolved to go to the duke and disclose the whole to him.

This false friend began his tale with many artful speeches to the duke, such as that by the laws of friendship he ought to conceal what he was going to reveal, but that the gracious favour the duke had shown him, and the duty he owed his grace, urged him to tell that which else no worldly good should draw from him. He then told all he had heard from Valentine, not omitting the ladder of ropes and the manner in which Valentine meant to conceal them under a long cloak.

The duke thought Protheus quite a miracle of integrity, in that he preferred telling his friend's intention rather than he would conceal an unjust action; highly commended him, and promised not to let Valentine know from whom he had learnt all his intelligence, but by some artifice to make Valentine betray the secret himself. For this purpose the duke awaited the coming of Valentine in the evening, whom he soon saw hurrying towards the palace, and he perceived something was wrapped within his cloak, which he concluded was the rope ladder.

The duke upon this stopped him, saying, "Whither away so fast, Valentine?" "May it please your grace," said Valentine, "there is a messenger that stays to bear my letters to my friends, and I am going to deliver them." Now this falsehood of Valentine's had no better success in the event than the untruth Protheus told his father.

"Be they of much import?" said the duke.

"No more, my lord," said Valentine, "than to tell my father I am well and happy at your grace's court."

"Nay, then," said the duke, "no matter; stay with me awhile. I wish your counsel about some affairs that concern me nearly." He then told Valentine an artful story as a prelude to draw his secret from him, saying that Valentine knew he wished to match his daughter with Thurio, but that she was stubborn and disobedient to his commands, "neither regarding," said he, "that she is my child, nor fearing me as if I were her father. And I may say to thee, this pride of hers has drawn my love from her. I had thought my age should have been cherished by her childlike duty. I now am resolved to take a wife, and turn her out to whosoever will take her in. Let her beauty be her wedding dower, for me and my possessions she esteems not."

Valentine, wondering where all this would end, made answer, "And what would your grace have me to do in all this?"

"Why," said the duke, "the lady I would wish to marry is nice and coy, and does not much esteem my aged eloquence. Besides, the fashion of courtship is much changed since I was young; now I would willingly have you to be my tutor to instruct me how I am to woo."

Valentine gave him a general idea of the modes of courtship then practised by young men when they wished to win a fair lady's love, such as presents, frequent visits, and the like.

The duke replied to this that the lady did refuse a present which he sent her, and that she was so strictly kept by her father, that no man might have access to her by day.

"Why, then," said Valentine, "you must visit her by night."

"But at night," said the artful duke, who was now coming to the drift of his discourse, "her doors are fast locked."

Valentine then unfortunately proposed that the duke should endeavour to speak with the lady at night by means of a ladder of ropes, saying he would procure him one fitting for that purpose, and in conclusion advised him to conceal this ladder of ropes under such a cloak as that which he now wore. "Lend me your cloak," said the duke, who had feigned this long story on purpose to have a pretence to get off the cloak; so, upon saying these words, he caught hold of Valentine's cloak, and throwing it back he discovered not only the ladder of ropes, but also a letter of Silvia's, which he instantly opened and read, and this letter contained a full account of their intended elopement. The duke, after upbraiding Valentine for his ingratitude in thus returning the favour he had shown him by endeavouring to steal away his daughter, banished him from the court and city of Milan for ever, and Valentine was forced to depart that night without even seeing Silvia.

While Protheus at Milan was thus injuring Valentine, Julia at Verona was regretting the absence of Protheus, and her regard for him at last so far overcame her sense of propriety that she resolved to leave Verona and seek her lover at Milan, and to secure herself from danger on the road she dressed her maid Lucetta and herself in men's clothes, and they set out in this disguise, and arrived at Milan soon after Valentine was banished from that city through the treachery of Protheus.

Julia entered Milan about noon, and she took up her abode at an inn, and her thoughts being all on her dear Protheus, she entered into conversation with the innkeeper (or host, as he was called), thinking by that means to learn some news of Protheus.

The host was greatly pleased that this handsome young gentleman (as he took her to be), who from his appearance, he concluded was of high rank, spoke so familiarly to him; and being a good-natured man he was sorry to see him look so melancholy, and to amuse his young guest he offered to take him to hear some fine music, with which, he said, a gentleman that evening was going to serenade his mistress.

The reason Julia looked so very melancholy was that she did not well know what Protheus would think of the imprudent step she had taken; for she knew he had loved her for her noble maiden pride and dignity of character, and she feared she would lower herself in his esteem, and this it was that made her wear a sad and thoughtful countenance.

She gladly accepted the offer of the host to go with him and hear the music; for she secretly hoped she might meet Protheus by the way.

But when she came to the palace whither the host conducted her, a very different effect was produced to what the kind host intended; for there, to her heart's sorrow, she beheld her lover, the inconstant Protheus, serenading the Lady Silvia with music, and addressing discourse of love and admiration to her. And Julia overheard Silvia from a window talk with Protheus and reproach him for forsaking his own true lady, and for his ingratitude to his friend Valentine; and then Silvia left the window, not choosing to listen to his music and his fine speeches; for she was a faithful lady to her banished Valentine, and abhorred the ungenerous conduct of his false friend Protheus.

Though Julia was in despair at what she had just witnessed, yet did she still love the truant Protheus; and hearing that he had lately parted with a servant, she contrived, with the assistance of her host, the friendly innkeeper, to hire herself to Protheus as a page; and Protheus knew not she was Julia, and he sent her with letters and presents to her rival Silvia, and he even sent by her the very ring she gave him as a parting gift at Verona.

When she went to that lady with the ring, she was most glad to find that Silvia utterly rejected the suit of Protheus; and Julia, or the page Sebastian, as she was called, entered into conversation with Silvia about Protheus' first love, the forsaken Lady Julia. She, putting in (as one may say) a good word for herself, said she knew Julia, as well she might, being herself the Julia of whom she spoke; telling how fondly Julia loved her master Protheus, and how his unkind neglect would grieve her, and then she with a pretty equivocation went on: "Julia is about my height and of my complexion, the colour of her eyes and hair the same as mine"; and indeed Julia looked a most beautiful youth in her boy's attire. Silvia was moved to pity this lovely lady, who was so sadly forsaken by the man she loved; and when Julia offered the ring which Protheus had sent, refused it, saying, "The more shame for him that he sends me that ring; I will not take it, for I have often heard him say his Julia gave it to him. I love thee, gentle youth, for pitying her, poor lady! Here is a purse; I give it you for Julia's sake." These comfortable words coming from her kind rival's tongue cheered the drooping heart of the disguised lady.

But to return to the banished Valentine, who scarce knew which way to bend his course, being unwilling to return home to his father a disgraced and banished man. As he was wandering over a lonely forest, not far distant from Milan, where he had left his heart's dear treasure, the Lady Silvia, he was set upon by robbers, who demanded his money.

Valentine told them that he was a man crossed by adversity, that he was going into banishment, and that he had no money, the clothes he had on being all his riches.

The robbers, hearing that he was a distressed man, and being struck with his noble air and manly behaviour, told him if he would live with them and be their chief or captain they would put themselves under his command, but that if he refused to accept their offer they would kill him.

Valentine, who cared little what became of himself, said he would consent to live with them and be their captain, provided they did no outrage on women or poor passengers.

Thus the noble Valentine became, like Robin Hood of whom we read in ballads, a captain of robbers and outlawed banditti; and in this situation he was found by Silvia, and in this manner it came to pass.

Silvia, to avoid a marriage with Thurio, whom her father insisted upon her no longer refusing, came at last to the resolution of following Valentine to Mantua, at which place she had heard her lover had taken refuge; but in this account she was misinformed, for he still lived in the forest among the robbers, bearing the name of their captain, but taking no part in their depredations, and using the authority which they had imposed upon him in no other way than to compel them to show compassion to the travellers they robbed.

Silvia contrived to effect her escape from her father's palace in company with a worthy old gentleman, whose name was Eglamour, whom she took along with her for protection on the road. She had to pass through the forest where Valentine and the banditti dwelt, and one of these robbers seized on Silvia and would also have taken Eglamour, but he escaped.

The robber who had taken Silvia, seeing the terror she was in, bid her not be alarmed, for that he was only going to carry her to a cave where his captain lived and that she need not be afraid, for their captain had an honourable mind and always showed humanity to women. Silvia found little comfort in hearing she was going to be carried as a prisoner before the captain of a lawless banditti. "O Valentine," she cried, "this I endure for thee."

But as the robber was conveying her to the cave of his captain he was stopped by Protheus, who, still attended by Julia in the disguise of a page, having heard of the flight of Silvia, had traced her steps to this forest. Protheus now rescued her from the hands of the robbers; but scarce had she time to thank him for the service he had done her before he began to distress her afresh with his love suit, and while he was rudely pressing her consent to marry him, and his page (the forlorn Julia) was standing beside him in great anxiety of mind, fearing lest the great service which Protheus had done to Silvia should win her to show him some favour, they were all strangely surprised with the sudden appearance of Valentine, who, having heard his robbers had taken a lady prisoner, came to console and relieve her.

Protheus was courting Silvia, and he was so much ashamed of being caught by his friend that he was all at once seized with penitence and remorse, and he expressed such a lively sorrow for the injuries he had done to Valentine that Valentine, whose nature was noble and generous, even to a romantic degree, not only forgave and restored him to his former place in his friendship, but in a sudden flight of heroism he said, "I freely do forgive you, and all the interest I have in Silvia I give it up to you." Julia, who was standing beside her master as a page, hearing this strange offer, and fearing Protheus would not be able with this new-found virtue to refuse Silvia, fainted and they were all employed in recovering her, else would Silvia have been offended at being thus made over to Protheus, though she could scarcely think that Valentine would long persevere in this overstrained and too generous act of friendship. When Julia recovered from the fainting fit, she said, "I had forgot, my master ordered me to deliver this ring to Silvia." Protheus, looking upon the ring, saw that it was the one he gave to Julia, in return for that which he received from her, and which he had sent by the supposed page to Silvia. "How is this?" said he, "this is Julia's ring; how came you by it, boy?" Julia answered, "Julia herself did give it me, and Julia herself hath brought it hither."

Protheus, now looking earnestly upon her, plainly perceived that the page Sebastian was no other than the Lady Julia herself; and the proof she had given of her constancy and true love so wrought in him, that his love for her returned into his heart, and he took again his own dear lady, and joyfully resigned all pretensions to the Lady Silvia to Valentine, who had so well deserved her.

Protheus and Valentine were expressing their happiness in their reconciliation, and in the love of their faithful ladies, when they were surprised with the sight of the Duke of Milan and Thurio, who came there in pursuit of Silvia.

Thurio first approached, and attempted to seize Silvia, saying, "Silvia is mine ". Upon this Valentine said to him in a very spirited manner, "Thurio, keep back; if once again you say that Silvia is yours you shall embrace your death. Here she stands, take but possession of her with a touch! I dare you but to breathe upon my love." Hearing this threat, Thurio, who was a great coward, drew back, and said he cared not for her, and that none but a fool would fight for a girl who loved him not.

The duke, who was a very brave man himself, said now in great anger, "The more base and degenerate in you to take such means for her as you have done, and leave her on such light conditions." Then, turning to Valentine, he said, "I do applaud your spirit, Valentine, and think you worthy of an empress's love. You shall have Silvia, for you have well deserved her." Valentine then with great humility kissed the duke's hand, and accepted the noble present which he had made him of his daughter with becoming thankfulness; taking occasion of this joyful minute to entreat the good-humoured duke to pardon the thieves with whom he had associated in the forest, assuring him, that when reformed and restored to society, there would be found among them many good and fit for great employment; for the most of them had been banished, like Valentine, for state offences, rather than for any black crimes they had been guilty of. To this the ready duke consented; and now nothing remained but that Protheus, the false friend, was ordained, by way of penance for his love-prompted faults, to be present at the recital of the whole story of his loves and falsehoods before the duke, and the shame of the recital to his awakened conscience was judged sufficient punishment; which being done, the lovers, all four, returned back to Milan, and their nuptials were solemnised in presence of the duke, with high triumphs and feasting.

Cymbeline

During the time of Augustus Caesar, Emperor of Rome, there reigned in England (which was then called Britain) a king whose name was Cymbeline.

Cymbeline's first wife died when his three children (two sons and a daughter) were very young. Imogen, the eldest of these children, was brought up in her father's court; but by a strange chance the two sons of Cymbeline were stolen out of their nursery, when the eldest was but three years of age, and the youngest quite an infant; and Cymbeline could never discover what was become of them, or by whom they were conveyed away.

Cymbeline was twice married; his second wife was a wicked, plotting woman, and a cruel stepmother to Imogen, Cymbeline's daughter by his first wife.

The queen, though she hated Imogen, yet wished her to marry a son of her own by a former husband (she also having been twice married); for by this means she hoped, upon the death of Cymbeline, to place the crown of Britain upon the head of her son Cloten; for she knew that if the king's sons were not found the Princess Imogen must be the king's heir. But this design was prevented by Imogen herself, who married without the consent or even knowledge of her father or the queen.

Posthumus (for that was the name of Imogen's husband) was the best scholar and most accomplished gentleman of that age. His father died fighting in the wars for Cymbeline, and soon after his birth his mother died also for grief at the loss of her husband.

Cymbeline, pitying the helpless state of this orphan, took Posthumus (Cymbeline having given him that name, because he was born after his father's death) and educated him in his own court.

Imogen and Posthumus were both taught by the same masters,

and were play-fellows from their infancy; they loved each other tenderly when they were children, and their affection continuing to increase with their years, when they grew up they privately married.

The disappointed queen soon learnt this secret, for she kept spies constantly in watch upon the actions of her daughter-in-law, and she immediately told the king of the marriage of Imogen with Posthumus.

Nothing could exceed the wrath of Cymbeline when he heard that his daughter had been so forgetful of her high dignity as to marry a subject. He commanded Posthumus to leave Britain, and banished him from his native country for ever.

The queen, who pretended to pity Imogen for the grief she suffered at losing her husband, offered to procure them a private meeting before Posthumus set out on his journey to Rome, which place he had chosen for his residence in his banishment. This seeming kindness she showed the better to succeed in her future designs in regard to her son Cloten; for she meant to persuade Imogen, when her husband was gone, that her marriage was not lawful, being contracted without the consent of the king.

Imogen and Posthumus took a most affectionate leave of each other. Imogen gave her husband a diamond ring which had been her mother's, and Posthumus promised never to part with the ring; and he fastened a bracelet on the arm of his wife, which he begged she would preserve with great care as a token of his love; they then bid each other farewell, with many vows of everlasting love and fidelity.

Imogen remained a solitary and dejected lady in her father's court, and Posthumus arrived at Rome, the place he had chosen for his banishment.

Posthumus fell into company at Rome with some young men of different nations, who were talking freely of ladies, each one praising the ladies of his own country and his own mistress. Posthumus, who had ever his own dear lady in his mind, affirmed that his wife, the fair Imogen, was the most virtuous, wise and constant lady in the world.

One of these gentlemen, whose name was Iachimo, being offended that a lady of Britain should be so praised above the Roman ladies, his country-women, provoked Posthumus by seeming to doubt the constancy of his so highly-praised wife; and at length, after much altercation, Posthumus consented to a proposal of Iachimo's that he (Iachimo) should go to Britain and endeavour to gain the love of the married Imogen. They then laid a wager that if Iachimo did not succeed in this wicked design he was to forfeit a large sum of money; but if he could win Imogen's favour, and prevail upon her to give him the bracelet which Posthumus had so earnestly desired she would keep as a token of his love, then the wager was to terminate with Posthumus giving to Iachimo the ring, which was Imogen's love-present when she parted with her husband. Such firm faith had Posthumus in the fidelity of Imogen, that he thought he ran no hazard in this trial of her honour.

Iachimo, on his arrival in Britain, gained admittance, and a courteous welcome from Imogen, as a friend of her husband; but when he began to make professions of love to her, she repulsed him with disdain, and he soon found that he could have no hope of succeeding in his dishonourable design.

The desire Iachimo had to win the wager made him now have recourse to a stratagem to impose upon Posthumus, and for this purpose he bribed some of Imogen's attendants, and was by them conveyed into her bedchamber, concealed in a large trunk, where he remained shut up till Imogen had retired to rest and had fallen to sleep; and then, getting out of the trunk, he examined the chamber with great attention, and wrote down everything he saw there, and particularly noticed a mole which he observed upon Imogen's neck, and then softly unloosing the bracelet from her arm, which Posthumus had given to her, he retired into the chest again; and the next day he set off for Rome with great expedition, and boasted to Posthumus that Imogen had given him the bracelet, and in this manner Iachimo told his false tale: "Her bedchamber," said he, "was hung with tapestry of silk and silver, the story was *the proud Cleopatra when she met her Antony*, a piece of work most bravely wrought."

"This is true," said Posthumus; "but this you might have heard spoken of without seeing."

"Then the chimney," said Iachimo, "is south of the chamber, and the chimney-piece is *Diana bathing*; never saw I figures livelier expressed."

"This is a thing you might have likewise heard," said Posthumus, "for it is much talked of."

Iachimo as accurately described the roof of the chamber, and added, "I had almost forgot her andirons, they were *two winking Cupids* made of silver, each on one foot standing." He then took out the bracelet and said, "Know you this jewel, sir? She gave me this. She took it from her arm. I see her yet; her pretty action did outsell her gift, and yet enriched it too. She gave it me, and said, *she prized it once.*" He last of all described the mole he had observed upon her neck.

Posthumus, who had heard the whole of this artful recital in an agony of doubt, now broke out into the most passionate exclamations against Imogen. He delivered up the diamond ring to Iachimo, which he had agreed to forfeit to him if he obtained the bracelet from Imogen.

Posthumus then in a jealous rage wrote to Pisanio, a gentleman of Britain, who was one of Imogen's attendants, and had long been a faithful attendant to Posthumus; and after telling him what proof he had of his wife's disloyalty, he desired Pisanio would take Imogen to Milford Haven, a seaport of Wales, and there kill her. And at the same time he wrote a deceitful letter to Imogen, desiring her to go with Pisanio, for that, finding he could live no longer without seeing her, though he was forbidden upon pain of death to return to Britain, he would come to Milford Haven, at which place he begged she would meet him. She, good unsuspecting lady, who loved her husband above all things, and desired more than her life to see him, hastened her departure with Pisanio, and the same night she received the letter she set out.

When their journey was nearly at an end, Pisanio, who, though faithful to Posthumus, was not faithful to serve him in an evil deed, disclosed to Imogen the cruel order he had received.

Imogen, who, instead of meeting a loving and beloved husband, found herself doomed by that husband to suffer death, was afflicted beyond measure.

Pisanio persuaded her to take comfort, and wait with patient fortitude for the time when Posthumus should see and repent his injustice; in the meantime, as she refused in her distress to return to her father's court, he advised her to dress herself in boy's clothes for more security in travelling; to which advice she agreed, and thought in that disguise she would go over to Rome and see her husband, whom, though he had used her so barbarously, she could not forget to love.

When Pisanio had provided her with her new apparel, he left her to her uncertain fortune, being obliged to return to court; but before he departed he gave her a phial of cordial, which he said the queen had given him as a sovereign remedy in all disorders.

The queen, who hated Pisanio because he was a friend to Imogen and Posthumus, gave him the phial, which she supposed contained poison, she having ordered her physician to give her some poison to try its effects (as she said) upon animals; but the physician, knowing her malicious disposition, would not trust her with real poison, but gave her a drug that would do no other mischief than causing a person to sleep with every appearance of death for a few hours. This mixture, which Pisanio thought a choice cordial, he gave to Imogen, desiring her, if she found herself ill upon the road, to take it; and so, with blessings and prayers for her safety and happy deliverance from her undeserved troubles, he left her.

Providence strangely directed Imogen's steps to the dwelling of her two brothers, who had been stolen away in their infancy. Bellarius, who stole them away, was a lord in the court of Cymbeline, and having been falsely accused to the king of treason, and banished from the court, in revenge he stole away the two sons of Cymbeline, and brought them up in a forest, where he lived concealed in a cave. He stole them through revenge, but he soon loved them as tenderly as if they had been his own children, educated them carefully, and they grew up fine youths, their princely spirits leading them to bold and daring actions; and as they subsisted by hunting, they were active and hardy, and were always pressing their supposed father to let them seek their fortune in the wars.

At the cave where these youths dwelt it was Imogen's fortune to arrive. She had lost her way in a large forest through which her road lay to Milford Haven (from which she meant to embark for Rome), and being unable to find any place where she could purchase food, she was with weariness and hunger almost dying; for it is not merely putting on a man's apparel that will enable a young lady, tenderly brought up, to bear the fatigue of wandering about lonely forests like a man. Seeing this cave, she entered, hoping to find someone within of whom she could procure food. She found the cave empty, but looking about she discovered some cold meat, and her hunger was so pressing that she could not wait for an invitation, but sat down and began to eat. "Ah!" said she, talking to herself, "I see man's life is a tedious one, how tired am I! for two nights together I have made the ground my bed; my resolution helps me, or I should be sick. When Pisanio showed me Milford Haven from the mountain-top, how near it seemed!" Then the thoughts of her husband and his cruel mandate came across her, and she said, "My dear Posthumus, thou art a false one."

The two brothers of Imogen, who had been hunting with their reputed father, Bellarius, were by this time returned home. Bellarius had given them the names of Polidore and Cadwal, and they knew no better, but supposed that Bellarius was their father; but the real names of these princes were Guiderius and Arviragus.

Bellarius entered the cave first, and seeing Imogen; stopped them, saying, "Come not in yet; it eats our victuals, or I should think it was a fairy."

"What is the matter, sir?" said the young men "By Jupiter," said Bellarius again, "there is an angel in the cave, or if not, an earthly paragon." So beautiful did Imogen look in her boy's apparel.

She, hearing the sound of voices, came forth from the cave, and addressed them in these words: "Good masters, do not harm me; before I entered your cave I had thought to have begged or bought what I have eaten. Indeed, I have stolen nothing, nor would I, though I had found gold strewed on the floor. Here is money for my meat, which I would have left on the board when I had made my meal, and parted with prayers for the provider." They refused her money with great earnestness. "I see you are angry with me," said the timid Imogen; "but, sirs, if you kill me for my fault, know that I should have died if I had not made it."

"Whither are you bound?" asked Bellarius, "and what is your name?"

"Fidele is my name," answered Imogen. "I have a kinsman, who is bound for Italy; he embarked at Milford Haven, to whom being going, almost spent with hunger, I am fallen into this offence."

"Prithee, fair youth," said old Bellarius, "do not think us churls, nor measure our good minds by this rude place we live in. You are well encountered; it is almost night. You shall have better cheer before you depart, and thanks to stay and eat it. Boys, bid him welcome."

The gentle youths, her brothers, then welcomed Imogen to their cave with many kind expressions, saying they would love her (or, as they said, *him*) as a brother, and they entered the cave where (they having killed venison when they were hunting) Imogen delighted them with her neat housewifery, assisting them in preparing their supper; for though it is not the custom now for young women of high birth to understand cookery, it was then, and Imogen excelled in this useful art, and, as her brothers prettily expressed it, Fidele cut their roots in characters, and sauced their broth, as if Juno had been sick and Fidele were her dieter. "And then," said Polidore to his brother, "how angel-like he sings!"

They also remarked to each other that though Fidele smiled so sweetly, yet so sad a melancholy did overcloud his lovely face, as if grief and patience had together taken possession of him.

For these her gentle qualities (or perhaps it was their near relationship, though they knew it not) Imogen (or, as the boys called her, *Fidele*) became the doting-piece of her brothers, and she scarcely less loved them, thinking that, but for the memory of her dear Posthumus, she could live and die in the cave with these wild forest youths, and she gladly consented to stay with them till she was enough rested from the fatigue of travelling to pursue her way to Milford Haven.

When the venison they had taken was all eaten, and they were going out to hunt for more, Fidele could not accompany them, because she was unwell. Sorrow, no doubt, for her husband's cruel usage, as well as the fatigue of wandering in the forest, was the cause of her illness.

They then bid her farewell, and went to their hunt, praising all the way the noble parts and graceful demeanour of the youth Fidele.

Imogen was no sooner left alone than she recollected the cordial Pisanio had given her, and drank it off, and presently fell into a sound and deadlike sleep.

When Bellarius and her brothers returned from hunting, Polidore went first into the cave, and, supposing her asleep, pulled off his heavy shoes, that he might tread softly and not awake her; so did true gentleness spring up in the minds of these princely foresters; but he soon discovered that she could not be awakened by any noise, and concluded her to be dead, and Polidore lamented over her with dear and brotherly regret, as if they had never from their infancy been parted.

Bellarius also proposed to carry her out into the forest, and there celebrate her funeral with songs and solemn dirges, as was then the custom.

Imogen's two brothers then carried her to a shady covert, and there laying her gently on the grass, they sang repose to her departed spirit, and covering her over with leaves and flowers, Polidore said, "While summer lasts and I live here, Fidele, I will daily strew thy sad grave. The pale primrose, that flower most like thy face; the blue-bell, like thy clear veins; and the leaf of eglantine, which is not sweeter than was thy breath—all these I will strew over thee. Yea, and the furred moss in winter, when there are no flowers to cover thy sweet corpse."

When they had finished her funeral obsequies, they departed very sorrowful.

Imogen had not been long left alone, when, the effect of the sleepy drug going off, she awakened, and easily shaking off the light covering of leaves and flowers they had thrown over her she arose, and imagining she had been dreaming, she said, "I thought I was a cave-keeper, and cook to honest creatures; how came I here, covered with flowers?" Not being able to find her way back to the cave, and seeing nothing of her new companions, she concluded it was certainly all a dream; and once more Imogen set out on her weary pilgrimage, hoping at last she should find her way to Milford Haven, and thence get a passage in some ship for Italy; for all her thoughts were still with her husband Posthumus, whom she intended to seek in the disguise of a page.

But great events were happening at this time, of which Imogen knew nothing; for a war had suddenly broken out between the Roman Emperor Augustus Caesar and Cymbeline the King of Britain; and a Roman army had landed to invade Britain, and was advancing into the very forest over which Imogen was journeying. With this army came Posthumus.

Though Posthumus came over to Britain with the Roman army,

he did not mean to fight on their side against his own countrymen, but intended to join the army of Britain, and fight in the cause of his king who had banished him.

He still believed Imogen false to him; yet the death of her he had so fondly loved, and by his own orders too (Pisanio having written him a letter to say he had obeyed his command, and that Imogen was dead), sat heavy on his heart, and therefore he returned to Britain, desiring either to be slain in battle, or to be put to death by Cymbeline for returning home from banishment.

Imogen, before she reached Milford Haven, fell into the hands of the Roman army; and her presence and deportment recommending her, she was made a page to Lucius, the Roman general.

Cymbeline's army now advanced to meet the enemy, and when they entered this forest, Polidore and Cadwal joined the king's army. The young men were eager to engage in acts of valour, though they little thought they were going to fight for their own royal father, and Bellarius went with them to the battle. He had long since repented of the injury he had done to Cymbeline in carrying away his sons, and having been a warrior in his youth, he gladly joined the army to fight for king he had so injured.

And now a great battle commenced between armies, and the Britons would have been defeated, and Cymbeline himself killed, but for the extraordinary valour of Posthumus, and Bellarius, and the two sons of Cymbeline. They rescued the king and saved his life, and so entirely turned the fortune of the day, that the Britons gained the victory.

When the battle was over, Posthumus, who had not found the death he sought for, surrendered himself to one of the officers of Cymbeline, willing to suffer the death which was to be his punishment if he returned from banishment.

Imogen and the master she served were taken prisoners, and brought before Cymbeline, as was also her old enemy Iachimo, who was an officer in the Roman army; and when these prisoners were before the king Posthumus was brought in to receive his sentence of death; and at this strange juncture of time, Bellarius, with Polidore and Cadwal, were also brought before Cymbeline, to receive the rewards due to the great services they had by their valour done for the king. Pisanio, being one of the king's attendants, was likewise present.

Therefore there were now standing in the king's presence (but with very different hopes and fears) Posthumus and Imogen, with her new master the Roman general; the faithful servant Pisanio, and the false friend Iachimo, and likewise the two lost sons of Cymbeline, with Bellarius, who had stolen them away.

The Roman general was the first who spoke, the rest stood silent before the king, though there was many a beating heart among them.

Imogen saw Posthumus and knew him, though he was in the disguise of a peasant; but he did not know her in her male attire, and she knew Iachimo, and she saw the ring on his finger which she perceived to be her own, but she did not know him as yet to have been the author of all her troubles, and she stood before her own father a prisoner of war.

Pisanio knew Imogen, for it was he who had dressed her in the garb of a boy. "It is my mistress," thought he; "since she is living, let the time run on to good or bad." Bellarius knew her too, and softly said to Cadwal, "is not this boy revived from death?" "One sand," replied Cadwal, "does not more resemble another than that sweet rosy lad is like the dead Fidele." "The same dead thing alive," said Polidore. "Peace, peace," said Bellarius, "if it were he, I am sure he would have spoken to us." "But we saw him dead," again whispered Polidore. "Be silent," replied Bellarius.

Posthumus waited in silence to hear the welcome sentence of his own death; and he resolved not to disclose to the king that he had saved his life in the battle, lest that should move Cymbeline to pardon him.

Lucius, the Roman general, who had taken Imogen under his protection as his page, was the first (as has been before said) who spoke to the king. He was a man of high courage and noble dignity, and this was his speech to the king:

"I hear you take no ransom for your prisoners, but doom them all to death; I am a Roman, and with a Roman heart will suffer death. But there is one thing for which I would entreat." Then bringing Imogen before the king, he said, "This boy is a Briton born. Let him be ransomed. He is my page. Never master had a page so kind, so duteous, so diligent on all occasions, so true, so nurse-like. He hath done no Briton wrong, though he hath served a Roman. Save him, if you spare no one beside."

Cymbeline looked earnestly on his daughter Imogen. He knew her not in that disguise; but it seemed that all-powerful nature spake in his heart, for he said, "I have surely seen him, his face appears familiar to me. I know not why or wherefore I say, Live, boy; but I give you your life, and ask of me what boon you will, and I will grant it you. Yea, even though it be the life of the noblest prisoner I have."

"I humbly thank your highness," said Imogen

What was then called granting a boon was the same as a promise to give any one thing, whatever it might be, that the person on whom that favour was conferred chose to ask for. They were all attentive to hear what thing the page would ask for; and Lucius her master said to her, "I do not beg my life, good lad, but I know that is what you will ask for." "No, no, alas!" said Imogen, "I have other work in hand, good master: your life I cannot ask for."

This seeming want of gratitude in the boy astonished the Roman general.

Imogen then, fixing her eyes on Iachimo, demanded no other boon than this, that Iachimo should be made to confess whence he had the ring he wore on his finger.

Cymbeline granted her this boon, and threatened Iachimo with the torture if he did not confess how he came by the diamond ring on his finger.

Iachimo then made a full acknowledgment of all his villany, telling, as has been before related, the whole story of his wager with Posthumus, and how he had succeeded in imposing upon his credulity.

What Posthumus felt at hearing this proof of the innocence of his lady cannot be expressed. He instantly came forward, and confessed to Cymbeline the cruel sentence which he had enjoined Pisanio to execute upon the princess, exclaiming wildly, "O, Imogen, my queen, my life, my wife! O, Imogen, Imogen, Imogen!"

Imogen could not see her beloved husband in this distress without discovering herself, to the unutterable joy of Posthumus, who was thus relieved from a weight of guilt and woe, and restored to the good graces of the dear lady he had so cruelly treated.

Cymbeline, almost as much overwhelmed as he with joy at finding his lost daughter, so strangely recovered, received her to her former place in his fatherly affection, and not only gave her husband Posthumus his life, but consented to acknowledge him for his son-in-law.

Bellarius chose this time of joy and reconciliation to make his confession. He presented Polidore and Cadwal to the king, telling him they were his two lost sons Guiderius and Arviragus.

Cymbeline forgave old Bellarius, for who could think of punishment at a season of such universal happiness? To find his daughter living, and his lost sons in the persons of his young deliverers, that he had seen so bravely fight in his defence, was unlooked-for joy indeed!

Imogen was now at leisure to perform good services for her late master, the Roman general Lucius, whose life the king, her father, readily granted at her request, and by the mediation of the same Lucius a peace was concluded between the Romans and the Britons, which was kept inviolate many years.

How Cymbeline's wicked queen, through despair of bringing her projects to pass, and touched with remorse of conscience, sickened and died, having first lived to see her foolish son Cloten slain in a quarrel which he had provoked, are events too tragical to interrupt this happy conclusion by more than merely touching upon. It is sufficient that all were made happy who were deserving, and even the treacherous Iachimo, in consideration of his villany having missed its final aim, was dismissed without punishment.